*THE PAWNBROKER*

# THE PAWNBROKER

Edward Lewis Wallant

*A Harvest/HBJ Book*
*HARCOURT BRACE JOVANOVICH*
*New York and London*

Copyright © 1961 by Edward Lewis Wallant

All rights reserved. No part of this publication may be reproduced or transmitt
in any form or by any means, electronic or mechanical, including photocopy,
recording, or any information storage and retrieval system, without permission
in writing from the publisher.

Printed in the United States of America

Library of Congress Cataloging in Publication Data

Wallant, Edward Lewis, 1926–1962.
  The pawnbroker

  (A Harvest/HBJ book)
  I. Title.
[PZ4.W195Paw   1978]      [PS3573.A434]      813'.5'4      78-7101
ISBN 0-15-671422-1

First Harvest/HBJ edition 1978
A B C D E F G H I J

*For Joyce, Scott, Leslie, and Kim*

# THE PAWNBROKER

His feet crunched on the hard-packed sand. On his left was
the Harlem River, across the street to the right was the Community Center, and beyond was the vast, packed city. At
seven thirty in the morning it was quiet for New York. In
that relative silence, his footsteps made ponderous, dragging
sounds that were louder and more immediate in his own
ears than the chugging of the various river boats or the
wakening noise of traffic a few blocks away on 125th Street.

*Crunch, crunch, crunch.*

It could almost have been the pleasant sound of someone
walking over clean white snow. But the sight of the great,
bulky figure, with its puffy face, its heedless dark eyes distorted behind the thick lenses of strangely old-fashioned
glasses, dispelled any thought of pleasure.

Cecil Mapp, a small, skinny Negro, sat nursing a monumental hangover on the wooden curbing that edged the river. He gazed blearily at Sol Nazerman the Pawnbroker and thought the heavy, trudging man resembled some kind of metal conveyance. Look like a tank or like that, he thought. The sight of the big white man lifted Cecil's spirit perceptibly; the awkward caution of his walk indicated misery on a different scale from his own. For a few minutes he forgot about his furious wife, whom he would have to face that night, forgot even the anticipated misery of a whole day's work plastering walls with shaky, unwilling hands. He was actually moved to smile as Sol Nazerman approached, and he thought gaily, That man *suffer!*

He waved his hand and raised his eyebrows like someone greeting a friend at a party.

"Hiya there, Mr. Nazerman. Look like it goin' to be a real nice day, don't it?"

"It is a day," Sol allowed indifferently, with a slight, sidewise movement of his head.

As he plodded along, Sol watched the quiet flow of the water. Ironically, he noted the river's deceptive beauty. Despite its oil-green opacity and the indecipherable things floating on its filthy surface, somehow its insistent direction made it impressive.

He narrowed his eyes at the August morning: the tarnished gold light on receding bridges, the multi-shaped industrial buildings, and all the random gleams that bordered the river and made the view somehow reminiscent of a great and ancient European city.

No fear that *he* could be taken in by it; he had the battered memento of his body and his brain to protect him from illusion.

Oh yes, yes, a nice, peaceful summer day; quiet, safe, full of people going about their business in the rich, promising heat. A dozing morning in a great city. He looked idly at the intricate landscape, his eyes lidded with boredom as he walked.

Suddenly he had the sensation of being clubbed. An image was stamped *behind* his eyes like a bolt of pain. For an instant he moved blindly in the rosy morning, seeing a floodlit night filled with screaming. A groan escaped him, and he stretched his eyes wide. There was only the massed detail of a thousand buildings in quiet sunlight. In a minute he hardly remembered the hellish vision and sighed at just the recollection of a brief ache, his glass-covered eyes as bland and aloof as before. Another minute and he was allowing himself the usual shallow speculation on his surroundings.

What was there here, in this shabby patch on his journey to the store each morning, that eased him slightly? Just a large, sandy triangle, perhaps two blocks long, a waste that seemed to wait for some utilitarian purpose, or a spot where something had once existed, whose traces were now covered by the anonymous, thin layer of beach sand. It was a block out of his way, too. Eh, go figure the things a person reacts to! He liked to come this way, that was enough. Maybe it was the lovely *scenery,* the charming, lovely type of people you might see strewn along the way, like Cecil Mapp. Whatever—the dreams of night lost their sharp edges for him at this particular distance in time from his sleep. He glanced idly at the bright-painted tugs, the weathered, broad barges carrying all manner of things. Gradually, as he walked, he drained himself of the phantoms of his sleep, and the multiple tiny abrasions he got from his sister and her family lost their soreness. Perhaps, then, this brief part of his walk was a bridge between two separate atmospheres, a bridge upon which he could readjust the mantle of his impregnable scorn.

As he reached the apex of the sandy area and turned to the pavement, he allowed himself a moment's recall of his troubled sleep. Not that he could remember what he had dreamed, but he knew the dreams were bad. For years he had experienced bad dreams from time to time, but lately they were occurring more frequently.

My age, I guess. At forty-five the nerves lose some of their elasticity, he thought. "Agh," he said aloud, and shrugged, to throw dirt over the introspection; in the diplomatic delicacy of truce there was no sense in displaying your dead.

But when he got to the store, he could not resist a grimace at the sight of the three gilded balls hanging over the doorway. It was no more than a joke in rather poor taste that had led to this. Still, he could never evade the foolish idea, each morning when he first looked at the ugly symbol of his calling, that the sign was the result of some particularly diabolic vandalism perpetrated during the night by an unknown tormentor.

The grimace turned to a wintry smile; he still had a thin sense of humor for certain little vulgarities. So what if the onetime instructor at the University of Cracow could now be found behind the three gold balls of a pawnshop? It was by far the mildest joke life had played on him.

And the joke wasn't entirely at his expense, either, he mused as he unfastened the elaborate series of locks, disconnected the two burglar alarms, and took down the heavy wire screening that protected the show windows during the night. No indeed, he thought, taking a slow, smug look around him. This much-maligned calling had bought him the one commodity he still valued—*privacy*. He had bought the large house in Mount Vernon in which he lived with his sister, Bertha, and her family, and by continuing to support them (no big houses in Mount Vernon on his brother-in-law Selig's teacher salary), had earned his own room and bath, decently cooked meals, and best of all, his privacy from them. And, as they owed their sustenance to him, so he in turn owed Albert Murillio. Trace anything far enough and it leads to filth. Even rescuing angels must have some grime on their wing tips. He had been working for the United Jewish Appeal in Paris, and through them had gotten to America on the strength of a job offer by the pawnbroker Pearlman. He had worked two years for that half-decent man when someone told someone else that Sol Nazerman was a man with no allegiances. One day a cold, monotonous voice on the telephone had outlined a plan: one Albert Murillio would channel unreportable income through a pawnshop which Sol would manage, and be the ostensible owner of, at least on paper. The financial arrangements were unbelievably generous for Sol, and he hadn't hesitated to accept. With mechanical ease, the deal had been consummated. Sol had worked out the details with an envoy of the unseen Murillio, an accountant had established a business structure and paid all the bills, and, lo, a new pawnbroker had been established! All in a purely logical progression; from the lofty, philanthropic people of the U.J.A. in Paris, down through the not-so-good, not-so-bad Sam Pearlman, finally to Albert Murillio—a dull, heartless voice on a telephone. And all of it was fine for Sol Nazerman. He wasted no time worrying about the sources of money; let the Murillios of the world do what they wanted as long as they made no personal demands, as long as they left his privacy inviolate. The immediate moment, and maybe the one right next to it, was as far as he cared to go.

Now, in the small, insulated chamber he dwelt in, Sol began his informal morning appraisal of the store. He derived a bleak comfort from just touching and moving the various objects a little, from hefting and studying the great and patternless conglomeration of the things people had pawned.

He plucked the strings of a warped violin, blew the dust from the lens of a Japanese camera, turned the knob of a dead radio on and off a few times. With the furtive air of an adult trying to hide interest in a child's toy, he played lightly with the keys of an old typewriter for a few seconds before turning to plonk his fingernail against a floral china plate.

In a corner under the counter he found a pair of mother-of-pearl opera glasses, and, looking in the wrong end, scanned the store, so that the place looked vast and ancient, like a museum dedicated to an odd history. And all the while, half consciously, he got a perverse pleasure from the sense of kinship, of community with all the centuries of hand-rubbing Shylocks. Yes, he, Sol Nazerman, practiced the ancient, despised profession; and he survived!

At the sound of footsteps he looked up. His assistant, Jesus Ortiz, moved toward him wearing his dazzling, bravo's smile.

"*Guten Tag,* Sol, I'm here! You could let the business commence now," he said, moving with that leopard-like fluidity that made it hard to say where bone gave way to fine muscle.

"If I depended on you . . ." Sol frowned to cover the feeling of awe he always experienced when he first saw the brown-skinned youth each morning. The boy's face was formed with exquisite subtlety; straight, narrow nose, high cheekbones, a mouth curved and mobile as a girl's. He always seemed to flaunt the perfection of his face when he spoke, to offer it in a sort of spiteful compensation for whatever it was he had failed at.

"It is past nine thirty already," Sol said, turning his attention sternly to the pile of bills on the counter.

"I know, I know," Jesus said regretfully, shaking his sleek, narrow head so that one shiny strand of black hair flopped over his forehead. "I jus' have the biggest trouble gettin' out of bed mornings." He jerked his head back with a practiced movement to toss the strand of hair into place. Then he scowled at one of the multitude of clocks, a grandfather clock that both of them knew was fixed in permanent paralysis at nine twenty. "Well now, I told you I want this all to be real businesslike. That clock say twenty minute past nine, so I gonna insist you dock me for exactly . . ."

"You are a real wise guy, Ortiz."

"Aw, come on, Sol, you don't have to worry a bit. I gonna work so goddam hard the next few hours you probably offer me time-and-a-half."

He was only half joking, because he did feel a strange dedication to the job that his sense of logic told him was a fool's vocation. Jesus Ortiz had earned three and four times his present salary in riskier and more remunerative pursuits, enterprises that had called upon his wits and his reflexes. For ten months he had sold marijuana cigarettes, and once, two years before, when he had been eighteen, he had shared in the loot from a robbed warehouse. But there had always been a deep-rooted nervousness in him, a feeling of fragility and terror. He had never wanted to account for this feeling, because that would have been like succumbing to it. But if he had, he might have connected it with the memory of being left alone at night as a child while his husband-deserted mother went off to work as a scrubwoman in a downtown office building. She had always left the door of the apartment open for some neighbor woman to "listen in," but Jesus had known there was no one to hear his heart-cries, so he had practiced a horrid silence amidst the barbaric voices of all the neighborhoods they had lived in. Night was emptiness, dark was nothingness. Later on, that dreadful hollow had come to hide even from his memory, but he had its residue, and it had left him with peculiar mannerisms. He would laugh at the most inappropriate moments, and once, when a group of white boys had seized him, pulled his pants down, and pretended to emasculate him with a harmless little twig, he had shrieked with a sound of such mad glee that they had released him and run away. Now, when he was "restless" (his own word for those strange, dizzying moods), he sometimes went to the Catholic church where his mother was a parishioner, to kneel without prayer before the crucifix and indulge an odd daydream. He would imagine the bearded figure was the father he had never seen, and, kneeling there, he would smile cruelly at the thought of his imagined father's riven flesh. And yet, strangely, at those times he would feel the anguish of love, too, and his body would seem to contain a terrible, racking struggle. So that when he got up to leave the church, he would be exhausted and listless, and it would appear to him that he had banished the "restlessness."

Several months before, he had seized on the idea of "business." He had visualized solidity and immense strength in it and had even, in his wilder moments, begun to daydream a mercantile dynasty, some great store with *his* name emblazoned in gold on its sign. And so he had answered Sol's ad for a "bright, willing-to-learn young man to assist in pawnshop. Opportunity to learn the business." Once there, in the presence of the big, inscrutable Jew, he had become even more obsessed with the magic potential of "business," for there had seemed to be some great mystery about the Pawnbroker, some secret which, if he could learn it, would enrich Jesus Ortiz immeasurably.

"Meanwhile, I see you still standing there," Sol said. "You who are going to work so hard."

But Ortiz wasn't listening; he was staring raptly at the papers spread out before the Pawnbroker.

"You pay all your bills by check, do you?" he asked. "I mean that's the most businesslike way, ain't it? What do you do, just fill out how much and to who on that little stub like and then . . . "

Sol exhaled a deep breath of exasperation.

"Well Christ, man, I s'pose to be learnin' the business, too, ain't I? You ain't done much learnin' of me, far as I could see."

"All right, all right, tomorrow, remind me tomorrow. When it gets quiet, late tomorrow afternoon, maybe we'll go over a few things," Sol said dully.

"*Okay,*" Ortiz said, flashing that sudden, almost shockingly irrelevant smile that sometimes affected Sol like a quick painful scratch against his skin. "I gonna rearrange them suits upstairs *efficient!* I been thinkin' to break 'em down into type of suit an' by price. They's a shitload of summer suits. . . . You waste a good hour just gettin' to the type suit somebody wants. I got me a bunch of cards an' I'm gonna label . . . "

"You have a lot of plans. So how come you are still standing with your nose in what I'm doing?"

Ortiz dazed him with the peculiar beauty of his smile again. There was something dangerous and wild on his smooth face, a look of guile and unpredictable curiosity; and yet, oddly, there was an unnerving quality of volatile innocence there, too. He seemed to have some . . . what— a cleanness of spirit? Oh sure, the boy had sold marijuana, according to old John Rider, the janitor, and had probably stolen and pandered and God knew what else. And yet . . . somehow Sol had the vague feeling that there were certain horrors this boy would not commit. In Sol Nazerman's eyes, this was a great deal; there were very few people to whom he attributed even that limitation of evil.

"Go already with your big plans, with your *labeling!*"

"You right, Sol, no question, you got my number. Take me time to get me a start on. But here I go, watch me move, I'm atom-power, shh-ht." And with that he was around the corner and on the steps leading up to the loft, moving with the amazing litheness that so startled Sol. For a moment, as he heard the footsteps ascending and then on the floor over his head, he stared at the last point at which he had seen the boy, his eyes faintly bemused, his face seemingly caught on a shelf of ease. Briefly, he tried to recall the distant sensation of youth. With his head tilted a little, his expression became vapid, loose, and vulnerable looking. All the clocks ticked or buzzed an anonymous time. But then he suddenly wiped at his face as though at some unseen perspiration. A jagged darkness closed around his casting back, and he began frowning over the bills again.

There were only a few business bills; most of them were

the personal expenses incurred by his sister's family. Here was a staggering telephone bill, an electric bill twice the size of the store's, and a bill for a new rug bought by Bertha. There were, in addition, several clothing bills incurred by his niece, Joan, a dermatologist's bill and an internist's bill for Selig, and a bill from the art school his nephew, Morton, attended. His lips hardened as he began making out the checks.

He heard a heavy jingling and looked up to see Leventhal, the policeman, standing and rocking on the balls of his feet.

"What d'ya say, Solly? How's business?"

"You could be my first customer of the day. You want to hock the badge, or maybe the gun?"

"Can't do that, Solly; need them to protect you."

"Oh yes, to protect me," Sol said sarcastically. Leventhal had been making it increasingly evident that he imagined Sol had something to hide, that he, Leventhal, might be in a position to expect some kind of favors from Sol.

"Speaking of protection, what the hell time were you here till last night?" Leventhal asked, with an expression of affectionate admonishment on his tough, blue-jawed face.

"Why do you ask?"

"Why! I'll tell you why. Because you're asking for trouble staying open so late in this neighborhood, all by yourself. All the other Uncles close up at six o'clock. What are you trying to do, get rich fast or what? Maybe you think you're like a doctor, hah? Gotta be on call in case some nigger suddenly runs out of booze money or needs dough for a quick fix. I mean you got to wise up, Solly. You get some kind of trouble here and pretty soon the department starts poking their nose in your business and . . . " He shrugged suggestively.

"I appreciate your concern. I know what I am doing. Just do not trouble yourself worrying about me," Sol said coldly, lowering his attention pointedly to the checks again.

"Aw now, don't take that attitude. That's my business to

worry about you. Where would you be without law and order?"

"Oh yes, law and order."

"I mean you ought to be more co-operative, Solly. Take my advice in the spirit it's given. Look, we're landsmen, got to stick together against all these crooked goys," Leventhal said with a loose smile.

"Is that a fact?" He stared at the policeman with an icy, inscrutable expression. "Well thank you then. Now if you will excuse me, I have work to do." A landsman indeed! And where was the heritage of a Jew in a black uniform, carrying a club and a revolver? Sol had no friends, but his enemies were clearly marked for him.

"Okay, Solly, we'll leave it at that . . . for now." Leventhal shrugged, looked slowly around with the pompous, constabulary warning, and walked slowly, insolently out, trailing a toneless whistle behind him.

And then, at ten o'clock, the traffic began.

A white man in his early twenties walked stiffly up to the grille. He had wild soft hair that rose up and was in constant motion from the tiniest drafts and crosscurrents of air, so that, with his drowned-looking face, he seemed to float under water. His clothing was threadbare but showed the conservative taste of some sensible, middle-class shopper. He held a paper bag before him under crossed arms, and he stared with cautious intensity at the Pawnbroker before even entrusting his burden to the edge of the counter.

"How much will you give me?" he asked in a low, breathless voice.

"For what?" Sol twisted his mouth impatiently.

"For this," the man answered, his black eyes gleaming above the big blade of nose. There was something histrionic and a little mad in his manner, and he clutched at the bag as though against Sol's attempt to steal it.

"This, this . . . what in hell is *this?* All I am able to see is

a paper bag. What are you selling? I am no mind reader."
Sol's voice was harsh but his face was professionally bland
behind the round, black-framed glasses.

"It is an award for oratory," said the wild-haired young
man. "I won it in a city-wide oratorical contest nine years
ago."

Sol took the bag, which was greasy-soft and made up of
a million shallow wrinkles. He wondered where they got
those bags or what they did to ordinary bags to make them
feel like thin, aged skin. He opened it with an attitude of
distaste. Inside was a bust of shiny yellow metal on a black-
lacquered wooden base. A plaque in the same yellow metal
was inscribed:

*DANIEL WEBSTER AWARD*

*New York Public School Oratorical Contest for 1949*

LEOPOLD S. SCHNEIDER

"It's gold," Leopold Schneider said.

"Plate," the Pawnbroker corrected, tapping Daniel Webster's shiny skull. "Look, I'll loan you a dollar on it. The
devil what I could do with it if you didn't come back for it."

"A dollar!" Leopold Schneider pressed his starved face
against the bars like a maddened bird. "This is an important
award. Why, do you know there were two thousand quarter-
finalists out of twenty thousand, only fifty semifinalists. And
*I* won! I recited 'The Raven,' and I won, from twenty
thousand. I was the best of twenty thousand."

"Good, good, you are one in twenty thousand, Leopold,
maybe one in a million. That's why I will loan you a dollar
. . . because I'm so impressed."

"But one in *twenty thousand*. You don't think I would
part with that glory for a miserable dollar, do you!"

"There is a very small market for oratory awards with
your name engraved on them. One dollar," Sol said, lowering his eyes to the checks again.

"Look, I'm hungry. I'm busy writing a great, great play.

I just need a few dollars to carry me. I'll redeem it, I swear it. It's worth more than money . . . "

"Not to me, Leopold."

"I'll give you triple interest. . . . "

"One dollar," the Pawnbroker said without looking up. He had added one column of numbers three times now.

"What's the matter with you?" Leopold Schneider shrilled suddenly in the quiet store. Upstairs, Ortiz' footsteps stopped for a moment at the sound, as though he might be considering coming down to see what was happening. "Haven't you got a heart?"

"No," Sol answered. "No heart."

"What a world this is!"

Sol ran his finger deliberately down the column of numbers again.

"Five dollars at least?" Leopold whined, breathing the sour breath of the chronically hungry on the Pawnbroker.

Sol finally totaled the first column, carried a seven to the second.

"All right, three dollars, at least three miserable dollars. What is it to you?"

Sol raised his gray, impervious face. All the clocks ticked around his unrelenting stare. "I am busy. Go away now if you please. I have no use for the damned thing anyhow."

"All right, all right, give me the dollar," Leopold said in a trembling half-whisper.

Sol reached into the money drawer and took out a bill as greasy and battered as Leopold's paper bag. He tore off a pawn ticket, wrote up the description of the award, and gave the claim ticket to Leopold Schneider. Then he continued his adding of the numbers. Leopold stood there for a full minute before he turned and went out of the store with the awkward tread of a huge, ungainly bird.

Only several minutes later did the Pawnbroker look up to stare at the empty doorway. He rubbed his eyes in a little gesture of weariness. Daniel Webster caught a tiny dart of sunlight, and it disturbed Sol's corner vision. He picked the award up and shoved it into a low, dark shelf where the light never reached.

Mrs. Harmon might have seemed a relief after Leopold Schneider. She was big and brown, and her face had long ago committed her to frequent smiling; even in repose it was a series of benevolently curving lines. Mrs. Harmon was convinced you could either laugh or cry, that there were no other alternatives; she had elected to go with the former.

"Come on, Mistuh Nazerman, smile! You got some more business comin' at you. Here I is with a load of pure profit for you." She held up two silver candlesticks, the latest of her diminishing, yet never quite depleted, store of heirlooms. Her husband, Willy Harmon, was a janitor in a department store and came home with occasional delights for her in the form of floor samples, remains of old window dressings, and various other fruits of his modest thievery. Still, their needs were greater than his timid supplying. They had constant medical bills for a crippled son and were trying to put their daughter through secretarial school, so Mrs. Harmon was a steady client. "Genuine Duchess pattern, solid silver-plate silver. I'll settle for ten dollars the pair." She had really been fond of the candlesticks; they made a table *look* like a table. But she was the type of woman who could have cut off her own snake-bitten finger with great equanimity, for she believed mightily in salvaging what you could.

"I can only give you two dollars," Sol said, flipping over the pages of his ledger, looking for nothing in particular. "You've left an awful lot of things lately, haven't redeemed anything."

"Aw I know, but Mistuh Nazerman! Why, my goodness, these candlesticks is very high quality, costed twenny-five dollars new." She chuckled indignantly, shook her head at his offer. "Why I could get fifteen dollars *easy* down to Triboro Pawn."

"Take them to Triboro, Mrs. Harmon," he said quietly.

Mrs. Harmon sighed, still shaking her great smiling face as though in reminiscence of an atrocious but funny joke. She clucked through her teeth, shifted heavily from one foot to the other. Her dignity, that much-abused yet resilient thing, suffered behind her rueful smile as the Pawnbroker kept his face of gray Asian stone averted indifferently from her. Like a child forced to choose between two unpleasant alternatives, she stared thoughtfully through the window, furrowed her brow, tried on a few uneasy smiles. Finally she muttered, "Ah well," and leaned her plump brown face close to the barred wicket behind which Sol worked on all the papers.

"Les jus' say five dollars the pair and forget it, Mistuh Nazerman," she said, breathing hopefully on him.

"Two dollars," he repeated tonelessly, frowning over a name in the ledger which suddenly intrigued him.

She laughed her indignation, a bellowing *wahh-hh* that struck the glass cases like the flat of a hand. "You a *merciless* man for sure. Now you don't think I is reduce to being insulted by that measly offer. Two dollars! Why, my goodness, Mistuh Nazerman, you cain't even buy a *sinful* woman for that nowadays." She grabbed up her candlesticks and looked craftily to see what response that drew from the cold, gray face. But there was nothing; the man truly was made of stone. She sighed a sad but good-natured defeat. "*All* right, I jus' too pooped to haggle." She plunked the candlesticks down and exhaled noisily. "Make it foah dollars."

Sol took a deep breath and looked up with an expression of mild suprise, as though he hadn't expected her to still be there.

"The devil, Mrs. Harmon, I'll give you three dollars just to get this over with."

"Three fifty?" she tried timidly.

He just looked at her without expression.

"Sold," she said tiredly. Then she giggled her fat woman's laugh and cocked her head to one side. "You a hard man,

Mistuh Nazerman, no two ways about it. Well, God pity you . . . he d'ony judge after all." She took the silently proffered money and tucked it delicately into her huge, cracking plastic pocketbook, shaking her head and with a pensive grin on her wide lips. "Ohh my, hard times, always hard times. Well . . . " She brightened her smile for farewell. "I see you again, Mistuh Nazerman, that for sure. Take care now, hear?"

"Goodby, Mrs. Harmon," he said, tying a ticket to the candlesticks and sliding them under the counter next to Daniel Webster. After she was gone, he stole a furtive look at the clock nearest him. "Ten forty-five," he murmured in irritated surprise; it disturbed him to be so tired that early in the day.

Several customers came and went, but they remained anonymous to him because they were disposed of quickly and easily.

He began studying some of the more recent additions to his stock. There was an old Kodak Autographic, a zither of ancient make, an almost new electric traveling iron. The things people lived by! But it was no use trying to recall the owners by the shapes of the things they had pawned. The objects were dead and characterless, had been unique and part of life only while they were in use. Oh, he was so tired, and it wasn't even eleven o'clock. Forty-five wasn't old . . . but he was old.

The young Negro wore gaudy clothes whose vividness was obscured by the grime and grease that made it look as though he had been wearing them without letup for years. He had the terrified, twitching face of a jackal, with pupils like tiny periods in his ocherous eyes. Under his arm was a small white table radio.

"Whatta you gimme, Unc, how much? Hey, dis worth plenty rubles. Dis a hot li'l ol' radio, plenty juice. Got short wave, police call, boats from d'sea. Even get outer space on a clear night. Yeah, *space,* real-far space like from satlites an' all. C'mon, Unc, make a offer. Hey, dis a hundred-dollar radio. How much you gimme? C'mon, dis powaful, clear tone, clear like a . . . a mother-f——n ol' bell." The saliva flew from his mouth as from a leaky old steam engine, and he kept snuffling through his nose and making queer jig steps for emphasis.

Sol took the radio and plugged it into the socket under the counter. He watched the light glow brighter as it warmed up, his face impassive while the young Negro in his filthy Ivy League cap twitched and muttered encouragement, as though the radio could redeem *him*.

"C'mon, baby, show d'man you *power* . . . blast him . . . Give him dat *tone!* Man, dat radio . . . O, dat mother . . . "

There came a few whistles, a loud electrical gibberish, and then the nerve-racking sound as of stiff cellophane being steadily crumpled by many hands. The youth stopped twitching and aimed his pin-point gaze at the radio. His mouth dropped open at the sound of his betrayal.

"Give you four dollars," Sol said. Ah, our youth, the progenitor of our future. Maybe the earth will be lucky, maybe they will all be sterile.

"Hey, dat dere radio always play better dan dat," he accused. "It mus' be 'count of d'weather. Make it eight bucks. I mean, man, dat my mother's radio!"

"Four dollars, take it or leave it."

"Oh say, you tryin' to bleed me, you suckin' a man's guts. I takin' a awful chance hockin' my mother's radio. She *sell* me when she fin' out."

She ought to sell you. Sol massaged the bridge of his nose as he fumbled in his mind for the profit to all this.

"Six bucks?"

"Four."

"C'mon, at least five skins, you bloodsuckin' Sheeny!"

Sol felt a dangerous blue flicker behind his eyes. He began to move menacingly toward the little gate that led from behind the counter. "All right, animal, get out of here! Come on, out! Go peddle your junk in the street!"

"Okay, okay, mister, don' go gettin' all hot like. Gimme the four rubles, I take the four," he said, his hands trembling and flying around with his need. "Hurry, hurry up, man, please." His face showed the agony of some inner burning, an unbearable expression that filled the Pawnbroker with rage.

"Go on now," Sol said, pushing the money at him. "And don't go bothering me with your foul mouth any more. This is a place of business. I don't have to have human rubbish in here."

"Yes, man, O yes," the youth said, not even hearing the Pawnbroker's words. He took the money and gave it a quick kiss before stuffing it into his pocket. Then he cool-stepped out of the store with a beatific, lost smile on his writhing face. He left the pawn ticket on the floor behind him.

Sol felt the throbbing start of a bad headache. "It is getting hot," he said aloud, as though to excuse the pain. He began rolling up the sleeves of his shirt for the first time that summer, disturbed at this first concession to the heat.

Jesus Ortiz came downstairs with a pair of suits on hangers. All morning he had sorted and stacked and labeled. He had looked at the clothing stacked in dusty hundreds to the ceiling of the stifling loft and each suit had seemed a building block for some odd edifice he was erecting without conscious design. Now he had reached a point where he was obsessed with perfection, and two ordinary suits had seemed to mar the aesthetic daze he worked in.

"These here suits, Sol," he began, and then stared in puzzlement at the crudely tattooed numbers on his employer's thick, hairless arm. "Hey, what kind of tattoo you call that?" he asked.

"It's a secret society I belong to," Sol answered, with a scythelike curve to his mouth. "You could never belong. You have to be able to walk on the water."

"Okay, okay, mind my own business, hah," Ortiz said, his eyes still on the strange, codelike markings. How many secrets the big, pallid Jew had! "I mean, like these here suits is like brand new," he went on in an absent voice, no longer concerned with his mission. "They worth thirty-five, forty bucks easy. Got Hickey-Freeman labels inside."

"I leave it to you, Ortiz. Be creative, use your own intiative," the Pawnbroker said sardonically.

Ortiz just looked steadily at him for a minute before turning away with an equally secluded expression. He had secrets, too; secrets gave you a look of vast dignity, a feeling of power.

Just before twelve, as was his habit, Ortiz went out. He ate his own lunch in the cafeteria diagonally across the street and then bought Sol's never-varying cheese sandwich and coffee, and brought them back to the store. He handled the traffic alone for some fifteen minutes while Sol sat in the little windowed office eating and staring out sightlessly through the glass like some exhibited creature from another clime. And while Ortiz worked, treating the predominantly Negro customers with a show of better-humored hardness than his employer's, he was constantly aware of the odd, blind gaze on his back. He felt tense with a mysterious excitement, for the sense of his apprenticeship assumed an unfathomable importance then, seemed to possess the key to Sol's buried treasure.

At least half the clocks hovered near one when three men came in pushing a motorized lawn mower. Sol stared at it for a moment, reminded of how incredible and silly his atmosphere was. Then he nodded in mild disgust, as though bowing to some nasty omnipotence. "Oh yes, here's an item, fine, fine."

He had seen two of the men around the neighborhood; the gaudy little Tangee in a wide-shouldered, checked suit, and Buck White, with his majestic tribesman face of almost pure black, who appeared elemental in his dignity until you noticed the foolish, childish dreaminess of his eyes. But it was the third man who took Sol's attention. He was an oddly plain-clothed Negro in a shapeless, ash-gray suit and with a battered, styleless hat square on his head. With his clean white shirt and drab brown tie, he might have been some poor but discreet civil servant of decent education who was determined to avoid the Negro cliché in dress. Until you looked at his face, which was bony and gaunt and dominated by blue eyes filled with restless, darting menace. And in the presence of that face, the ridiculous transaction suddenly became oppressive out of all proportion.

"What's this here worth, Uncle?" Tangee asked with a smile that was all flash. "Brand new, never been use. S'pose to have a real strong engine. I mean what do they get for these?" As he talked, his eyes, like those of his companions, roved over the vast assortment of merchandise with an insolent and covetous look.

"Where'd you get it?" Sol asked, rubbing his cheek.

"What kind of question is that? Why, it was a gift, man, a gift! I woulda return it to the store my friend bought it, on'y I was embarrass to ask him where. Didn't want to let on I had no use for it, hurt his feelin's and all. Can't look a gift horse in the mouth." Tangee's tiny mustache twitched over the ivory display of smile. "Yeah, this here friend give it to me for housewarmin' present like."

"Amazing how stupid some people can be, isn't it?" Sol said. "I mean that he shouldn't have noticed that there wasn't a blade of grass within two miles of your house. Your friend, that is."

"Oh well, yeah," Tangee agreed, beginning to tire of the badinage, his eyes licking more hungrily at the great collection around him, darting occasionally toward his companions as though for some agreement. "You know how it is."

"Yes, I know very well," Sol said flatly. "Where did you get it?"

"Hey, man, I don't see where you come off askin' like that. I got it, that's all. I mean that there my business, ain't it?"

"Look, my friend, the police have lists of stolen merchandise. I am obligated to list all the items taken for pawn. For myself, I don't give a care if you stole it from Macy's window. All I am concerned with is that I would be out my money if they appropriated it."

Three other customers came in while he struggled with Tangee and his silent companions. He pressed the little signal button that called Ortiz down from the second floor.

"I ain't stole it, man; you don't have to worry. Some guy give it to me, figure I make *some* use out of it."

"A lawn mower?" The Pawnbroker's sarcasm was a bland poison that acted only on himself. He had a faint sensation of suffocation as he watched the loose rubbery lips of Tangee and the nightmarishly blue eyes of the Negro in the ash-gray suit.

"Sure, a lawn mower! I hock the friggen thing and get money. That useful enough, ain't it?" Tangee said with a roving, marble-eyed study of the Pawnbroker's face, an expression of cold appraisal, as though he were figuring how to go about taking Sol's face apart.

Buck White stared at Sol's tattooed arm, and the blue-eyed Negro kept his gaze on the rear of the store, his face like a burned bone. There was, in their idle patience, the murderous quality of hunting dogs so sure of their prey that they rest, panting, in a confident circle around it. Sol held himself motionless, trying to be as patient and cool as they. Across the store, Ortiz was crowded with customers, moving busily, waiting on two or three at once, disposing of them quickly and efficiently. And he stood there before the three strange men, imprisoned in their mood of menace, the silly lawn mower in the middle of the floor like some grotesque totem they were urging on him.

"Even if it isn't stolen . . . a *lawn mower!* No one comes in here for a lawn mower. Even at auction . . ."

"Take it, Pawnbroker, take the goddam thing," the blue-eyed Negro said suddenly, his voice amazingly low, sub-terranean even, like an echo from a distant depth.

Sol looked at him bleakly for a moment, went on to the inhuman ox-glance of Buck White, the insolent appraisal of Tangee. Suddenly he just wanted them out of there; they were like bands around his chest. He nodded.

"I'll give you seven dollars," he mumbled. "Take it or leave it."

"Why sure, man, *sold!* See, I ain't no trouble . . . pleasure to do business with, ain't I?" Tangee turned to his two companions like a performer. Buck White grinned, a shy expression forming as he shifted his huge, powerful body. The blue-eyed man just bent his mouth and took his eyes reluctantly from whatever they had been fixed on at the rear of the store.

Tangee took the money and then, his eyes mockingly on the Pawnbroker, crumpled up the pawn ticket and tossed it lightly against the Pawnbroker's hands.

"We be in again, Uncle. I like to do business with you," he said, and then walked out with his retinue like one of those strange little chieftains who are so impressive because they do not see anything ridiculous in their air of power.

All afternoon Sol's head pounded. It seemed very important for him to keep busy. Tangee's quiet, haggard wife came in like her vivid husband's drab shadow. She pawned some of her husband's castoff finery without attempting to bargain, took the money with the trace of a polite smile, and walked out stiffly, as though she feared she might be called back for some reason. Cecil Mapp's wife came in, covering her shame with righteous scorn for all men, Sol included. She offered a silver-plated tray. "You can be happy to know, Mr. Pawnbroker, that you is at least helpin'," she said sourly, waving the money he had just given her. "You're feedin' the children that Cecil Mapp's whisky is robbin' of food!" With that, she stalked out like a huge avenging angel, and Sol could see her take a small child's hand and move off like a liner with a tug; she wouldn't corrupt her child with the air of the pawnshop. One of the prostitutes from the masseur-fronted brothel down the street brought in a fancy sterling-backed brush and hand mirror. She was a handsome, light-skinned girl named Mabel Wheatly, and she had a surprisingly clean and unsullied look. But she wore boredom like armor and didn't look at Sol once during their brief transaction. A plumber with dented, cheerful features and battered ears came in to redeem the shiny nickle-plated Stillson wrench on which Sol had been loaning him money for almost three years; two dollars to him when he brought it in, something more than that to Sol when he redeemed it— a cycle as pointless as the following of the surface of a metal ring. A laborer, a schoolgirl, a sailor, a swarthy gypsy woman with shiny pots. An old man, a young man, a man with a hook for a hand. A dim-witted ex-fighter, a student, a deadpan mother. In and out, and back again in another guise. And all the while the Pawnbroker maintained that long-mastered yet precarious equilibrium of the senses. It was as though his nerves and his brain held on to the present and the immediate like some finely balanced instrument. If it ever broke down . . . he murdered that thought at birth for the thousandth time. The shop creaked with the weight of other people's sorrows; he abided.

He faced the depraved and the deprived, the small villains, the smaller victims. And his battlements were his hard assaying eyes, his cool voice that offered the very least. Through the hours, others besides Jesus Ortiz found time to wonder at the peculiar ragged numbers etched like false veins under the skin of his arm, or to speculate on the graven cast of his fleshy, spectacled face. But the Pawnbroker kept his secret, for while some of them might surmise some of the facts of his history, none of them could know its real truth. And as he plied his trade, each of them took away only a feeling of something quite huge and terrible.

At six forty-five in the evening the phone rang, and Sol answered, knowing who it was.

"Murillio?" he said with only the slightest intonation of question.

"You got to spend five thousand bucks, Nazerman." The voice in the receiver had the depthless timbre of a recording. "A contractor comes over tomorrow. He gives you an estimate of five thousand for general repairs. Give him a certified check on the store account."

"I see. What is his name?"

"Savarese."

"Yes, very well."

"How is business, Nazerman? Are we making money?" A dry chuckle had the same recorded quality as the spoken word.

"As always, we spend more than we make."

"Very good, Uncle. Pretty soon Uncle Sam will have to pay *us* money. Subsidize *us,* hah? Can't expect taxes from a losing business, can they? Hey, that's a good idea, subsidize. Sponsor us. Like they use to do in Italy durin' the Renaissance. The Medici, you know. They was patrons to the artists, Michelangelo, da Vinci. Hey, how about that. Why not us, too! The hell, Uncle, we're artists, too, ain't we? *Gyp artists!*" The dehumanized, mirthless chuckle sounded again. "Okay, okay, partner, I'll talk to you in a day or so. You take care of that little matter then. And keep your nose clean, hah?"

He looked up from the phone to see Ortiz studying the engraved plaque under Daniel Webster's bust. The store was dim even with the lights on, so it seemed the quality of light was at fault, not the intensity. Outside, the evening sun made the street shimmer in a golden bath through which the passers-by moved like dark swimmers in no hurry to get anywhere. He breathed, with his assistant, the dust of the much-handled merchandise, the imaginable odors of sweat and pride and weeping; and it was an indefinable yet powerful atmosphere, which gave them an intimacy neither desired.

"All this junk," Ortiz said musingly. "Still an' all, it's business. A solid thing, oh a real solid thing—business. You got records an' books an' papers, everythin' down in black an' white. Take like you people, how it carry you along no matter what."

"What people?" Sol asked, numbly admiring the almost poreless skin over his assistant's delicate features.

"Jews, all the Jews."

"Yes, yes, certainly, you have it all figured out," Sol said dryly, as he drew his eyes from the young man's face to fish for more substantial catches among the brass tubas, the cameras and radios and silver trays.

"Niggers suffer like animals. They ain't caught on. Oh yeah, Jews suffer. But they do it big, they shake up the worl' with they sufferin'."

"You tell them, Ortiz, go spread the word. You have it all figured out, a regular professor is what you are."

"I know, don't worry, I know," Ortiz said smugly. "I know the way things is."

"You know nothing, absolutely nothing."

"That's all right, jus' don't worry about what *I* know."

"Nothing, nothing, nothing."

"You go around with that poker face, think you the only one what know. Don't fool yourself. I got eyes and ears, I figure, I know."

"Nothing," the Pawnbroker hollowed out of himself in a sigh.

"An' what I don't know, I find out."

Sol turned cold, denying eyes on his assistant. "You're a pisher, that's all you are," he said. "It's after seven; why don't you go home now?"

"All right, sure, *boss,*" he said sourly. He put Daniel Webster down regretfully, a calm anger on his dark, ivory face. "Good night, *boss,* a very good night to you."

*"Gay in draird!"*

Ortiz bowed himself out with a mocking smile, his shiny black hair bobbing over his forehead with each bow.

"Good night, good night, good night . . ."

Sol hissed at the empty store. What is it, what is it? He was shaken with a minute trembling, like an aspen in an almost invisible breeze. A fever, could I have perhaps a fever? Oy, the season; every year it gets like this. Some people have hay fever, I have my *anniversary!* What, it's about two weeks away, the twenty-eighth. I'll get through it like always. Maybe I'll go to Tessie tonight? No, too tired. I'll go home and read in my bed. Oh yes, I have a *wonderful* two weeks ahead of me. Oh what nonsense, what nonsense this all is!

After a while he began readying the store for the night. He closed the safe and twirled the dial a few times. He turned on the one light in the little glassed-in office and flicked off the fluorescents one by one. Then he put up the heavy screens over the windows and switched on the two burglar alarms. Finally, with a brief look around at all the conglomerated stock, lying submerged in the dimness he had brought about, like some ancient remains half buried in the muck of an ocean bottom, he closed the door and locked it.

His mouth widened in a grimace that a passing man took for a smile and returned. He closed his eyes for a moment and leaned against the coarse metal screen that covered the window. The warm evening air played over his blinded face and the mingled homely smells of a poor neighborhood assaulted his nose. He stood there as though dead while the world continued its Babel-like conversation in car motors and boat whistles from the river, in distant shouts, in laughter, in the frayed yet gaudy music from some jukebox. Finally he touched the bridge of his glasses in a habit of adjustment and began walking toward the river, to his car, and ultimately to his cool, immaculate bed.

But there were obstacles between him and his bed.

He parked the dusty Plymouth in the driveway and walked past the stone barbecue, across the flagstone patio with its expensive, yellow-painted garden furniture and the round table with the flowery umbrella in the middle. And suddenly, as he approached the back door of the house, he was burdened with his weight. For a moment he worried about the state of his health, tinkered carefully, but with eyes averted, with that inner mechanism which maintained his equilibrium. Until he opened the screened door and smiled wryly at the creak of it. Maybe it is my menopause, he thought, my change of life come early.

His sister rushed at him as he entered the kitchen.

"Ah, look at him, all worn out. Sol, *totinka.* Sit, sit.

Bertha will get you a nice cool lemonade," she said with stagy affection, her gray eyes reckoning slyly as always. "You should conserve, not work so hard, Solly." A heavily built woman in her early fifties, she dressed too youthfully, and her hair was hairdresser-aged, the ends tipped with silver. "Sit. Let Bertha make you comfy with some lemonade." She prodded him toward a kitchen chair with patting motions of her soft hands.

"I do not want lemonade, Bertha. Stop pushing me to sit! I am dirty—let me wash my hands. Do not concern yourself so much with my comfort all of a sudden," he said. He saw, in his sister's generosity, those sticky fingers that came away with more than they gave. "What do you want?" he asked coldly.

"Oh, Solly," she scolded. Then she shrugged as though resigned to his lack of understanding. "Well, you know how bad the television has been working. So I figured if you start spending money repairing, it doesn't pay." She looked at him timidly for a moment. "I put down a little deposit on a new R.C.A. But I can get it back. If you object, I can get the deposit back. I just thought that . . ."

"All right, all right. Buy it," he said indifferently. "If the others are ready, let us have dinner. Otherwise give me a bite of food now. I'm tired. I would like to go to bed soon."

"Certainly, I'll call them right away," she said. "Selig is resting. His back is bothering him again. Ah, he's so delicate, my husband." Bertha spoke with a little smile of pride. "Thank God he has a brain, that he's a schoolteacher. He's so delicate, really," she sighed, pretending wistfulness.

"He has a good appetite with his delicacy," Sol said with the same unrevealing blandness of tone and expression.

For a moment Bertha's face revealed her. Her eyes grew hard and her lips drew back slightly; she knew very well the shape and sound of a taunt. But she also knew which side all their bread was buttered on as well as who bought the bread. So, while her dislike of her brother grew a shade bigger, she smiled even more dotingly under her hostile eyes and ventured another intimate touch of his arm.

"Have I got a delicious piece of brisket for you, Solly; nice black roasted like Momma used to make," she said warmly. "So go, you go wash up and I'll call them all."

Her smile didn't fade when he left the room; it flicked off electrically. "And tell my big *artist* upstairs that supper is ready," she called after him. She couldn't say what she would have liked to her brother; he had them bound in a chain of money. But her son, Morton, was vulnerable to her irritation. In some ways, her son and her brother were two of a kind, both sullen, unattractive creatures who dampened her "Happy American Family" setting. Oh, she supposed it wasn't Sol's fault that he had gone through what he had. But it *had* been a prison, and the degradation and filth had rubbed off on him. God knew what had so soiled Morton!

When they all sat down to dinner, Bertha unhappily compared Morton and Sol with her husband and her daughter. Joan was talking to her father, and the two of them were smiling in a glow of intellectual rapport. You wouldn't even guess they were Jews, Bertha thought proudly. Joan had thick, straight brown hair and even features. Her clear, shining skin was a testimonial to her mother's care and feeding, her easy smile an open proof of family love. And Selig—rosy and fair, with the same straight brown hair his daughter had. What a contrast between his clean, pink face and Sol's leaden grayness! And the dignity and cleverness with which he spoke. Why, he hardly moved his hands at all, and his voice was crisp with a delightfully Midwestern accent; so *American!*

But her faint smile slipped away when she turned back to her son. Morton ate with his thin face close to his plate, shoveling in the food with quick darts of his fork like a Chinese plying chopsticks. His dark, unattractive face resembled those of the young ghetto scholars she remembered from her childhood, morose, intense, despising appearance.

It depressed her just to look at him, made her feel a melancholy guilt which invariably turned to anger. He was not there enjoying the family meal, but, like his uncle, only hurrying toward his own solitude.

Sol ate slowly and deliberately. Eating was something he had to do, and the tastes made no difference to him. Despite Bertha's cajoling promise about the brisket, he ate only the vegetables, as always. He never ate meat, because it sickened him; it just never seemed important to remind his sister of that distaste.

". . . and Sid is taking me to that new Japanese film, Daddy."

Joan liked the aspect of the typically American family, which Bertha tried to develop, in spite of the intellectual pretensions that sometimes obligated her to scorn Americanism. Somewhat more generous and good-natured than her mother, she was even able to include her Uncle Sol in that rosy-tinted picture. She referred to Sol as being an old-fashioned bachelor, a very learned European ex-professor, and intimated to outsiders that his taciturnity was only a guise for a shyly affectionate nature.

"The thing is," Selig said, "Hollywood is just interested in making money." His fresh, youthful face was good-natured but not very mobile or expressive, as though too much animation might belie his alleged delicacy. Now he sighed in wan regret. "No, to Hollywood, culture is just a dirty word. Callow, that's the word for American culture. They have so much to learn from the Europeans."

"That's what Sid was saying, Dad, exactly that. He said that we live in a cultural vacuum here."

"Hey, that's good—cultural vacuum. Perfect. He sounds like a bright young man, your Sid." He smiled affectionately at his daughter and patted her arm.

"He *is* a nice boy," Bertha interrupted. "But is he serious? I mean I don't want you to get too . . . intimate," she said, casting her eyes down in an attitude of daintiness. She knew what she meant, too, how hot in the pants you could get at that age—how well she remembered! She glanced at Selig with a little throb of reminiscence. But then, when she looked at Sol next to him, she felt an inward shudder of disgust like the hidden, other side of her feelings about her husband, and for a moment she imagined her brother naked and wondered how a woman ever could have loved him. "I mean," she went on, "it can be a problem with young people. You get all emotional like, you know. Maybe you lose your head a little. . . ."

"Oh, Mother, you sound so old-fashioned," Joan said.

"She's right, Bertha," Selig said with a little chuckle. "You don't understand youth today. They're sensible enough but they have different standards."

The voices filled the room, rang on the cut-glass bowl of salad, the sideboard of good mahogany, with its bronze mortar and pestle, its framed picture of the long-forgotten Nazermans, father and mother of Sol and Bertha. Morton kept his eyes on the food like some searcher for gold, and Sol chewed slowly beside him, his eyes flat behind the black-rimmed steel-sided glasses.

Selig and Joan went back to talking about movies, and Selig observed that another trouble with Hollywood was that they were unwilling to face life. Suddenly noticing his silent brother-in-law, Selig smiled sympathetically and decided to include him in the conversation.

"Does that make sense to you, Solly, that the Europeans are more willing to face life?"

"Oh yes, they are willing to face life," Sol answered, without intonation, as he went on eating, chewing and swallowing, eating with his numbed taste in the midst of all the meaningless talk.

Selig shrugged at Joan and Bertha. "What could you do?" his face said. Friendliness rolled off that man like water off porcelain.

Joan indicated with a wink that she would give it a try.

This was almost a regular after-dinner game with them, trying to "draw Sol out," and they considered it a sort of amusing demonstration of their own good will and charity.

"Uncle Sol, I'm going to buy you a decent pair of glasses whether you like it or not. Maybe tortoise shell, those heavy, movie-producer kind."

"Thank you, but my own will do very well," Sol answered without looking up.

"Don't you want to look interesting, maybe like a man of destiny?" Joan said.

He just glanced at her with cold disdain.

"And Ivy League clothes? You have a big frame, you'd look just fabulous, Uncle Sol."

"Sure, Ivy League," Sol said with a thin smile. "Many of my customers wear the little caps with the buckle in the back." And he went on eating, wiping out the remains in his plate with a piece of bread, in a stilted imitation of unsatisfied hunger.

His retort had the power to cast a pall on their game; none of them liked to be reminded of where their money came from.

"Those *Shwartsas*," Bertha said in disgust. She always avoided telling people about her brother's business, feeling they would visualize some crafty old, hand-rubbing Yid with a big nose.

"Mother," Joan admonished.

"Please, Bertha," Selig said in pedagogical reproof. "You know I don't like to hear you refer to Negroes like that."

"Oh yes, I forgot," Bertha apologized. "*Negroes,* I mean." They were so intelligent and so liberal, her husband and her daughter. It seemed to be the style to be liberal nowadays. She really ought to keep up with things. Sometimes she felt like such a dope.

Suddenly her eye fell on her son, still eating silently and voraciously. She turned a half-guilty cruelty toward him, as though, with some compulsive pecking-order instinct, she knew he was the only victim for her there.

"And you, the big picture drawer, my *artiste*. You have nothing to say for yourself?" She waited a moment, watching how he ignored her, ignored all of them, his skinny, misanthropic face scowling at the food. Sometimes she felt she hated him; he embarrassed her deeply. "Couldn't be that we don't interest you?" There was no response from her son. "Look at you! Like an animal wolfing the food, scowling. I know why you got those pimples, that bad skin. It's your nature—you poison yourself."

"She's right, son," Selig said. "Maybe Mother is a little harsh on you, but the truth is that you just let yourself go. That attitude isn't going to make you an artist. A man needs some self-discipline no matter what his calling is."

"They're right, Mort," Joan said, as though she regretted the necessity of agreeing.

"Sometimes I'm ashamed for the neighbors," Bertha said. "My own son walking around, acting and looking like a bum."

Suddenly Morton jerked his head up and glared savagely around at them, as though just finding himself surrounded by enemies.

"Why the hell don't you all leave me alone?" he snarled, his sallow face desperate and defiant.

"Now, Morton!" Selig sat erect in spite of his delicate back. "That will be just about enough."

"Ah, there's a runt in every litter," Bertha said. "I don't know what I did to deserve . . ."

"Don't blame yourself, Mom," Joan said. "He's a neurotic. I honestly think it would be a good idea for him to pay a visit to an analyst."

Morton pushed away from the table and stood up, a rigid, aged-looking youth with brooding, dark-circled eyes. As a child he had had tantrums and used to spit at them.

He had no friends and stayed away from girls because he felt that if they ever insulted him he might be tempted to kill them. Several years before, his teachers had discovered his talent for drawing and, upon their advice and with his Uncle Sol's financing, he had been allowed to go to an art school, which he was still attending. Without the drawing and the painting, he sometimes thought, he might have considered suicide. He rarely thought about his uncle, only harbored a vague feeling of gratitude, not for his uncle's largesse, which was something they all shared in without gratitude, but rather because Sol was the only one who left him alone.

"All right," he said to them. "I can't take any more of this. You make me feel like vomiting everything I ate. Well, I'm sorry to spoil your fun, but I'm going upstairs. You'll have to find something else to crap on." He swept them with a final look of hatred before turning and leaving the room.

"Now I ask you," Bertha said to her brother, calling on the silent witness to her tribulation. "Can you blame me?"

Sol got up then, too, his head full of pain, the food leaden in his stomach. "Do not bother me with your squabbles, Bertha," he said. "Eat each other up, for all I care, but do not bother me! I will go upstairs now. I will shower and turn on my fan and then read until I sleep. My door will be closed. For my part, you can do what you want; do you understand?"

With that, he left the room, appreciating at least the silence he could impose on them when he displayed anger; *that* he had been able to buy from them.

In the private bathroom adjoining his bedroom, he stood under the cool shower with his eyes closed. The sound of the water drove their voices from his ears. He filled the glass-doored shower stall. The water, running over the puffy, inarticulate structure of his face, seemed to be dissolving his features. It ran over the bulky, subtly deformed body, the body he never looked at, with its peculiar unevennesses, its inexplicable collapses and thickenings. There was a piece of his pelvic bone missing, two of his ribs were gone, and his collarbone slanted in weird misdirection. Seeing him, one might wonder what kind of bizarre accident had malformed him so shrewdly, with such perverse design. But when he dried and covered himself with a robe, it became apparent that, by some coincidence (or queer design), each distortion had been compensated for by another, and nothing untoward showed in his clothed body except perhaps the careful awkwardness of his walk, in which he observed his delicate balance with each step.

For a long time he lay on his bed reading, beside the open window. The fan swung cool drafts on him; little billows of summer scent fell over his face, smells of flowers and cut grass. From the surrounding yards came voices, the clinking of glasses, the hiss of hoses and sprinklers. From above came the restless movements of his nephew, drawing or painting or just pacing out his sick and furious misery. It was all nothing to Sol Nazerman. He was reading *The Memoirs of Henri Brulard* in French and he made his brain dwell on the intricacies of a distant past.

When the light had been gone from his window for a long time and the crickets were as loud as the random sounds of the few people still outside in their yards, he laid the book down on the night table and turned off the light. Then he convinced himself that he was sleepy; it worked and very quickly, too, and he slept.

*His face was pressed against the wood. His eyes were in the open part between the slats of the cattle car. The plains of Poland moved by monotonously, almost repetitively, as though the train were still and the same landscape were being displayed over and over again. His son David squealed with a rodent sound of helplessness somewhere down near Sol's leg. "I'm slipping in it, Daddy, in the dirty stuff. I can't stay up." But what could he do about it? He was pressed into that one position by two hundred other bodies. So he studied the tidal landscape. Yes, it was the same view over and over. There, that house, low and black, with a broken stone chimney, he had seen that at least a dozen times. They were just standing still and, by some odd circumstance, the earth was being unrolled for their view. "Do something for him," his wife, Ruth, cried harshly beside him. She had little Naomi up against her chest, held there without her arms, for the crush of bodies held them all as in ice. "Sol, don't let him fall down in that! All our filth is down there. It would be terrible for him to lie in it!" Just moving his nose down an inch toward the carpeting of feces nauseated Sol. The child would turn his insides out. He tried to move a little more than his fingers, felt the soft, damp hair of David's head as it slid slowly downward. "I can't," he complained peevishly. "What do you expect of me? I cannot move a muscle." In the dim, slatted light he saw his wife's grim face. She seemed to hate him for all this. "But I can't, I can't. I can do nothing." His voice sounded flat and unconcerned and he tried to put more passion into it. "I am helpless, do you hear?" She continued looking at him with burning eyes and motionless features, like one of those startlingly lifelike wax figures. "I can do nothing." His voice still came out in the same dispassionate, soulless way. There came the sound of the boy at his feet making savage, empty retches, vomiting and slipping around in the bottomless filth. The roar of the train, the endless wailing of all the crushed people, and his wife's burning glass eyes in a waxen face. "Nothing, nothing, nothing," Sol shrieked in the awful din.*

The Pawnbroker moaned in his sleep without waking. No one stirred in the house; they were used to his noisy sleep.

## ❊ *T H R E E*

The morning was gray and cool, and the air, even along the
Harlem River, lay still and dense; nothing broke clear of the
edge-softening light. Sol looked at the numerous bridges,
flat against their increasing distances, and their various textures of steel and brick and concrete were as insubstantial as
drawings on tinted paper. He sighed heavily.

There seemed to be few people on the streets as he unlocked the store, and those few moved slower, too, as though
their vitality were reduced by the unreality of the light. For a
moment he believed some weird blight had carried off the
millions, and he made unnecessary noise with the iron
screens and slapped at the counters as he passed them. He
flicked on the fluorescents, and as he watched them shudder
into light he was startled by the voice.

"An' d'Lawd say, 'Let dere be Light.'" John Rider chuckled from the doorway, a more or less perpendicular figure in faded railroad denims and a high-crowned, long-beaked engineer's cap. "Good mornin', Sol. Hah, you shoulda seen you jump. Bad nerves, all you young fellas got bad nerves."

Sol's heart slowed from its brief tattoo; he managed a faint bend to his lips. "John," he said. No significance there; the old man came every other morning to sweep out or wash the floors or windows. Stop looking for omens.

"You late, Sol. I been waitin' across d'street a half hour now. Oversleep, hah? Ah, you youngsters, hell-raisin' all night, I know, I know. Den ya cain't shake youself out of bed in d'mornin'. Pay no heed to d'Book, that's d'trouble. Dere a time to sow an' a time to reap . . . a time to wuk an' a time . . ."

"Don't bother to wash the floor today, John. Just sweep out a little." Oh yes, I have been hell-raising all night, that is the truth.

*"Guten Morgen,* Sol. Hey, how's this for prompt? Not even eight thirty," Ortiz said, cat-walking in and then spinning around to stare back at the street. "Man, it's a funny day outside," he said with a sudden change of tone. "I got a feelin' we gonna be very quiet today; I got a feelin' a lot of people crawl off an' die someplace during the night."

Sol looked up at him. He felt the strange sensation of having his thoughts pried into.

But the ivory-dark face was bland and innocent, admitted to no trespassing. "Well, it give me a chance to catch up some more on them suits. I was talking to that George Smith, you know, that kook comes in here to talk to you sometimes. Got the hots for young girls, that guy, but he intelligent, too. I think he been to college one time. Well, anyway, he give me a idea over in the restaurant this morning. I tellin' him what I doing with the suits and all and he say I should *cross-index!"* He leaned over the counter, his eyes shining and provocative. And then, in spite of Sol's unmoved expression, he supplied his own motivation. "I make a list of the suits accordin' to size first. Then I make another list of all the suits accordin' to condition, and then I make a third list of all the suits accordin' to the type suit it is; like summer, or serge or gabardine. And on each list I refer to where it is on the other lists and like that. Pretty soon I can put my finger on a suit, just the one I want, quick as a flash." He stood grinning before Sol's little cage, triumphant and pleased with himself, his teeth whitely perfect in the smooth tawny face, his own medal of accomplishment, perfect and delicate, like something carved by a dreamer.

"All right," the Pawnbroker said, his voice rough and old. "If it's quiet, you can fool with that. Just don't make too big a project. There are other things besides that, you know." He was huge and ugly, and he wished his ugliness to pierce the smallest of dreams. And there *were* other things besides that lovely ordering and tabulating, that creating; there were grubbier, more joyless things, which his business depended on. "I want you to go over the junk in the cellar, too; see what we have for auction next month. There's all kinds of filth down there. I want you to get to that when you finish with your playing upstairs."

For a moment Ortiz's face hardened. But his plans had deep roots, could survive mere words. "Oh, that cross-index going to increase efficiency. You gonna thank me. You get busy, don't hesitate to call on your-friend-and-mine, Jesus Ortiz. I'm available." He smiled again, and Sol couldn't look at his smile.

"In d'sweet bye an bye," John Rider crooned, following the dirt out to the sidewalk behind his wide push-broom, "We will meet on dat beautiful shore."

Sol had an idea it *would* be quiet that day. Clairvoyance? Well, not to dignify it with scientific jargon, but there were things you anticipated with illogical confidence. Never important things, useful things, just little moods and colors. You walked down a certain road and as you approached a farmhouse you *knew* there would be a smooth-skinned beech tree heavy with leaves. Things like that, never things that saved you any pain. Ah, he didn't know whether he preferred it quiet or busy. His customers oppressed him, but then, he oppressed himself, too. "The menopause," he said, shaking his head with sour humor.

Half the clocks read ten when the woman came in. He looked up, and his impassiveness showed a few cracks. She didn't look like his kind of customer. Still, you got all kinds; he had had them in here with mink coats on, too. She had shiny sandy hair, an immaculate full face, the clear, forward blue eyes of a woman at home in her own country; an *American* face.

"Madam?" he queried with stony courtesy. She had nothing with her to pawn. Perhaps she had seen something in the window she wished to buy. Someplace, buried in the New York ordinances, there was something forbidding you to sell retail in a store where things were taken for pawn; no one observed it. "Is there something I can do for you?"

"How do you do. My name is Marilyn Birchfield." She seemed to flaunt her health in her even smile, and held her hand out like a man. "I'm introducing myself around among the merchants. In a sense, I'm a new neighbor."

Sol touched her hand uneasily; he could never get used to the aggressive confidence of some American women. What were they trying to prove, that they were as good as men? Well, that was no great accomplishment. "You are in business around here?" he asked.

"You might say that." She was a heavy-set woman, in her early thirties, he guessed, yet she moved her rather thick body with an adolescent awkwardness, a sort of touching, coltish animation quite different from the movements of a stout matron. "Actually, I'm with the new Youth Center down the block. I thought I'd just make myself known to the local merchants and perhaps get some kind of help, support, you might say, in certain activities. Some of the merchants have become sponsors of the children's teams, contributed both money and time to the Center."

"I see," he said, not seeing at all, fascinated, rather, by the fantastic shine and color of her. Where did they get skin like that, so pink and gold, so *healthy?* You couldn't imagine anyone who looked like that ever dying.

"I'll tell you, quite frankly, your business provokes my curiosity more than any of the others. Actually, I don't know a thing about pawnbroking. I'm sure there must be several pawnshops in my own home town, but until I came to New York I never even noticed them. It's just that I'm so interested in my children's environment, and the pawnbroker is apparently an integral part of their landscape and . . . Oh, here I go again, talking like a house on fire as usual. I suppose I shouldn't have burst in on you like this."

He nodded, slightly stunned by her.

"To get down to it, Mister . . ."

"Wha . . . Oh, Nazerman, Sol Nazerman."

"Mr. Nazerman," she said, with a wide smile. "What I would like is your permission to put you down as a tentative sponsor. Later on we can decide just what you would be willing and able to give or do. Oh, you might see your way clear to backing one of the teams, supplying uniforms and the like. Or perhaps you would be interested in devoting your time, perhaps an evening a week at the Center, directing some activity. Have you had any experience with basketball, or possibly one of the crafts?"

For a moment he was only able to shake his head in confusion. She was such a medley of sunlight and tawny pink skin. But then he was reminded of himself again.

"Look here, Miss . . ."

"Birchfield," she supplied. "Now you don't have to make up your mind right away. Perhaps you'd like to think about it. I just thought I'd introduce myself around, like a neighbor." She smiled into his surliness; it was part of her self-discipline. "That's always the hardest part for me. I find myself getting very tense when I have to solicit people. Oh, I would have made a miserable saleswoman."

"I wouldn't say that," he said sourly.

"But then, we all have to do things alien to our nature sometimes," she went on. "Anyhow, I think it's important for me to know all about the climate my children live in."

"Wait a minute, Miss Birchfield, hold on. This is a lot of talk. Forgive me if I try to simplify it according to my experience. If you are looking for some kind of handout, all well and good. I am solicited every day in the week; I am used to it. Tell me how much and I will answer you straight out. Otherwise, all the other, I have no time or inclination for it."

Her smile faded. She looked oddly like a child in spite of her full, matronly body and the little lines around her eyes; as an old woman, she would have that look, he guessed, an expression of credulity and unmanageable innocence.

"I don't think of these contributions as *handouts,* Mr. Nazerman. I'm sorry you do. I think what people can do for these children is, in a sense, for themselves, too—an investment in their own future."

"I am not concerned with the future."

She looked at him questioningly. "I don't understand. . . ."

"There is no sense talking about it. Let us deal on my terms, if you please. You are soliciting me. You have a job with the city, you work with the children, collect money for them, whatever. Fine, you do your job, let me tend to mine. I am willing to, how they say, 'kick in.' I am used to it, as I have said. Just tell me how much."

Her mouth tightened a little and there was a barely perceptible whitening under her scrubbed, bright skin. A Yankee, brave and stubborn and stupid, he thought with a scorn that held a bare trace of admiration.

"Let me say this then, Mr. Nazerman; I'll take any amount you're willing to give, regardless of the spirit in which it is given. I'm quite willing to sacrifice my personal feelings, because I know the money will be well spent." She took out a little pad of receipts with the imprint of the Youth Center on top, made a great show of impersonal efficiency about taking out a ball-point pen and ejecting the little nib. But then her demeanor failed her. "I'm still new at this. Perhaps you can tell me if I will meet such heedlessness often. You, for example, do you think the worst of everyone?"

"See here, Miss Birchfield," Sol said heatedly, "I resent having to explain to you. I do not wish to get involved in a philosophic argument first thing in the morning. But I will be as gracious as I can. I will explain. They are always coming around to me, collecting; phony nuns, people jingling cans with a slot on top and holding the can around so I can't see who they are supposed to be collecting for, blind men with twenty-twenty eyes, deaf ones who could hear the tumblers in my safe when I dial the combination. This is my experience, and much more. So, on this basis, I say, why not you?" Her face was beginning to irritate him; he had outgrown that kind of face.

"All right, why not me?" she agreed, with that peculiar stubbornness. "If you will give me something, then . . ." She held her hand out, her face flushed with embarrassment. And when he silently put a five-dollar bill in her hand, his eyes challenging, as though looking to see what change would be wrought by the touch of the money, she smiled rigidly. "There, you see I have no pride, Mr. Nazerman. And since you have been so co-operative, I will be back again and again." The smile twitched off, then came on again, for courtesy was an instinct with her.

"I will look forward," he said as she wrote out the amount on the little receipt and handed it to him. She gave him no answer, but walked her schoolgirl heaviness out of the store, leaving behind only a thin scent of sweetness that seemed to irritate his nostrils.

She had added to the peculiarity of the day. Something dug into him just under the skin, not steadily, not even with real pain. Rather, it was like some small sliver of rusty recall, a thing that made itself felt only in occasional moments, as though brought on by movements for which he could find no pattern or consistency and so could not avoid.

Customers began coming in, not as many as the day before, but enough to keep him occupied and many of these seemed anonymous to him, cast as he was in the strange daze.

Tangee came in alone. He had an electric drill to pawn. "Make me a offer, Uncle," he said, flashing an absent grin as he ran his eyes greedily over the store. He wore a shiny black silk suit and a harlequin-patterned tie of black and red which seemed to glow electrically. "No reasonable offer refuse . . ." Tangee's face was toward Sol but his eyes were a few inches to the left of Sol's head. It gave the Pawnbroker an odd sensation, a feeling that someone was behind him.

He turned, embarrassed for his instinct. He almost cried out; Jesus was close enough to him to touch.

"What are you pussyfooting around here for?" he shouted in the irritation of shock. But his assistant stared past Sol, too, as though affected by the same cast of eye as Tangee. He was looking directly into the eyes of Tangee, and in the seconds before Ortiz found a smile and moved it to the Pawnbroker's face, Sol had the feeling that he was invisible to the two of them.

"I was on my way to the cellar, figured to get at it now," Ortiz said. "I got it going pretty good upstairs, pick up where I left off any time." He darted a swift, expressionless glance at Tangee again, said, "What do you say, man; how they going?" and then slipped into the back room and down to the cellar.

Sol turned back to his customer. "Three dollars," he said as he pulled the drill toward him. His face was taut and harried looking, and Tangee smiled at the sight of him.

"Ain't you even gonna try it, see it works?" he asked with heavy-lidded amusement.

"Oh, I trust you implicitly," Sol answered. "You want the three dollars, take it. Otherwise do not waste my time, I have things to do." He found he had to hold his arm rigid against a sudden trembling.

"Okay, man, calm down. Three dollars fine. *Relax* Uncle, take it slow." He shifted his shoulders under the extravagant padding, cast another chillingly covetous look at the tawdry treasures all around, and then swaggered out.

Sol heard him call cheerily to the old man, John Rider, out on the sidewalk with the boxes of wastepaper he was bringing up from the outside cellar entrance.

"Take care, dad, don't strain your nuts now, hear?"

And the thin, preacher-voice of the old man answered, "Slothfulness casteth into a deep sleep an' a idle soul shall suffah hungah."

In the rich, heedless laughter of Tangee, the Pawnbroker shivered and felt old and put upon. And, aged that much more, he looked up at his next assailant.

George Smith had the face of an old Venetian doge, the features drawn with a silvery-fine pencil, the excesses reproduced in the shallowest, most subtle of creases. Only his eyes mirrored the wrestling starvation. He carried a rather dented, battery-powered hurricane lamp which Sol recognized as having been in for pawn several times before.

Sol offered him a dollar and waited with the patience that was a habit between them for George to ponder the offer with elaborate thoughtfulness; it was the preface to the conversation he intended. George Smith would have paid the Pawnbroker outright for a half-hour's talk except that it would have violated that frail diplomacy he practiced, and which the Pawnbroker countenanced for some unknown reason.

"A dollar, well . . . I don't know," he said in his diffident, gentle voice. His growth had been twisty and far darker than his skin color, and his surface was a strenuously polished, brittle thing. In here, he buffed that surface to a bright gleam, which blinded even himself to the mutation he was. "It's really worth considerably more," he said, checking the Pawnbroker's face cautiously against the rules of the game.

"Well, George, I don't know. . . ."

"I *would* like at least three dollars for it," George said, trying not to demonstrate too much enjoyment while he looked around at the stock, as though he found himself in some great, rich citadel. At one time he had attended a Negro college in the South, but too many twistings and turnings had been engraved in him and he had been expelled from there after a discreetly hushed outrage. Now he worked in the post office, read many fine books in his room at night, and abandoned himself to fantastic dream-ravishing of young boys and girls. Thank the books and the towering aspiration of his intellect for the fact that, so far, his rapes were confined to his dreams. Thank the weekly visits to the Pawnbroker for the nourishing of his wistful discipline. Sol had appeared to him one day three years before, when he had been wandering in a maddened daze of lust, had answered him in that heady language he had formerly encountered only in the books, had thus lent a reality to words he had been losing contact with. Every few days he brought a token article for pawn, and Sol Nazerman had been unable to deny him that, had, in spite of a deep exasperation, played the strange, sad game with the frail Negro, as though it were some unwelcome yet necessary tribute he paid.

"I might go to two dollars, tops," he said tiredly.

"Well . . ." George allowed a decent interval and then gave a smile of casual reminiscence. "Say there, Sol, just in passing," he said with offhand ease, "I just happened to be reading that 'Genesis of Science'—Herbert Spencer. You probably know it."

"I read it in the German when I was in Paris, while I was waiting for a visa," Sol said thoughtfully, leaning hard upon his hands for patience. "A good book, as I remember it."

"I'll say *good*," George emphasized with too much enthusiasm. "I particularly got a kick out of what he says when he points out that science arose from art. He says, 'It is impossible to say when art ends and science begins.' Now to me that is a very refreshing thing to come from a man whom a lot of modern thinkers find old-fashioned." His thin-skinned, self-scored face pressed close to the barred cage. "That supports what we were talking about last time. You remember how you said the scientists try to make themselves so aloof, so far above the so-called *soft-headed* artists?"

"Spencer did not come up with anything really new. Thinking people knew of that a good six centuries before Christ," Sol said, tinkering with the hurricane lamp, the symbol of the transaction that made their exchange tolerable. The lamp only glowed dimly each time he switched it on. "You may know that Pythagoras was a great lover of music. In fact, he made the discovery that the pitch of sound depends on the length of the vibrating string."

"It goes without saying. All the great scientists have had imagination and emotion. I mean, they are not mechanics." George chuckled with the mellow exultation of someone responding to a glass of wine. "Particularly in philosophy— there you see where the two fields overlap."

"Socrates was really on the borderline of drama," Sol said, running his eyes over the ledger for appearance's sake. Appearance for whom? For George Smith or Sol Nazerman? What was the difference? So he gave the poor beast a few minutes of talk!

"I wouldn't be at all surprised if his philosophy wasn't an

outgrowth of the Greek drama, a direct outgrowth. Why Herbert Spencer goes on to say . . ."

The Greek drama! What was all this, a madhouse? And yet he let himself form words that made brilliant sense to the incubus-ridden creature before him.

And in spite of everything, their talk created a small, faintly warming buzz in the pawnshop. It did nothing to disturb or alleviate the abandoned wreckage of the stock; nothing profound or original was arrived at, no conclusions were even dared. Just so might the conversation of two prisoners talking late at night in their cell ease the talkers; because of nothing more than the sounds of another voice that did not importune or demand. Only, perhaps, the burned spirit of the colored man was warmed in the bright, myriad reflections of the big names and words, and possibly also, in some lesser, more remote way, the consciousness of the rock-colored Pawnbroker, who put a proper face on their vagary all the while by thumbing in a businesslike fashion through the big ledger.

Until finally a point was reached beyond the Pawnbroker's discretion. Someone outside studied the assortment of cameras and musical instruments in the window, threatened to come in to buy. Sol, all business again, wrote out the record of their transaction, put the lamp under the counter, and solemnly gave George Smith the ticket. George studied the little piece of cardboard with a regretful yet hopeful sigh, knowing his visit was over beyond appeal; but knowing, too, that he had at least the rain check for another time.

Some minutes after he had gone, a curse of anger and pain erupted from the lips of the Pawnbroker. "That damned fool with all his talk—crazy *Shwartsa* bastard! What does he want from me?" And all of it was no more than a whisper, so that Jesus Ortiz only turned curiously toward the sibilance for a moment on his way out to get their lunches.

In the evening, Ortiz took his pay from Sol's hand and then stood blowing dreamily over the edges of the bills.

"I got a uncle lives out in Detroit," he said, staring now at the sleeve that covered Sol's tattoo. "He been in business for forty years—clothes he sell. My old lady tell me that man solid as the Rock of Gibraltar in that town. All the time he plow the profit back in, get better capitalize all the time. They have race riots, depressions out there, but that business of my uncle get stronger and stronger all the time, no matter what. The cops even call him Mister. He belong to merchant organizations and all. He got him a son 'bout my age, and that kid in the store gonna get it all when my uncle kick off. See, that business make him *solid*. Hey, like a king a little, pass his crown on down to the kids. My mother tell me we was out there to visit when I was around four years old. I *think* I remember him; it's hard to tell. I seen pictures of him so I don't know if I remember seein' *him* or just *seem* like I do from all the times I look at his picture." He snatched his eyes from the empty space and took a deep, resolute breath. "I'm gonna get me a business, I got that in mind for sure," he said almost fiercely to Sol. "All I need is the money, the goddam loot!" He flicked contemptuously at the little sheaf of bills and then put it into his pocket.

"Save your pennies," Sol said with all the warmth of a carnival shill.

"I gonna do that, Sol," he said with a level, ruthless stare. Then his face performed that mimelike change to smile. "Anyhow I learnin' something about business from a master, meantime." His eyes were flat with his undeniable curiosity, and there was something reminiscent of Tangee's dissecting gaze as he looked at Sol. "Tell me one thing," he demanded in a voice shaded by whispering intensity. "How come you Jews come to business so natural?"

Sol looked at him with harsh amusement.

"How come, how come. You want to steal my secret of

success, hah. Well, *Jesus,*" he said ironically, "I will do you a favor; it is part of my obligation to you as an apprentice. Really it is very simple. Pay attention, though, or you may miss something."

Jesus held out against the stinging humor for whatever might slip from his employer's scornful monologue, his eyes as clear and receptive as those of a cat searching the dusk for nourishment.

"You begin with several thousand years during which you have nothing except a great, bearded legend, nothing else. You have no land to grow food on, no land on which to hunt, not enough time in one place to have a geography or an army or a land-myth. Only you have a little brain in your head and this bearded legend to sustain you and convince you that there *is* something special about you, even in your poverty. But this little brain, that is the real key. With it you obtain a small piece of cloth—wool, silk, cotton—it doesn't matter. You take this cloth and you cut it in two and sell the two pieces for a penny or two more than you paid for the one. With this money, then, you buy a slightly larger piece of cloth, which perhaps may be cut into three pieces and sold for *three* pennies' profit. You must never succumb to buying an extra piece of bread at this point, a luxury like a toy for your child. Immediately you must go out and buy a still-larger cloth, or two large cloths, and repeat the process. And so you continue until there is no longer any temptation to dig in the earth and grow food, no longer any desire to gaze at limitless land which is in your name. You repeat this process over and over and over for approximately twenty centuries. And then, *voilà*—you have a mercantile heritage, you are known as a merchant, a man with secret resources, usurer, pawnbroker, witch, and what have you. By then it is instinct. Is it not simple? My whole formula for success— 'How to Succeed in Business,' by Sol Nazerman." He smiled his frozen smile.

"Good lesson, Sol," Jesus said. "It's things like that make

it all worth while." All right, you are a weird bunch of people, mix a man up whether you holy or the worst devils. I figure out yet what's behind that shit-eatin' grin. "I thank you for the lesson, boss, oh yes. So much better listenin' to you than goin' out for the quick dollar. I can't hardly wait for tomorrow's classes." He whirled around like a dancer, at least capable of that reminder, that taunt of his grace and youth. "You all heart, Solly, all heart," he said over his shoulder as he sauntered out with his leopard walk in the cold light of Sol's smile.

"Go, *Jesus,* go in peace," the Pawnbroker murmured, his hand resting on the phone, which he expected to ring at any moment.

And that pose, which might have suggested only arrested motion in anyone else, in him had a different connotation. One hand extended to the phone, the other on the counter, he was like one of those stilted figures in old engravings of torture, hardly horrible because of its stylized remoteness from life; just a bloodless, black-and-white rendition, reminiscent of pain.

The policeman Leventhal found him like that.

"*Vas macht du,* Solly? Where's all the business? Slow today, I bet. Seemed like the whole damn city was out of town."

He ignored Sol's silence, began roving around the store, touching things lightly with the tip of his club. "Boy, the stuff you got here." He shook his head in exaggerated awe. "These shines buy stuff at the drop of a hat. They got the newest cars, the latest models of television. Easy come, easy go. They buy on installment and end up here with it; you get it all. It's a good business. Hey Solly," he said, looking up with an idea on his gross face, "my wife been looking for an electric mixer. You got one here?"

Sol nodded and bent down to a low shelf where several appliances stood in the dust. "I got here a Hamilton Beach, last year's model."

"Hey, that would be great. How about billing me for it?" Leventhal said, pulling it possessively over to him.

"This is a cash business," Sol answered.

"Ah, I'll pay you when I get my check. How much is it?"

"To you, nine dollars. Come in when you have the money; I'll reserve it," Sol said impassively as he pulled the mixer back and returned it to the low shelf.

Leventhal's face went hard but he bent his mouth in a minimal smile to cover the shock of his anger. "Okay, Solly, you do that." He slapped his palm menacingly with his club and began looking around the store with narrowed eyes. Suddenly he noticed the lawn mower. "Who the hell would have a brand-new power mower around here? I think I'll just mark down the serial number, if you don't mind."

Sol shrugged; he felt a sardonic amusement. Here he was in the classic role of the interrogated again, and Leventhal was playing the part of the oppressor. It was getting confusing; soon you wouldn't know the Jews from their oppressors, the black from the white.

"It's not on the list; otherwise, I can't know," Sol said, his palms out in caricature.

"Okay, Solly, okay for now. Just keep your nose clean."

Sol raised his eyebrows at the familiar warning.

"And keep in mind what I said about staying open so late. There's been a couple of stick-ups in the neighborhood. I wouldn't want my landsman to get hurt now, would I?"

Sol nodded. "I will keep it in mind," he said, and watched the uniformed figure stroll out of the store.

And then the phone rang.

"It's me, Uncle," said the recorded voice.

"That Savarese didn't come in today," Sol said.

"No? Well that's all right, I'll take care of that," the lifeless voice of Albert Murillio said. "He will be in tomorrow. Nothing else new?"

"Nothing important. That cop, Leventhal, is nosing around for a handout. He would like to make trouble."

"Leventhal?" There was metal laughter. "That son of a bitch. He don't know what's going on. Don't worry about *him*."

Sol agreed in silence; there was never any small talk on his end of their conversations.

"Okay then, Uncle, look for Savarese tomorrow. Otherwise, keep your nose clean. I'll be in touch." And then the voice was gone.

So that was where Leventhal picked up his phrase. They were all around him like so many guards.

He kept the store open until eight thirty out of a childish feeling of spite against someone unnamable. It was a perverse thing, too, for he was unnaturally tired and shaky-feeling.

As he moved about doing petty, unnecessary chores, he sensed the beginning of a deep, unlocalized ache, a pain that was no real pain yet but only the vague promise of suffering, like some barometrical instinct. No one came in, and only occasionally did a person pause outside before the windows jammed with merchandise. As he fumbled needlessly with papers that suddenly resembled bits of ancient papyrus loaded with hieroglyphics, he forced plausible reasons on himself for that odd oppression. In little fragments of unspoken words, he told himself that he might be coming down with some minor disease, that he was overworking and hadn't been getting enough sleep, that he was going through a *phase*.

> *I grow old . . . I grow old . . .*
> *I shall wear the bottoms of my trousers rolled.*

He chuckled hoarsely, and the sound of his voice shocked him. I think I will go over to Tessie tonight. Yes, that is what I will do. "All right, all right," he said aloud, as though to someone's urging. And he gave in then to the sudden failure of his body. He closed and locked and bolted, and put the heavy screens over the windows. Then he walked toward the subway that would take him to Tessie Rubin's apartment. As he walked, he had the feeling he had narrowly escaped one thing and was now treading precariously the edge of countless other dangers.

And as he descended the grimy steps of the subway, it seemed as if the gray, humid air fell on him like a solid, crushing mass, so that even the roar of the buried train was a sound of escape.

Tessie Rubin opened the door to Sol and gave him access to a different kind of smell from that of the hallway of the apartment house. The hallway, with its tile floors and broken windows, smelled of garbage and soot; Tessie's apartment gave forth the more personal odors of bad cooking and dust.

"Oh, it's you," she said, opening the door wider. The immediate apprehension on her yellowish face settled down to the chronic yet resigned look of perpetual fear. "That Goberman has been bothering me for money. He curses—imagine—*curses* me for not giving money to the Jewish Appeal. Is that any way to get charity from people, to curse!"

Sol walked past her, down the hall whose walls were so dark and featureless that they seemed like empty space.

"He pockets it himself," he reassured her as she followed him to the living room.

"He's a devil is what he is. Says to me, 'You of all people should contribute to saving Jewish lives.' What does he want from me, blood? Can't he see how I live? Maybe he doesn't know I don't have a single penny in the house. Every week he comes, and when I give him something he looks at it like it's *dreck*. 'Is this what you call a contribution?' he says. What does he want from me, I'm asking you." She fell wearily into an armchair which leaned swollenly to one side under its faded cretonne covering, like an old sick elephant under shabby regal garments. She had a large, curved nose, and her face was very thin; there were hollows in her temples, and her eyes, stranded in the leanness of all the features, were exceptionally large and dismal. She threw her arms outward, splayed her legs in exhaustion: their thinness was grotesque, because her torso was heavy and short, with huge breasts. "Why doesn't he look around how I live? How can he think I'm a Rothschild, a Baruch! Maybe he should know that I made bread soaked in evaporated milk for supper for me and the *alta*."

"I gave you fifty dollars last week. Why bread and milk?" Sol said angrily as he reclined on the sofa, which was as shapeless as the chair she sat on.

"Why, why! I had to have the doctor twice for him, the old man—*house calls*. Ten dollars each time."

"So, thirty dollars in five days. Not a fortune, but you should have more than bread and milk from it."

"Oh, I go crazy, too, you know. So I took in one little movie, so I bought one little house dress I shouldn't walk around with holes showing. It's a crime?" She glared at him savagely, as though to make up for her unaltered position of repose.

Sol waved his hand to dismiss the subject. "I'll leave you a few dollars before I go. Remind me." He turned his head toward the doorway that led to the two bedrooms. "How is he, the old man?"

"Eh, he lives. How can he be?"

Sol nodded and slid lower on the couch, so that he was lying almost horizontal. He exhaled slowly through his teeth and crossed his arms over his eyes. The ugly grotto of the room permeated him with all its stale, musty odors; and yet oddly, as always, his body went limp with relaxation. He heard Tessie sighing quietly across the small room, seemed to see, even through his covering arms, the crowding, unattractive mementoes she had reclaimed or imitated from her past life: a brass samovar, a twin-framed ornate picture of herself and her late husband, Herman Rubin, a brown depressing tapestry which depicted a waterway in Venice, a fluted china plate teeming with iridescent-green tulips, a picture of her father and her mother in the frozen poses of a half-century ago, an oval-framed portrait of a fat-faced child with slightly crossed eyes—her late son, Morris. The sink in the kitchen leaked steadily, not drops, but in a persistent trickle. From above came the sound of many footsteps, the heavy ones of men and women, the dance of the young. The old man groaned in the bedroom, called out a complicated Yiddish-Polish curse, and then subsided into high, womanish moans, which gradually diminished to little respiratory grunts. There was a smell of sour milk and cauliflower and an all-pervading odor of sweat, as though the building were a huge living creature. Gradually, Sol's body lightened, his breathing came more deeply and regularly. He lay there listening to the sound of his body drifting toward sleep, observing the numbing peace of his limbs, until he slept, deeply and peacefully.

When he woke he couldn't remember where he was for a moment. The room was dark except for the thick beam of light cast on the floor from the kitchen. He lay without moving, listening to the clattering of pots and pans, savoring the nerveless ease of his body.

"Vat is to eat? *Ich bin kronk.* I need strength, *kayach,*" the old querulous voice said. "I eat bread and milk and you . . . vat do you hide and eat ven I sleep? Hah, vat—lox and herring, some juicy smoked fish? *Ich bin kronk, dine aine tata.* You would starve me. Ah, it is all up vit me," he whined.

"Shh, you will wake him, let him sleep. He is so tired, that man, he needs to sleep. I took some money from his pocket and bought some nice fresh eggs, some cream cheese. You like cream cheese, Pa," she said.

"I dream about smoked butterfish. Why can't we have smoked butterfish?" the old man complained.

"I'll fry the eggs hard, the way you like them," the woman's voice said. "Just don't talk so loud, please. He gets his best sleep here."

Sol lay without moving. The smell of the frying eggs came to him, the sounds of the other people in the building. All around him life of various sorts, stone hollowed out and filled with the insect life of humans, the whole earth honeycombed with them. In another pocket of stone or brick or wood, Jesus Ortiz, Morton, George Smith, Murillio, billions. Insects ruining the sweet, silent proportions of the earth. Undermining, soiling, hurting. Where was the gigantic foot to crush them all? Where was blessed silence? Footsteps, pots clanking, voices of strangers, of the old man, the woman in the kitchen. He drifted off to explore a last little void of dreamless sleep.

"Sol, Sol, wake up. I have supper. Come, before it gets cold."

He peered up at her gaunt, bleak face. She nodded to tell him he was awake; she had much experience with the violated borders between reality and dreams, knew enough to take the time to reassure a sleeper. "Eggs and rolls, coffee. Yes, yes, it is only Tessie . . . come."

Slowly he unrolled himself, sat up, then stood. She touched his arm, and he followed her. In the kitchen, the old man shrugged at him.

"Hello Mendel," he said.

"Sure, sure," the old man said bitterly. "What do they

care? Yeh, don't esk qvestion, it's a Jew—gas him, burn him, stick him through vit hot needles."

"Eat, Pa, while it's hot," Tessie said, looking at Sol over her father's head.

They sat down together at the porcelain-topped table. Sol reached for a roll, and Tessie poured coffee while the old man muttered the prayer over the food sullenly, his face like an arid relief map of some forgotten valley. He was seventy-five but he looked a hundred. He had many dents in his bald head, his nose was crushed; but he had been of durable stock, so he was still alive.

"Her husband died in Belsen," the old man said suddenly, pointing a crooked accusing finger at his daughter. "And vat they did to her, yes, yes. And she sits there like a *lady. Oy vay, ich bin zayer kronk.*" He began to weep and dab at his eyes.

"I know, Mendel. Stop that now. Let us eat in peace, for Christ's sake," Sol said. Mournfully, he himself began to eat, as though to set an example. Tessie shrugged and ate, too, with her eyes on the food. She had a tattoo similar to Sol's on the dead-white skin of her arm. The sink dripped, the neighbors pounded on the ceiling, shouted occasionally in Spanish or Yiddish. Someone screamed in the street, and a police siren sounded, going away from all of it. Here, Rubin, here is your lovely widow, your stately father-in-law; I watch over them for you, keep them in a manner befitting their station. Let your bones lie easy in the earth— you are missing nothing, nothing at all.

Finally they were through. Tessie herded the old man into his room and closed the door. She came back into the kitchen and cleared the dishes away. Sol went into the living room and sat down. He closed his eyes and waited. Soon he heard her come into the room and sit down beside him. He opened his eyes; the room was still lit only by the light from the kitchen. She looked at him with glittering, dismal eyes.

"So what do we have in this life?" she said.

"We have, we have. We live."

"I feel like screaming all day long. I feel like screaming myself to death," she said.

"But you don't and I don't and the old man doesn't. We live and fight off the animals."

"They're better off, the dead ones."

"I won't argue. I don't want to talk about it. It is ridiculous to talk about it. I don't feel so good the past week or two anyhow. Don't talk about nonsense."

"So I won't talk," she said.

They sat there in silence for about ten minutes, in the pose of two peaceful people seated on a cool veranda watching the country scene.

After a while she said, "Do you want to?"

"All right," he said.

She took off her dress in the dimness. He lay back on the couch. Finally she pushed her heavy, hanging breasts in his face and lay against him. "You're not too tired?"

He shook his head against her warm body, which smelled old. They turned into each other with little moans. And then they made love on the lumpy couch with the sounds of the old man's groaning madness in the other room, and there was very little of passion between them and nothing of real love or tenderness, but, rather, that immensely stronger force of desperation and mutual anguish.

When it was over, they said nothing to each other. After a few minutes, Sol got up and straightened his clothing. Then he took some money from his pocket and wedged it under the samovar. With his hand on the door, he spoke without turning.

"Maybe Monday, Tuesday I will come again," he said.

"What shall I do about that torturer Goberman?" she asked dully, expecting no illusion of grace from him. Her collapsed body lay wraithlike in the darkened room.

"All right, I will come Monday night. Tell Goberman to

come then, that you will settle with him then. I will be here, I will deal with him."

She sighed for answer.

He closed the door on her and her father; it was like administering a drug to himself, that closing of the door, an opiate locking off a corridor of his mind. He went out through the tiled hallway, with its smell of garbage and its resemblance to some ancient, abandoned hospital, until he was on the street, which was erratically lit and smoky with the increasing heat.

Then he walked like a man in a dream toward the subway, sagging with tiredness again at the prospect of the distance between him and his bed.

## ❋ F I V E

Mabel Wheatly hung on Jesus Ortiz's arm like a bride; he suffered her possessive embrace because it made him feel manly to walk through the crowd that way. The counterfeit exoticism of the dance hall, garish and frenetic, fell over them as they walked. There was a huge babble of voices, the feathery rustling of dresses. The savage farce of light that came from a rotating prism on the ceiling bathed Jesus and the girl in green, in red, in yellow, in blue. The orchestra crashed rhythmically, with a minimum of tune. Dark faces, white teeth, and fluttering clothes made a shifting corridor for them as they shoved their way along one side of the huge room toward an empty table.

Ortiz plunked the two bottles of beer on the table, and they sat. He scanned the teeming hall with cool, faintly bored eyes, liking the picture of them; him sitting like a man who had been around, Mabel half leaning over the table, holding his hand, her eyes fixed on him. Her expression was a naïve attempt at sultriness; it was her stock in trade, but also the only way she knew how to show emotion. She had on a dress of metallic green, cut low to reveal the tops of her full, brown breasts. Her face was softly curved, wide-nostriled, long-eyed; she offered the best of herself to her companion, but he sat in a sullen reverie, casting his eyes around for something he had no hope of finding there.

"You want to dance, hon?" she asked timidly, brushing her fingers against the back of his hand.

"Let's just sit . . . talk a while. I'm tired. That Jew had me working my *cojones* off all afternoon. Let's just talk," he said idly, his eyes everywhere but on her.

"What you want to talk about, honey?" she asked. She clung to him hungrily with her eyes, yearning toward some odd, bright cleanliness she imagined in him. Half consciously she saw a hope of escape in him. Not that she actually thought her prostitution was a bad way to earn a living. Only she became drugged with hopelessness at times, experienced boredom of such an intense degree, as she indulged the queer fears and lusts of her paying customers, that she had even considered suicide, and passed it by only because of some inexplicable curiosity about what the next day would bring. This boy was so cool, so sweet to look at. He seemed to know something, have some marvelous answer in him. "You got somethin' special in mind, sweety? What?"

"Talk?" He turned to her as though she had brought up the suggestion. "Well now, what could you and me have to talk? Business, you want to talk about what kind of business I should go into?" he said sarcastically. "You an expert or something? All right then, tell me. Should I go into the clothing business like my uncle in Detroit? Or tombstones, or baby carriages, or groceries, or . . . or a pawnshop?"

"Good money in that pawnshop business," she said, pretending he hadn't been teasing her with the question. "The Jew teachin' you that business, ain't he?"

"Yeah, he teachin'." Suddenly his eyes went hard with the gleam of desire. "Oh, if I had the f——g dough, the loot . . . "

"You serious about that business kick, ain't you, hon?" she asked, wondering how to connect herself with his desire.

"I'm serious."

She looked at him cautiously for a moment. "Could I maybe go in with you?" she blurted out.

He looked at her with scornful amusement.

"You sayin' how you need the money so bad. Well, what if I chip in with some? How would that be?"

He smiled and ran his fingers up her arm. He was flattered at being offered money by a whore. How many men got offers like that? Wasn't that evidence that he was a man among men?

"It might be; you never know, Mabel. I like you good enough, you a sweet baby to be with. Of course, I figure my plans for me alone, but you never know. You show me the money, and we could see."

"You see. I get me some money together, gonna start squeezin' for it. I don't want to do what I'm doin' forever either, you know. I get some *gifts,* extra, you know. I already got a load of stuff to hock. You see, honey, I gonna surprise you."

"Yeah, you do that, fine, fine," he said, searching the crowded hall. All around were the myriad, elusive colors, the thumping music entwined with the hundreds of voices and the whispering slide of the many dancers on the floor. The colors played over his delicate head like the reflection of all his fleeting ideas, of his strange, desperate daydreams. He was big and had hands of great brawny power, a face that was tough and brutal and inspired fear and awe; and everyone, himself included, knew his name, for it was graven on the wall of some huge and imposing edifice—JESUS ORTIZ.

Tangee and Buck White sat down at the next table. Tangee was with some strange woman, not his wife, a black, fulsome woman with purple lipstick. Buck White watched his wife shyly. She was a light-skinned girl of frail and tinselly beauty who demonstrated by her bored sullen expression that she had been bought by her slow-witted husband but that her price was going up, right before his despairing eyes.

"Hey man," Tangee called over. "How the pawnbrokin' business?"

"Makin' out," Jesus answered blandly.

"Aw listen to him, *makin' out!* That place *coin* money."

Jesus shrugged. "Ain't mine."

"Whyn't you and the gal come on over to sit with us," Tangee offered. "Be sociable."

Jesus looked at Mabel, then got up and went over. She followed him, a shy smile on her face. There was some shifting of chairs, little darts of smile.

"Billy an' Thelma, say hello to Jesus Ortiz an' . . . I didn't catch your gal's name. . . ." Tangee leaned over, the diplomatic link between all their dissimilarities.

"Mabel," Jesus said, and endured the giggling salutations, the embarrassed shifting of Buck, to whom amenities were complex and better avoided. Buck's wife, Billy, stared blatantly at Jesus over her conversation with the other two women, and Buck dreamed of the sacks of gold with which he could earn his wife's febrile attention.

"Now I been wonderin' somethin', Ortiz. I don't want you to take it bad. I'm just curious." Tangee looked at Jesus' small, hairless hands, with their delicate, thin fingers, and noted how he balled them up into little fists under his scrutiny. "How come a smart boy like you got to work in that pawnshop? I mean you used to have faster games than that. I happen to know you worked for that pusher, Kopey, one time. Even numbers a couple years ago. How come you go for that nigger job? What could you make—thirty, forty bucks? You just don't figure like for a janitor."

"That my business, Tangee."

"Okay, but it don't make no sense to me."

"I got my plans."

"Sure you do; ain't we all?" Tangee toyed with the ash tray, his eyes on the clenched, childish fists. After a decent interval, casually, he asked, "Say, tell me, that there pawnshop a goin' thing?"

"Much cash," Jesus said, staring hard at Tangee's face to force him off the study of his hands.

"Yes man, that what I thought," Tangee said. "That what Robinson say, ain't it, Buck? Just them same words, 'Much cash.' "

"He say like dat den when he . . . " Buck confirmed, stopping before the words got him out of his depth.

Billy White frowned disdainfully at her husband and began running her eyes from Jesus' hair to his mouth to his hands.

"It somethin' to think on, all that cash," Tangee said.

Jesus looked at him with a flat, unreadable expression while the orchestra pounded the beat on walls and floor, pulling at the smoky-sweet air so people's hands and feet followed the rhythm. The woman Thelma tapped her large, black hand and hummed indistinguishably. The turning prisms on the ceiling swung the phosphorescence of color over faces and bottles. There was, in all the hubbub, the clear sound of the three men's careful, speculative breathing.

"He's cute," Billy White said suddenly. They all turned to look at her. "I mean look at how cute he is," she said, gazing at Jesus' mouth. "Got a face like a girl. And look at his hands—pretty, like a girl's. I like fellas with like delicate hands and all."

Jesus felt his throat close, his whole body go rigid with fury and pain. All the hands seemed displayed on the table; Buck's mammoth ones, Tangee's, Thelma's, even Mabel's were slightly larger than his. Tangee smiled slyly. Buck just lifted his hands with mild amusement; he had never considered them before. Suddenly Jesus felt his arms twitch, as though pulled by someone. A glass turned over and fell to the floor without breaking. Mabel gave a little gasp, bent to pick it up, and then stopped, remembering some devious propriety.

"You just like fellas, period, Billy," Tangee said after a little laugh. But his own gaze followed the chiseled line of the Ortiz features, noted the lovely oversized eyes, the shapely lips, now compressed by some odd tension, and the hands bunched up at the very edge of the table. And his scrutiny was for something he could use, something perhaps too devious for him to seize on, but *there,* there all the same. "Don't pay her no attention, Ortiz; she just tryin' to embarrass you is all."

Jesus spread his mouth in a rigid smile and stared insolently at Billy. "Why, she like my type. That's no insult."

Buck stared at his new-found hands and began rubbing their knuckles together, his massive face perplexed, fermenting.

Jesus pushed back his chair and stood. "We got to cut out now," he said softly, the pale smile still in place. Mabel stood up with him.

"It somethin' to think about, all that cash," Tangee said.

"Well then, I think about it," Jesus answered. He gave a little wave to all of them. He looked at Tangee a moment longer, took the other man's veiled, suggestive expression, and returned it unopened.

"Maybe we talk some more, another time, Tangee," he said.

"That be fine if we do, *very* fine," Tangee said after them, and he watched Jesus' slender back with a flat yet avid gaze until it disappeared among the thronging men and women in a last reflection of blue and red from the prismatic light.

Mabel preceded him up the stairs to the Ortiz apartment. His mother would be long gone for her night job downtown, where she still worked as a scrubwoman in a big office building. They walked into the three-room apartment, and Mabel turned on the little radio while Jesus went into the kitchen with the bottle of gin he had bought. She hummed the tune as she waited, her eyes wandering absently over a familiar place, familiar in its resemblance to the ten thousands like it all over the city. She knew that Jesus and his mother had lived in a dozen different places in the last ten years, and that each flat was as like another as if they had all been the rooms of one gigantic house. Her gaze was uncritical of the paint-swollen walls, which were lumpy because of the many layers of pigment, as though poverty itself dented the rooms beyond any attempts at concealment. In one corner a little lantern flickered on a saccharine Mary, and farther away a gold-colored crucifix picked up the Mother's light. Shapelessness infected the modestly covered bed and the tired stuffed chairs. You sensed that the peculiar odor of poor living was somehow held slightly at bay by the desperate cleanliness of the woman who lived there. There was a picture of Jane Ortiz, Jesus' mother, a dark-skinned woman with pronounced Negroid features who smiled self-consciously, as though shy at the proximity to her husband in the twin frame. The father, long absent from their lives (Mabel had always been afraid to ask Jesus what had happened to him, well aware of his strange, inexplicable sore spots), looked almost white, a thin-nosed, narrow-lipped man with large, sensuous, slightly goiterous eyes like those of an ancient Spanish grandee.

"Here you go, Baby," Jesus said, handing her a glass full of gin with clumsily broken chunks of ice in it. He put the bottle down on the end table and sat beside her on the couch. There was a light in the kitchen, but the only light in the living room came from the little altar in the corner. The radio played a rock-'n'-roll tune, and Mabel hummed to it, occasionally inserting a string of words she remembered. Her head rested comfortably on his shoulder. Jesus sipped at the drink and stared at the dim colors reflected on the window shade from the scattered neons and street lights. Side-stepping his fearful rage, he placed himself on a great, flat plain with no one in sight, no house or tree, no rise of ground. And then he imagined himself approaching a great light in the earth, filled with an immense trembling excitement, not knowing the source of the light, moving toward it and wondering whether it would be fearsome or exalting.

"Penny for you thoughts, hon," she offered timidly, willing to go infinitely higher.

"Nazerman say to me one day, 'You know how old this profession is?' " His voice was soft and musing, almost as though he talked aloud to himself. "I say no, how old? And he say *thousands of years.* He say one time the Babylon . . . some crazy tribe, they use to take crops and even people for pawn. A man make loans on his family—wife, kid, anything. I mean you see what a solid business that is—thousands of years. Hard to think on thousands of years, people back then . . . " He laid his head back against the couch, his eyes burning at the dimness. His mind reeled at the succession of rooms he had lived in. He remembered, a thousand times multiplied, those few times his name had been doubted, his paternity jeered at. He recalled the hundred times he had experienced the same humiliation he had felt that same night when the woman had called attention to his delicate face, his small, girlish hands. His home, his name, his gender—all a tenuous, unproved thing. The world had no up or down for him; he floated disembodied in a dark void and he was forever clawing at the random things he passed, seeking a handhold, a mystical history. Only the Pawnbroker, with his cryptic eyes, his huge, secret body, seemed to have some sly key, some talisman of *knowing.*

"Only for the money. I learnin' that business, estimatin', figurin'. If I had me a bundle . . . " He turned to her, and she, mistaking his intention, opened her lips to him. "You got any idea what that Tangee hintin' at, back there in the dance hall?" he asked.

"He didn't say much of anything."

"He didn't *say*. But you know what that man is, who he hangs out with."

"He got that friend Robinson. I know *him*. You smart you don't get mixed up with that man. He's a ex-con, a real bad, bad man." She studied him for a moment and then lowered her eyes. "Yes," she said solemnly, "I do know what he getting at. But honey, you don't *need* to get in with them. I told you I gonna raise some money, and you save some here and there. Pretty soon you get it—safe!" She looked at him again, and her anxiety was not just for his welfare but for the threat to her contribution, her only possible claim on him.

"Sure, sure," he said blandly, excluding her once more with a covering smile. "Don't worry about a thing, sweety."

Then he pushed her back roughly and began fondling her thighs. The recent rage returned to him, and he demanded she forget how small his hands were by crushing her full breasts with them. He delighted in her groans of pain, saw himself as a great rutting male, for the while, in his assumed brutality. She cried out many times, "I love you, I love you, I love you," ecstatic in the glamour of the unpaid-for love-making she endured under her unfathomable lover.

And later, while she sighed wistfully and cast about in her mind for sudden wealth with which to ensnare him, Jesus puffed on a cigarette as he lay, thoughtfully blowing his scrambling dreams at the ceiling in dim clouds of smoke.

Maybe I have a tumor, Sol thought with bitter amusement. He tried to visualize that peculiar knot of pressure, tried even to localize it. It would seem to be here, just below the breastbone and then . . . up here near his neck . . . no, more toward his back and down. . . . For a moment he thought of death, that old companion of his youth. Ortiz feather-dusted quietly, and he watched him. That sourly anticlimatic joke; it only made him feel cold, not fearful at all.

"Mail this on the corner," he said.

Ortiz took the envelope and studied the address.

Sol sighed mildly. "Just mail it, will you," he said. "Don't waste time. Maybe when you get back I'll tell you a few things, give you a *lesson* in pawnbroking. You are always after me to."

Ortiz smiled and walked swiftly out on his errand. Sol studied his debts while he was waiting. He made a dozen small calculations which proved he didn't make enough money to pay all his bills. Then he just let the pencil meander over the paper in small, amoebic doodles until his assistant returned.

"All right. That thing you just mailed was the list of yesterday's hocks, the things I loaned money on."

The eager acolyte leaned on the counter, his eyes on the Pawnbroker's mouth, all of him narrowed to that mundane information. It occurred to him that great secrets could come from tiny perforations, inadvertently. He must be patient and receptive.

"All the information about an item of jewelry, for example, must be on that list; the amount loaned on it, the complete description. In describing a watch, you must have the case and movement numbers, the size, any unusual markings, any engraved inscriptions. In jewelry, you use the loupe to . . ."

The store creaked under the grotesque weight of its merchandise, and the air was respectful of the teacher's voice. No customers came in; the street in front of their doorway seemed deserted and even the traffic sounded distant. It seemed to Jesus that all the city found the time suddenly hallowed, and he offered himself to the Pawnbroker's dark, indrawn voice with an unconscious sensation of privilege.

"To find the purity of gold in something, up to fourteen karat, you scratch a tiny mark. I say *tiny* in the ethical sense. Actually, this is an area for dishonest profit, too; the filings from a year's gougings can add up to a pretty penny. Anyhow, you drop nitric acid on the scratch. If there is brass, you will get a bright green, silver will show up a dirty gray, and iron will give you a blackish-brown color. Now if the gold is above fourteen karat, you must use these special gold-tipped needles and a touchstone. The acid we use for this is a secret to the trade. . . ."

"*Secret,* huh," Jesus echoed in a languid voice as the Pawnbroker gave him the barest outlines of the mysteries.

And it seemed to him that many things of great significance just lay in the quality of the big Jew's voice, that he might, at any moment, surprise the great complexity of his employer just in the ponderous breath that carried the droning words. Horror and exaltation seemed to reside in the Pawnbroker's mysterious history. Jesus Ortiz crouched in the imminence of revelation, oddly eased and enriched in the things beyond what he could form in thought, beyond what the older man said.

". . . so you must watch out for the professional confidence men, the gyp-artists. They are shrewd and practiced and they have a huge bag of tricks. In jewelry, for instance. Take a good-quality pearl which has been accidentally ruined by acid or sweat. The con man will peel the vital top layer to expose the second layer. This layer *will* have a similar appearance to the unspoiled pearl. For a few months! But then you will realize that you are stuck with a dull, worthless nothing. It is important to examine the apparently beautiful pearl, for only the original top layer is really smooth; the other layers are coarse by close comparison."

Sol's voice rolled on in the stillness, disdainful of this latter-day craft of his, echoing his vast bitterness for the things he had once considered important and which he now hated because in his loss of them he had been left deprived and ugly.

Yet, not knowing this (nor would he have cared if he had), the smooth-skinned youth with the sly, delicate face basked in his exposure to ancient, terrible wonders, things only faintly shaped by his scattered knowledge of the Pawnbroker's peculiar heritage, his strange survival of fantastic horrors. So he looked at the blue numbers on his employer's arm and tried to work back from that cryptic sum to the figures that had made it; and, more and more, he was involved in an odd current of emotions, softened and blinded and bound.

Until, finally, the Pawnbroker pushed at him almost gently and said, "Enough with the lessons. Get to work now, Ortiz."

And then, to make the severance complete, Mrs. Harmon came in with three suits; Jesus took them upstairs to the loft and went reluctantly back to his cross-indexing, which now must include Willy Harmon's two Sunday suits and the invalid younger Harmon's rare festive change. And Jesus Ortiz muttered about nothing, really cursing the elusiveness of the Nazerman spirit.

"Fee time at my Edith's secretary school," Mrs. Harmon said in her chuckling voice. Then she laughed out loud and shook her head in wonder at the precariousness of her life. "Man d'lifeboats again, another bill. Honest and true, it like bailin' out a leaky ol' boat fill with holes. Pawn somethin' to buy somethin' else, then pawn that. Each time it seem like the boat gettin' lower in d'water. Ain't it a *wonder* a body stay afloat long as it do?" She sighed at her ridiculous resignation. "But you do, somehow you do, one way or another. I declare, sometimes I don't know if the good Lord plan it all this way to test or if he jus' so busy he get to you again and again jus' in time to keep you from goin' under for the third time." And then her rich, imperishable laughter struck on all the objects in the place, stealing all their value by implying that nothing had value without human hands to coax life into it.

"Five dollars for the three suits," Sol said, feeling the buried pressure again. It sent a streak of apprehension through him; he recalled the power of a few blades of grass to grow through and split solid stone.

"I jus' ain't up to horse-tradin' today, Mistuh Nazerman. No use threatenin' to take my suits someplace else. Too tired to bother." She held out her hand for the money. As she buried the bills deep in the shabby purse, she muttered, "Jus' keep them ol' pawn tickets, these and the ones from the candlesticks, too. You an' me both know that what you bury might jus' as well stay dead." For a moment she looked at the gray, untouchable face of the Pawnbroker. "Ain't that right, Mistuh Nazerman?"

"I suppose it is," he answered, his face sightless and only coincidentally directed toward her.

Two women came in with wedding rings to pawn, apparently arrived at similar desperations at the same time. An old Orthodox Jew, wearing a long gabardine coat despite the heat, offered a tiny diamond stickpin; he argued feebly in Yiddish for a few minutes and then took the small loan with a little clucking noise. A Puerto Rican youth brought in a Spanish guitar and took the first price offered without a word; only he plucked a two-note farewell to the instrument on its own strings before abandoning it. A jet-black girl with the face of a fourteen-year-old and a pregnant body gave him her engagement "diamond," which was glass. The Pawnbroker sent her out with it in her hand, stunned and lost.

At noon a man with nut-colored skin and white hair came into the store. He walked over to the counter with an amiability that indicated he had nothing he wished to get a loan on.

"I'm Savarese," he said. He had black eyes and puffy, fighter's features. "I'm agonna giva you d'estimate."

"I expected you yesterday," Sol said.

"I wasa busy." He ran his eyes in mock appraisal over the store and grinned. "Well, after carefula study, I'ma estimate the complete redecoratin' gona costa you five G's."

"Who do I make the check out to?"

"Acame Contractin' Corporation," Savarese said, picking at his teeth with a toothpick.

"How do you spell it?"

"It'sa A C M E, *Acame!*"

As Sol began to write, Savarese looked furtively around for a moment, then silently took a thick envelope from his breast pocket and dropped it in front of the Pawnbroker. Sol pocketed it without looking up as he continued writing.

Savarese took the check from him with a parting chuckle.

"Give you a gooda job, Mr. Pawnabroker, paint the whole goddama place pink anda yellow."

Sol waved him away with the offhand gesture he would have used to brush a bug off the counter.

He opened the envelope, and the inside was greasy-green with money. Fifty hundred-dollar bills bulged out. As he stared dully at it, the steps behind him creaked. He turned quickly to see his assistant gazing innocently at the money.

"I guess Thursdays are paydays," Jesus said flatly.

"Mind your own business," Sol said. He took the money back to the huge safe and, hiding the combination with his body, locked it in. Later, as was his custom, he would take it to the night depository of the bank down the street.

A well-dressed woman, white with mortification, brought in a diamond watch. He loaned her ninety dollars on it, and she took the money with a little wince before hurrying out with the pawn ticket clutched in her hand.

"Now she not a virgin any more," Jesus said. "She been in to a pawnshop, sell her soul to the devil."

"I can do without your jokes," Sol said, involved with that peculiar kernel inside him. What was the matter with him, worrying invisible aches like his fearful brother-in-law, Selig? "You have time to be funny? Go instead to the cafeteria and get me some coffee."

Jesus raised his eyes in mocking surprise at his employer's unusual self-indulgence. "Next thing you be takin' afternoons off to go to the track."

"You must be patient with me," Sol answered sourly. "I am getting on in years." He flipped a coin to Jesus.

The youth snapped it out of the air with a dart of his

hand and then winked at Sol for his own prowess. "Black, no sugar?"

Sol nodded impatiently.

While Jesus was gone, Mabel Wheatly came in.

"This here a expensive locket," she said challengingly. "No sense foolin' around, I *know* it's gold."

It *was* gold, heavy and pure. Obligatorily, he scratched and tested, but he knew all the time by the very feel of it.

"Fifty dollars," he said.

"Gimme the locket."

"Seventy-five," he revised, offering the figure she would get from anyone else.

"That worth a hundred easy," she said, taking up her property with an assaying glance at his face, emboldened by his one retreat.

"Not to me," he said, looking into her face as though it were a hollow well.

She saw finality in his expression. For a moment she rubbed the gold with her thumb, massaging prodigious value into it. Then she nodded and dropped it on the counter before him.

As he wrote up the article and made out the pawn ticket, she talked her relief like a man who, after a hard day's work, takes satisfaction in his pay, in the money he thinks will advance him along the road to a particular aspiration.

"Ah, you know all about *me*, Pawnbroker," she said in an easy, confiding voice. "You know what I'm in. I don't have to tell you how hard *I* work for my money."

"It is peculiar work," he agreed without judgment.

"Oh brother, peculiar is right." She lit a cigarette and looked back with comfortable melancholy at those hardships already behind her. "Like a woman could go right out of her mind if she thinks on it too much."

"Then I suppose you should not think about it," he said with a little serrated edge to his voice.

"I suppose," she said. She watched her exhaled smoke as

it was caught suddenly by the fan and torn to pieces. "Got me a hard boss there, too."

"The woman in charge?" he inquired politely as he finished the little bit of paper work.

"Oh no, she all right. No, I mean the big boss, the owner. He one hard man. Not that he do anything I know of. Only the way he look at us girls, talk in a quiet weird voice. Like you just *know* what he threatenin', if you mess around. Big man, too, got lots of irons in the fire, you know."

Sol looked up for a few seconds to stare at the slow-moving cigarette smoke between them. He was teased with an almost imperceptible sense of recognition, of connection. But the smoke caught in the fan's arc and was wafted away, so he found himself looking at the girl's ordinary brown features, and whatever it was ducked down in his consciousness.

That night, before he left, Jesus asked Sol if he wanted him to accompany him to the bank. "I take one of them duelin' pistols and guard you, huh?"

"If you would only do those things I ask you to, I would be satisfied. Never mind volunteering; I do not appreciate it. Just go on home, I will ask you for what I want."

"You gonna smother my initiative," Jesus said with his wild smile.

"Good night already," Sol said, raising his hand and turning his head away in exasperation. And when he looked back, Ortiz was gone.

He went to the safe and took the money out. For the first time he found himself apprehensive over that half-block walk. Formerly, he had always had the policeman on the beat escort him the short way. But in recent weeks, since Leventhal had become so annoying, he had gone alone.

Anyhow, it was still quite light on the street. There were many people around and police were never more than a block or so away. He locked up the store and started down the street.

When he was almost to the bank, he noticed the three men on the far corner, recognized the ash-gray suit, Tangee, the great bulk of Buck White. He hurried the last few dozen feet, and his hands shook as he slipped the envelope into the brass, revolving chamber. But when he looked back at the men after the money was safely deposited, they appeared quite innocent, like any three men commenting idly on the passing scene. And he felt a growing rage at himself, as though his greatest enemy had invaded his body to leave him shaken and unknown to himself.

When he got home that night, everyone but Selig was out for the evening. His brother-in-law sat stiffly in the dim-lit living room. His usually ruddy face was sweaty and pale, and he looked pleadingly up at Sol.

"What is wrong, Selig?"

"I think I'm having a heart attack," Selig whispered in terror.

Sol sat down and took his brother-in-law's wrist to feel the pulse. Selig stared at him like a bewildered animal. The pulse was strong and steady, only a little fast.

"Why do you think you are having a heart attack?"

"I had these *stabbing* pains in my chest before. Then I got faint. No one was here. It seemed terrible that I might die alone. I'm afraid of dying, Sol. I was afraid to move." He spoke softly, without moving his lips, as though careful to avoid even that tiny strain. "I'm not like you, Solly. I haven't been through the things you have. Your life doesn't seem to interest you very much. Not like me, not like me. I must live! I *love* living—eating, talking. . . . Bertha and I still have . . . love . . . you know what I mean. I'm terrified, please Sol . . ."

"Does it hurt you now?"

"Noo-o," Selig said, his expression one of inward inspection. "I don't think so."

"And just how many *stabbing* pains did you have?"

"About three or four," Selig whispered, just turning his eyes.

"And that was all?"

"Yes, except that I got this *faint* feeling after that."

Sol smiled distastefully. "You will not die now, Selig; relax. You are a very healthy man." Surprisingly, there was a note of gentleness in his scorn.

"You think so?" Selig leaned very cautiously into hope. "What was it, then, the pains, the faintness?"

"The pains were nerves. You were perhaps thinking about the possibility of a heart attack for some reason?"

"A teacher in my school, just my age, fifty-four, keeled over today. Never had a sick day, and, boom, he keels over dead!"

"Aha."

"But the faintness?" Selig asked, not letting go of fear too easily, although a craven smile of relief was beginning.

"A natural reaction to fear. The blood leaves your head, you see things as through a smoked glass, sounds get distant and small."

"Yes, yes, that was it exactly." He breathed delightedly the sweet air of life and began looking around him with great pleasure, like a child drinking in the familiarity of his room after a nightmare. "Oh, Solly, thank you. I wouldn't say this in front of anyone else but . . . well, you are a comfort, a strange comfort to me. You're younger than I am . . . but it's funny, this will sound foolish, I feel as protected with you here as I did when I was a kid still living with my father. Protected . . . a strange thing to say, isn't it? Tomorrow I will want to forget all about this. But now . . ."

"First of all, you are a hypochondriac, Selig. But most of all you are a fool." Sol stood up. "Relax now; your crisis is over. You must take care of *yourself*. I have nothing to do with you. I am not your protector, nor am I your father or your doctor or your rabbi. I give you the courtesy of exposing your own foolishness to you, that is all. I am nothing to you, Selig. Now I am going to bed."

"Yes, Sol, thank you Solly," Selig said, still beyond insult.

And that night, Sol Nazerman was ravaged by dreams again. But mercifully, perhaps, they were torn out of recognition, because he kept waking all through the night, waking up with a strange, nameless alarm.

## SEVEN

Buck White sat in one corner, brooding in the sound of his wife's flirtatious laughter. When he had been younger, his great muscularity had been an impressive focus for women's attention, but now his laborer's body was just a hard, knotty joke. He had nothing else to offer. Words came out of him in careful couples or trios. When he tried to use more than he needed for request or simple answer, they came out in a garbled winding whose beginning and end were lost to him. Once, he had won seven hundred dollars in a crap game, and his winnings had adorned him in suits and an installment car; people had seemed to smile respectfully at the dazzle he made. He sat there yearning savagely for that affluence again, his huge Bantu face lowering and hard as he watched his wife, Billy, parade her face and body for Kopey, the numbers man.

Three other men, Cecil Mapp among them, sat in another corner laughing over their beer. Actually, Cecil was drinking lemonade, under the influence of his wife, who sat with the other women in the kitchen. Billy White was the only woman among the men, and her laughter kept them all swollenly conscious of their maleness; except for her husband, who dreamed furiously of barbaric splendor and kneaded his huge hands.

"I'm going to take a little business trip out to L.A. in a couple of weeks," Kopey said with a blasé expression on his sleek, yellow face. He studied the big star sapphire on his pinky. "Pro'bly run out to Malibu Beach while I'm out there. That L.A. really jumpin'."

"I'm just dyin' to get out there," Billy said, courting him with a smile. "Catch a look of the movie stars, you know. I got a idea it's real crazy out there, loads of fun and all."

"Oh they *move* out there, no question," Kopey said with a last, bored look at his ring.

Buck cleared his throat, and they turned toward him, surprised at that manifestation of life. Billy frowned in anticipation of stupidity.

"I almos' went there . . . once," he said, embarking on the treacherous sea of conversation; it suddenly appeared to him that he had need of greater complexity. "It was like I was in there the army but not befo', not when I was gettin' out like, ony this guy I don' remember which because he wasn't in like me the army, ony he said if . . ." His eyes cast around for something that would orient him, searched for anything but his wife's face. He felt himself drowning in the sea of words, but he continued to thrash around, making a great show of swimming. "I . . . if *I* want to go like in he place, not he—*I*," he emphasized as though some clarity were just out of his reach. His face beaded with sweat, and the sudden silence of everyone else in the room was like a sound. "See I still in but not he, he never in at all so he could go ahead to L.A. but only he wasn't able, so he got to get I . . . *me* . . ." It was all so simple in his mind, how a 4F had offered him a chance to go to L.A. to deliver a car because he could get the gas rations on his army papers. How did people get those things across to other people? He stared at all their dumb, pitying faces, and his mouth closed over air. Slowly, he lowered his eyes to his ponderous hands and surrendered.

"I almos' go. . . ."

Billy White flashed her seraglio eyes upward in exasperation, and Kopey commiserated with a good-natured shrug. Then the two of them went on with their devious courtship in talk of the grand and glittering L.A. while Buck returned to his gloomy invocation of legendary riches.

In the kitchen, the other women talked around the table over their glasses of fruit juice. Mrs. Cecil Mapp sat in righteous ease as she castigated the small, wistful sinner who was her husband.

"Church, *him?* Don' make me laugh, sister," she said to Jane Ortiz, the mother of Jesus. "That man so far from God he can't pronounce the word. A fritterin' spineless creature of evil ways. Don' matter to him me and his children wear rags an' tatters. 'What the use anyway,' he say. 'We miserable hopeless people anyway.' Imagine a man like that! So he give up long ago. Now he courts the bottle, completely lost in the ways of intemperance."

"My Jesus have some wild ways, I admit," Jane Ortiz said, plucking at the tablecloth with a musing expression. "But he never lost to God; that much I can say. 'Course we of a different faith than you, Mrs. Mapp; it's a little different all around. But no matter what kind of devilment he get into, he fin' time to get to church now an' again. He took his communion, makes a confession every so often."

"Well sure, that is somethin' to say for him. His heart in the right place at least, no matter what kind of church," Mrs. Mapp said condescendingly, no real friend of Catholics. (Might as well be weird as those colored who worshiped in a synagogue.) "But of course with us Baptists you can't just leave you sins on no priest, not so easy with us. We got to fight with the Devil all the time."

"Well, Mrs. Mapp, you might not understand how we works in the *Catholic* Church," Jane Ortiz said, quite proud of her affiliation with the un-Negro faith she had married up to. "You see with us . . ."

Downstairs, the Pawnbroker's janitor, John Rider, sat smoking his new chrome-stemmed pipe, distracted from his reading of the Bible by the shrill voices of the women upstairs.

"It is better to dwell in a corner of d'housetop then wid a brawlin' woman in a wide house," he muttered angrily, yet with a proud smugness, as he slammed the window shut.

"My Jesus is ambitious," Jane Ortiz said with proud irrelevance.

"You people jus' don' believe in d'existence of Hell is your trouble. You think you get everything off you back in them confessions."

"It happen Jesus Christ hisself was a Catholic," Jane Ortiz threw in as a clincher.

"It happen he was a Jew," Mrs. Mapp answered.

"Why, Mrs. Mapp, what a awful thing to say!"

Kopey had an expression of delighted anguish on his shiny yellow face as he talked to Billy White.

"And you should see them night clubs out there in L.A. There's nothin' here to compare. . . ."

Billy sighed with yearning while her husband knotted his immense hands, trying to wring treasure from them.

Jesus sat low in his seat in the dark theater. His knees were crammed up against the seat in front of him, and his eyes were narrow and intense on the movie screen, like slits of fire.

The scene was the patio of a great country house. People in handsomely tailored evening clothes strolled through the parklike grounds, and Japanese lanterns were reflected in a large, free-form swimming pool. An orchestra played sleepily from inside the opened French doors. In the foreground now, a white man murmured languidly against the face of a skinny white woman. The land fell away quietly in a swoop of luxurious privacy; everything was immaculate, rich, and fabulous.

Jesus Ortiz felt a vast shapeless desire, but it was too great and beautiful to attain shape. So he thought about money and the power of *business*.

Mabel Wheatly writhed fetchingly on the white sheets of the whorehouse as she waited for her third customer of the evening to finish undressing. She murmured lustful catch phrases to him, this fat, balding white man with girlish skin and tiny plump hands. The summer air came hot and smoky in through the cautiously opened window, and the man's hands trembled.

"I'll tell you what I want you to do," he said in a voice savage with shame. "First lie over . . . like this. And then keep saying, 'Do it to me, Richy, do it to me,' like that," he said, his shaky hand moist on her bare brown skin.

"Is your name Richy, hon?" she asked with a vampish smile.

"No, no, my name is Don. But you just do what I say and don't ask questions. Do what I say." He fell on her then and began a mad pantomime of mock virility.

"Do it to me, Richy, do it to me, Richy, do it to me . . ." she intoned in a dead voice, contorting herself according to that particular recipe of passion. But her eyes were up on the ceiling, staring at a desperate dream.

Tessie Rubin didn't open the door to the angry knocking of Goberman. She called from behind the closed door in a loud half-whisper she hoped would carry to Goberman and not to her father lying in his raging sleep in the back bedroom.

"What do you mean coming this time of night?"

"Does it make a difference to the slaves in Yemen, the Israelites in the ghettos of Algiers and Alexandria what time it is? Their blood is on you. You must give me money for the Jewish Appeal or your name will go down with Hitler in Hell," Goberman cried in the same wild half-whisper from the hall.

"I'll give, I'll give, you madman," she said. "Only I don't have, now. Come Monday night, come then, I'll take care of you then."

"I'll come then, I'll come like the Angel of Death to the Egyptians. God help you if you don't . . ."

"Monday, Monday," she wailed against the door.

"Vat is the pounding? Are they here again?" the old man roared from the bedroom. *"Ich shtab svai huntret yourn!* I haf died too many times already."

"It's nothing, Poppa, *gay shluphin;* it is just the man from the electric company," she called in a soothing voice as she leaned against the door. "It will all be taken care of, Sol will take care of it." She covered her face with her hands and pressed as hard as she could.

Goberman's footsteps clacked hollowly over the tile floor of the hall, receded out to the street, and then were gone from her ears but not from her head, never from her head.

Miles away, the Pawnbroker sat up rigidly in his bed to escape the long-drawn and endless moaning of his dreams.

## ❊ EIGHT

His Sundays were parodies of Sabbaths; hours to be got through without the insulation of work. He swung his feet to the floor of his bedroom and stared at the leafy shape of sunlight over them; it was like morning discovering the marble of a statue. Outside, there were the sounds of the Sunday gardeners and children's voices slamming at the quiet. A lawn mower chugged in the warm air a half-block away, and a few birds twittered weakly, obligated to August. He was in a warm, safe place. Why then did he creak under invisible weights? Why did he feel that phantom growth deep inside?

For a few minutes he studied the motionless curtains tapestried with sunlight. He began to recognize the edge of something soothingly rational.

"A week from Thursday is the twenty-eighth of August," he said aloud. Every year around the anniversary of his family's death he experienced that now vague sense of oppression. It was only natural; in fact in its mildness it was almost unnatural. He did not grieve or mourn them, because he had been cauterized of all abstract things. Reality consisted of the world within one's sight and smell and hearing. He commemorated nothing; it was the secret of his survival. But August was his bad month, the period of his own mistral, a time when he felt healed scars as a veteran might recall his wounds in damp weather. No more than that; August would come and go, and he would continue to exist. Bleakly comforted at having found a name for his ache, he got up and began to dress.

He put on a pair of fawn-colored summer slacks and an olive sport shirt his niece, Joan, had bought him the Christmas before, which made his complexion take on the yellowish translucence of old marble. In the bathroom, he ran the electric razor over the sparse stubble of his beard, his eyes indifferent to the rest of his pallid face. Then he brushed his teeth, which were his own except for two steel ones a little to the side of his mouth. Amazing that he hadn't lost them all. He spread his lips to observe his teeth and then continued the expression in a mirthless smile at that odd persistence; the teeth continued to manufacture calcium, as hair and fingernails continued to grow in the grave.

With his unique spectacles on, Sol went downstairs to where the odor of fresh coffee and rolls and smoked fish filled the rooms pleasantly. Bertha was in the kitchen, the rest of the family reading the different sections of the *Times*.

"Good morning, Uncle Sol. You slept late," Joan said brightly. In her yellow bathrobe, her skin tanned to a lovely maple, she was a bright spot in the sunny room. "And so formal. I wish you would let me buy you a dressing gown."

"Good morning, *Solly*," Selig said with conspiratorial

heartiness, reminding his brother-in-law of his lingering gratitude with raised eyebrows.

"Good morning," Sol said, walking over to the living-room window to gaze blankly at the shaded street.

Morton glanced up from his perusal of the advertised bosoms in the theater section. For a moment he looked at his uncle. Oddly, he felt himself loosen in the presence of the big, shapeless figure, felt certain cords of anguish go limp and become bearable in his uncle's stillness.

Bertha's voice broke into the rustling quiet of the room.

"Come eat," she called from the kitchen.

They went in and sat around the sumptuous spread of rolls, bagels, cheeses, sturgeon, smoked whitefish and lox, huge tomatoes and chunks of sweet tub butter; and what was real between them was the mutual hunger, the greed that lit up their faces with an ersatz amiability. Bertha poured coffee into each of their cups. Sol's was an oversized novelty inscribed "Grandpa," which Joan had bought the year before on the vacation she and her parents had taken at Sol's expense. It was part of the half-conscious campaign she and her mother waged to make Sol a family "character"; that at least could explain his indefinable personality, could ultimately, they hoped, reduce him to something they could work with and control.

For a while, they talked in little side courses about friends and news events and book reviews. Bertha dug with gleeful savagery at the small failure of one of her friends' children. But when Selig and Joan finished eating and sat back with cigarettes and a second cup of coffee, Joan suddenly noticed her brother's skinny hands.

"Your nails are filthy," she said comfortably, exhaling a twin stream of smoke from her nose. The observation was made without malice, for she was a healthy, unfrustrated girl. "You keep them too long."

Selig cast his face into a father's sternness. "I don't want to see you coming to the table like that," he said.

Morton ate more quickly, as though he expected his plate to be taken away before he was through eating.

"You don't answer people when they talk to you?" his mother said.

"Leave me alone," Morton said, continuing to eat.

Bertha stared at him viciously for a minute, searching for ammunition, feeding her bitter disappointment in him. She had a certain capacity for love, but it was not large. Her life in America had been bright and clean and pretty; she had become accustomed to clean prettiness. She had come to America thirty years before and had gotten the educated, "American-looking" Selig to fall in love with her wholesome good looks. Their first child had been a beautiful credit to her. And then Morton! She might have been able to shape a pitying affection for her son, but from early childhood he had been as sour and unreceptive to her condescending attention as he was now.

"I found some indecent pictures in your drawer," she said, not adding that she had studied them curiously for almost ten minutes.

"Ah, the solitary vice, very unhealthy," Selig said, belching the essence of smoked fish out with his cigarette smoke. "You're at the age where self-discipline is important, Morton."

"Talk about shame," Morton snarled, "haven't you people got any shame? How can you talk to a person like this? All right, you despise me and I despise you. Yes, let's get it out in the open—*despise!* Well, okay, I don't need you. I'll become an artist and get out on my own. Then you can all go to hell, for all I care!"

"That language in front of your mother and your sister!" Selig half stood in threat. And this, his namesake, his hope of immortality. He was too lazy about discipline. Well, from now on he would take a hand. For an instant he visualized a tall, broad-shouldered Morton with tanned, smooth skin and bright friendly eyes and himself, Selig, introducing this beautiful son to his principal, telling the man that his son had been offered any number of football scholarships but that Morton preferred a particular nonathletic college whose pre-med courses were said to be the best. Selig stayed, half standing, his eyes glazed and forgetful of the purpose of his posture. Gradually, he sank back into his chair as the daydream faded.

"Morton," Joan said, "we don't hate you. What an unhealthy attitude that is! You have many antagonisms against yourself and you try to put them on us. We just want to help you. Our criticism is meant to be constructive."

"That's what a family is for," Selig said.

"Well I certainly hate to see him get like this," Joan said. Then, with a glance at her uncle, the payer-of-fees, "Maybe some professional help would be in order. Mort, would you consider talking to Sid's friend Doctor Klebish? Just informally; the brightest people do it nowadays."

Morton didn't answer, just kept stubbornly eating.

"*Get* like this," Bertha cried scornfully, suddenly flooded with bitter recall. "He was always like this. He sucked my milk till there was blood. At three years old he was still crying for the titty."

"*Really,* Mother!" Joan spoke with delicate distaste. "Now, Mort, you know Mother is just angry—not that I blame her. You get her all upset. Honestly, you don't let anyone relax and be friendly with you. You're so violently antisocial, so . . ."

"He used to pee in his pants when he was already eleven years old, just to embarrass me," Bertha persisted, half enjoying the dim nausea she felt in this attack on her son. It seemed that if she continued it long enough and intensely enough, she would vomit all the sick anger she felt for him, that she might be soothed and eased and patient enough to love him as she should.

"Nowadays we have guidance people in the schools," Selig said. "Perhaps if the people at the school . . . I mean this drawing business is not a solution to all your problems, you know, son. Let's say you are pursuing some modest talent, all well and good, but . . ."

"You don't know anything about it!" Morton cried hoarsely, his eyes bulging and wild. "You people with your slimy, warped little brains, talking about *foreign films* and *book reviews*. What do you know? Beauty, do you really understand about beauty? No, just prettiness, nice clean little things, fashionable, crappy little nothings. And you have the nerve to tell me . . ."

"Those pictures in your drawer maybe, that's beauty?" Bertha said.

Morton snarled miserably, like a trapped animal.

Sol just sat drinking his coffee and contemplating the cold, living stone in his vitals, in a hurry for the hour to end, for the day, the week, the month to be gone. He forced himself to anticipate the peace that would follow his strange seasonal discomfort. The voices of his relatives snapped in a closing circle around the ugly weakness of their prey, but he heard them only distantly, like the sound of some far-off hunt. He squinted at the chrome sparkle of the stove, which threw needles of light into his eyes. He might even take a little holiday in October, walk in some New England wood and just breathe without regret or poignance the pleasant cold air so free of unnatural smells. He would take some books along and stay at a quiet inn and walk and eat and read and be quite content within the walls of his senses. He sat in an autumnal reverie, his face slack and idiotic, his body collapsed sideways in the chair.

But suddenly the noise intruded. Morton was standing with his hands up to his ears and screaming one steady tantrum note.

"That's just childish, Morton," his sister said. "You refuse to take criticism like an adult."

"He's a baby, a nasty baby," Bertha shrilled.

"Get a grip on yourself, boy," Selig shouted.

"Shut up, all of you!" Sol said in a thunderous voice. "Leave him alone!"

"Now, Solly, you must let us work out our parental problems in our own way," Selig said with polite reproof.

"I said be still, be still!" He towered over them with his anger, and they were reminded that he came out of unknown violences. Selig and Joan sat open-mouthed and intimidated.

But Bertha was made of tougher material.

"You are not yet the dictator around here, Solly," she said. "Maybe you think you can throw up to us the little help you have been willing to give us. But we didn't vote you the head of the house. After all, we give something in return. We have made a home for you, given you a family. What money could buy that?"

Morton forgot to scream. He lowered his hands from his ears and watched his uncle.

Sol turned to his sister with a cold, glistening stare.

"You will be still now," he said. "No more talk at all until I am out of this room. Silence, Bertha, silence. When I am gone from here, you may continue your cannibalism; I do not take sides or interfere with your miserable pleasure. But hear what I say. I do *not* need you for a family—that is *your* myth. If you wish to be able to continue it, be silent!"

Then he turned and went from the room.

Morton followed, a careful distance behind his uncle. Like his father, he was prone to imaginative reconstructions. He looked at Sol's wide, bulky back and had no need to create a new and perfect father; he was willing, in his dream, to settle for that one somber, harsh man, would have taken his chances on all the darknesses in the Pawnbroker that would be forever beyond his knowing. He felt, without evidence, that there were murkinesses those eyes could penetrate and understand.

But Sol was only soliciting silence. He went into the yard with a book of Chekhov's short stories. Settled on the plastic-webbed chair, he began to read. He soaked in a fictitious climate which isolated him from the warm sunlight and the voices of all the neighbors, dulled by the heavy summer foliage. And slowly he worked away from the minor irritant of the recent scene in the house. He read avidly, and although he projected himself to a certain extent to the late nineteenth-century Russian town, he derived pleasure mainly from the lucid familiarity of something he had loved and enjoyed in another time. He appreciated the emotions evoked, but he was not involved emotionally himself because his invulnerability allowed for no exceptions. He was stirred only to a reminiscence of sadness; he was like an archaeologist studying the historic ruins of an interesting civilization. Sometimes he smiled faintly, at other times his eyes narrowed slightly; breezes of life seemed to play over his bland, buried face.

During the morning the members of the family came out into the yard for various reasons; Bertha to dump the garbage, Selig looking for a pair of pruning shears, Joan just wandering aimlessly. Each of them skirted his reposing figure with cautious silence and stayed for the shortest time; they were intimidated by Sol's motionless face, stony in the yellow-green light, and by his eyes, obscured behind the thick lenses of his glasses.

Only Morton stayed for a long time in another chair, a good distance away from his uncle. He read intermittently from Gardner's *Art Through the Ages,* and every so often swung his eyes furtively from some Byzantine saint or Renaissance madonna to the motionless figure.

After a while, Sol, too, found himself swinging in and out of the balm of his reading, although he did not lift his eyes from the printed pages. His mind drifted with the apparent abandon of an oarless boat, bumping on this strand and that. His customers ranged through his thoughts, and he examined them harshly, as though he might find the thing responsible for his increasing unease. With his eyes on "A Day in the Country," he checked off Jesus Ortiz and Buck White,

Tangee and the blue-eyed Negro. He considered craftily the harsh, sonic whine of Murillio's voice, the sleazy delicacy of George Smith's importuning debate. And he wondered if any or all of them might have anything to do with the way he felt. The buzzing conjecture began to make his nerves tingle, and a slight dizziness came over him.

"But it's just the time of the year . . . an old superstition," he said aloud, gesturing, too, as though in answer to an unseen companion.

"What did you say, Uncle Sol?" Morton asked, as alien with his sallow face in that cheery sunlight as his uncle.

"What . . . oh, nothing, nothing. I was reading aloud . . . it meant nothing," he said softly.

Then he went back to Chekhov with his memory strangled in the grip of his will. And the soft summer sounds fell over him with the sunlight, as unfelt as the lightest rain of pollen.

## ✳ NINE

*They could see the whole thing from where they stood in the camp square. Sol stood with the others in a long, endless line, halted by their guard, as were the several other work groups. Outside the barbed-wire fence, the dogs snarled in a closing ring around Rubin. The black-uniformed men smoked and joked idly in the noon sunshine; even the dogs seemed in no great hurry as they backed the small crouched figure toward the fence.*

*A week before, they had taken Rubin's cross-eyed son to the "showers." Last night, Rubin had managed to slip out of the camp, God knew how. But the dogs had found him, and the commandant's edifying "example" was imminent. All night they had given Rubin his head, yet all the while they were slyly working him back toward the camp. Now,* at high noon, he was right outside the high fence for everyone to learn from; the morbid joke was revealed to Rubin at last.

If you kept your eyes off the small hunched figure, you might think a harmless animal hunt was in progress, some sport of so little intrinsic excitement that the guards tried to make it interesting by jokes and side bets.

The dogs bayed in the hot light. The air was emptied of birds and insects by the loud voices of the dogs, and the prisoners stood like shades, arrested on their shuffling journey to Hell. Sol felt dust flowing from him instead of sweat, a dry, powdery secretion which smelled stale and fiery.

One of the guards of Sol's column called over to the men with the dogs, "I hope the electricity is off now, otherwise you'll ruin it."

A black-clad man answered that it was. He touched the twisty knot of wire and made a face of mock agony, as though he were being electrocuted. They all laughed at his clowning. That was the extent of the sounds; a few men's laughter and the yapping, the trumpeting of the hounds.

Rubin was only a few feet from the fence when the dogs jumped him. For a minute his figure was obscured by their tumbling, hairy bodies. Their snarls were wetly muffled by what they were doing. Sol looked away, a strange dead feeling spreading through his chest, a feeling like boredom. All the men in the column were bony-gray profiles, death masks coated by the faint dustiness of the air. A pigeon appeared on one of the sludge-colored barracks roofs; not quite sure of its roost, it fluttered its wings as it stood, then rose again and disappeared over the monotonous horizon of the camp.

The vile chorus from the beasts' throats rose to an insane pitch. Sol looked back to see Rubin rise up far bigger than he had ever been. For a few seconds the dogs fell back, surprised at the deceptive quarry which had seemed so small. Rubin was screaming, one shining red figure of blood, only his mouth definable in all the torn body, and that so vivid *because it framed the scream. Everything else was dust-white, the dark figures of the guards and the dogs overladen with a cloudy, powdered light. Only Rubin had immense color, was a great crimson font that demeaned the whole day.*

*Suddenly Rubin turned and flung himself up on the thorny wire fence, where he clung just out of reach of the snapping dogs. One of the guards waved toward the guard tower. There came the rattly crack of electricity. The bloody figure went rigid, pulled away from the horrid life of the wires, and then seized it and pulled it tight in a lover's embrace. Then the body went limp. And the ragged bundle of blood and charred flesh, caught like some wind-tossed rubbish on the wires, was no longer Rubin or anything else.*

*Sol retched dryly as they ripped the ruined form from the wires. All around him he heard others doing the same, standing straight, with expressionless faces, as though the retching were something animated by their captors, too. And, like all the others, Sol brought forth only dust.*

He decided not to try for any more sleep. It was just past dawn as he fumbled around quietly, dressing, washing, and shaving. He couldn't have borne the sight or sound of any of the family then, so he walked with elaborate caution, felt for each creak and lowered his weight on each step like someone trying out a newly mended leg. Outside, he drew a deep breath of the dew-sweet air and felt securely hidden in the awakening din of the birds.

His car tires whined over the damp streets. The sunlight searched out the dirty night shadows. He imagined relaxation and blew a faint unknown melody in a hiss just short of a whistle.

Today was the eighteenth of August—a week from Thursday was the twenty-eighth. Merely one of three hundred and sixty-five days. All right, indulge the old superstitions, if you must. So the day rang in his head with a somber resonance.

In two weeks it would be over. Nirvana would return, he thought wryly. No doubt his dreams would come less frequently; someday they might cease altogether. The capacity for dreaming was like an ulcer, an ailment common to humans. It could be cured by blandness of diet. In a few weeks he would be impregnable again.

He had just finished unlocking the store when Marilyn Birchfield came in. She moved in out of the low sunlight, her face just a shadow at first, with the brightness behind her.

"Good morning, Mister Nazerman. May I come in?"

Now the fluorescents flickered on, and he saw her matronly figure, clad in an azure-blue dress. Her face appeared astoundingly innocent and young-looking.

Sol fixed his eyes on the flush of pink that ran across her round cheeks and over the bridge of her nose.

"A little sunburn," she said with a smile. "I often take my sandwich over to the river and eat it there. Perhaps one day you'll join me?"

"Thank you, but I take my lunch in the store," he answered, fussing with pencils and paper clips on the counter. Then, at a loss for occupation, he looked up at her with bland patience. "Was there something you wanted?"

"Oh, the same old things, really—money, signatures, sponsorships, knowledge," she said.

"I thought we had straightened all that out." His voice was frankly cold now. An odd twinge of disappointment puzzled him.

"I never give up. But, really, I found myself walking. It was so early. And then I saw you and I said to myself that it would be nice to visit. Neighborly, you might say."

A cool refreshing breeze seemed to have followed her into the store, and Sol just nodded uncertainly.

"I'm not a very good sleeper," she said musingly, leaning one elbow on the counter and staring at an ivory abacus. "It doesn't seem to matter what time I hit the hay—five o'clock comes and I'm through with sleep. Oh, I've heard jokes about what keeps spinsters awake," she said, blushing so the sunburn seemed to flow all over her face. "But the truth is I never had a night's insomnia until I came to New York and began working for the city. The way these people live! Misery, the misery. I feel it even in my own apartment, as though it were in the air. In Springfield, my father used to have to pound on the door to wake me. It's very strange. Do these people affect you that way?"

"No," Sol said. "They do not affect me at all." With pointed rudeness, he began studying the list of pawned items.

She looked at him for a moment and then composed her face to mildness.

"If you will forgive my curiosity, you are foreign born, aren't you?"

He looked up at her suspiciously, beginning to vibrate under her childlike examination. In his state, he could well do without this plump woman with the schoolgirl face and manner.

"Yes, I am foreign born. Now then, Miss . . . Miss . . . "

"Birchfield," she supplied.

"Miss Birchfield. I am not a socially inclined man. You force me to say this; you seem to have no sense of discretion, much like a silly child who has no instinct for her listener's unwillingness to talk."

"You would be surprised about children," she said quietly.

"I am not friendly. I have no patience with passing the time of day. You solicited me the other day and I gave you five dollars; a generous offering. Come back next week and I may give some more. Otherwise, I have nothing for you. I could not coach basketball or ping-pong or the baseball even if I wanted to. I have lived a life quite alien to the Boy Scouts and the basketball. . . . "

And then, just when he had her on the point of angrily humiliated departure, her eyes fell on the blue numbers on his arm. Her eyes went dreamy with pity, and she looked back up to his strange, ugly face with an exasperating humility, armored now beyond his insult.

"I am sorry, Mr. Nazerman," she said. "You're right, and I apologize. Surprisingly, there are times when even *I* recognize my tactlessness. I guess I was irritated by your manner when I first came in, and I probably decided, half consciously, to work you over."

"Why apologize? My manner has not changed for the better, has it?"

"Not really, I'm afraid," she said with a little laugh. "But now, somehow, it doesn't bother me any more."

He groaned in exasperation.

She leaned over the counter toward him, her face appearing bright through the bars of his little cage, her plump, scrubbed hands only inches from his.

"Will you accept my apology?" she asked.

"Yes, yes, I will accept it. Now leave me alone." He sounded petulant to himself and he wondered at the ridiculousness of this encounter he had done nothing to deserve. "Whatever you say is fine with me. Now if you please . . . "

"Then there is the possibility of our being friends?"

"Yes, *friends,*" he agreed, as to a lunatic, and raised his eyes to the dusty ceiling, where a nickel-plated tuba coiled like a strange serpent.

"And, that being the case, you will join me for lunch tomorrow by the river?" she said mischievously.

"All *right,* anything, please . . . "

"I'll be by at twelve tomorrow, then," she said, waved gaily, and took herself out with her peculiarly awkward walk, which made it seem that some eternal adolescent inhabited her full, womanly body.

The Pawnbroker stared at the empty doorway with a dazed look for some time. Finally he sighed a sound of great bewilderment. What kind of joke was this? He needed that crazy woman like a second nose. But, oddly, her delicate, laundered smell clung to his nostrils with insidious stubbornness, and he began his work still haunted by it.

His first customer had a slyly insane face full of open sores. He walked cautiously over to the counter, his arms wrapped around one of those greasy, skinlike bags.

"Valuable piece of goods here," the man said, his skinny little body exhaling a stench of old illness. "Got it off a rabbi friend of mine. Real authentic, valuable."

He reached into the bag and pulled out a velvet Torah cover, glittering with silver thread and with gold-embroidered collars that had fitted over the scrolls' handles.

"What are you doing with this?" Sol snarled.

"He *give* it to me, the rabbi," the little man whined. "Ain't it worth to you?"

"Take it out of here, you and it together," Sol said.

Jesus Ortiz came in, but before Sol had a chance to say a word to his assistant, the store was suddenly full of customers.

For a long time they were busy estimating, haggling, exchanging quick professional signals from time to time. They were a strangely matched team engaged in an even stranger performance, giving mercy with the backs of their hands, touching the odd flotsam of people's lives, removing old dreams for the loan of brief new ones, nodding to each other over the innocent heads, negating, winking coldly, holding up fingers in cryptic exchange.

Some people shouted, others laughed good-naturedly, a girl cried. The smells of poorly washed people, of cheaply perfumed bodies, of the poverty-stricken, of the diseased, all filled the store to crowd the Pawnbroker and his graceful, delicate assistant. The shelves grew a little more crowded with the assorted remains of people's idyls, and Sol's hands lost the feel of air from the greasy handling of money.

Only near noontime was the store suddenly empty. Jesus

looked over at his employer with a tiny conspiratorial smile, and Sol acknowledged it with a tight-lipped nod and a shrug.

While Jesus wrote up the descriptions of the merchandise he had taken in for pawn, Sol looked around with a puzzled frown. He was seeking a logical reason for a peculiar phenomenon; in the wake of all the ugly, dirty smells, he still had the scent of something sweetly laundered in his nose.

## ✳ *T E N*

That afternoon he barely managed civility for George Smith. But the obvious preparation in the little man's appearance made him feel too weak to be as brutal as his impatience demanded. He knew by some unseen evidence that George had a chart, drawn in pen and ink, which had the date of each pawn, the listing of prospective items for pawn, the tentative dates for redeeming things (allowing a discreet interval between pawning and redeeming). Sol just didn't have the courage yet to humiliate him and drive him away, as he wanted to.

"I've been reading this *Preface to Logic,* you know," George said, settling himself comfortably against the counter. "And I came to this one part that goes along with what we were talking about the other day. He's talking about the logic of fiction, this time. So he goes on to show how Aristotle in his *Poetics* says that poetry is truer than history . . . *truer than history,* mind you."

"That's the book by Morris Cohen?" Sol said, writing up the transaction without the usual gracious delay.

George nodded happily and went on talking. He could disguise quite well the frequent appearances of indifference in the Pawnbroker; a man who is hungry enough can subsist on the most meager nourishment. So he talked, a momentary scholar, the high, clean tower of his mind swept for now of all the writhing hungers, the lusts delegated to a dark cellar by the purity of his mind's desire. He would have been happy as some garrulous, mildly virile old professor, surrounded by books and occasional listeners, indifferent to his body, dreamless.

Sol stared at him deafly for several minutes, watched how the frail, tautly bound face changed expression, flashed, exhorted, conducted, reflected ideas and pleasures. And although he had no sense of rapport with the tan-skinned little man, no patience with George's feverish dusting of the great ideas, he suffered him for about ten minutes, allowing even those minimal shrugs and nods that made the monologue possible, until he could stand no more.

"Yes, I know . . . but look, George," he broke in softly, "could we continue this the next time? The truth is I am rather busy now."

George smiled wanly, his disappointment barely concealed. He had been there for only ten minutes or so. Well, perhaps he hadn't really brought anything exciting this time, just a rehash of their previous talk. And then, he usually came in later in the day, when it was apt to be less busy. Oh, but he had something in store for the Pawnbroker next time! He had been saving Spinoza for a real ideal time, some afternoon when he would have something quite valuable to pawn and thus deserve more time in the store, maybe a half or even three-quarters of an hour. What a richness of exchange would be between them then! He could hardly wait.

"I'm apt to be in early next week, maybe even the end of this week. Have something interesting for you then, Sol," he said.

Sol nodded with a trace of a smile, which faded the moment George Smith was gone.

He felt a need for air. He walked out to the street and stood facing the distant railroad bridge, framed by the perspective of the tawdry store fronts. The air was thick and hot, worse even than inside the store. People walked past him, cars moved and honked, the trains under the street shook the pavement, a boat hooted from the river a block away. There was no relief in sight. He looked up; the sky stared down at all the stone and brick, a pale-blue monstrous eye that lumped him and all the other ridiculous creatures with the filthy city.

He hissed slightly through his teeth and turned back into the store. He had almost reached the counter when he realized someone had come in while he was facing down the street. He turned into the unpleasantness of the blue-eyed Negro's flat gaze.

"What can I do for you?" Sol asked evenly.

The blue-eyed man just pointed toward the counter without moving his chilling glance from Sol's face.

A gleaming, oversized harmonica lay there in an opened, blue velvet case. Sol looked it over briefly, noted the button that made sharps and flats, the famous German name. Normally, he wouldn't bother with a harmonica, but this was a very good one, a professional instrument of considerable value, which might have sold for fifty dollars or more.

"It is a nice little mouth organ. I can loan you ten dollars on it."

"Gimme the ticket, I want the ticket," Robinson said in his dry basso. He stood absolutely still, his cadaverous face as icy and patient as a fine hunter's. Only a little tic in his jaw indicated the possibility of turmoil under the dark, motionless surface.

While the Pawnbroker wrote up the description of the transaction, Jesus Ortiz came down from the clothing loft. He stood for a moment at Sol's shoulder, exchanging a look with Robinson, and when Sol glanced up at the two of them, neither offered an excuse for what might have passed between them.

"Don't sell that horn, Pawnbroker," Robinson said in that bottomless voice, which betrayed its disuse and solitude. "I gonna be back for it."

"You just bring your ticket. It will be here," Sol said.

"I bring my ticket," Robinson rasped in somber promise, his eyes on Jesus Ortiz.

Sol watched the ash-gray suit move stiffly out of the store. Somehow, from the rear, the man looked only old and impoverished, so that he could almost forget the inhuman menace of the stripped face, the eyes that had nothing to lose.

"I have a funny feeling about that man, Tangee's friend. I do not trust him. That suit, it strikes me as the kind of clothing they give a man when they release him from prison."

"Well, you don' trust no one anyhow, Sol. Ain't that the secret of your success?" Jesus asked.

"Correct," Sol answered, his glance veiled from his assistant. "I trust no one."

For a few minutes there was an abrasive quality in the silence. Jesus did some wrapping of parcels in the little office while Sol worked over the list of things to go to auction.

But by degrees the harshness dissolved, and the fantastic conglomeration of the shop claimed their unconscious moods. Again they were riven by the complexity, the intricacy of the tools of people's survival. And each, in his own unthinking way, responded to a tiny, sad abrasion in his spirit. Each of them pitied, without knowing he pitied, the pathetic paraphernalia with which humans made walls. The glossy woods of old violins, the dented brasses of tuba and trumpet, the curving eye of camera, the wink of gold and silver from a thousand castoffs made a light for the Pawnbroker and his assistant to work by, to abide in, and so to become more complex themselves; for that light was of a unique and mysterious quality. What Jesus Ortiz aspired to, he sensed in the Pawnbroker even though he did not recognize the shape of his aspiration. And what the Pawnbroker wanted had nothing to do with desire; he apparently yearned toward nothingness and in the part of him not apparent there was still darkness and terrifying growth.

Mabel Wheatly was nervous when she came in. She waited for two customers in the store to leave before she approached the counter.

"Gimme whatever it worth," she mumbled to Sol, her eyes resting on Jesus.

It was a man's watch of recent design and with a solid-gold case. On the back was engraved "Seymor Epstein 1956."

"What do you expect me to do with this?" Sol asked. "You must understand that I must send descriptions of all the jewelry to the police."

"It ain't stole. The man give it to me for . . . for a private session," she said, barely moving her lips, as though to keep her words hidden from the youth at the end of the counter.

"Why are you acting so nervous then?" Sol studied her with distaste. Suddenly he felt enraged at her tawdry intrigues, furious, too, with the idea that his assistant might be somehow involved with all these people, conspiring, scheming. . . . No, no, he would have to get a grip on himself; this was the way of a breakdown. No one was conspiring against him; no one had anything to do with him.

"It just that the big boss don't hold with private dates. If it was to get out to him . . . " She managed a crooked smile, trying to make an accessory of him. But her eyes, meanwhile, rolled uneasily from the watch to Jesus and back again.

"All I dare loan you with that engraving on it is five dollars. I would rather not bother at all."

Mabel took the money unhappily but turned a timid smile on Jesus before leaving. Then she walked out with her professional rolling walk carefully modified for the cool surveyal of her lover.

"This *boss* of hers, he must be a brutal individual," Sol said curiously.

"A real big-shot guinea. Owns a few houses. Suppose to have a lot of things workin' for him. Oh, he look hard enough to me. One time he seen me talkin' to her. Look at us like we spit layin' in the street. I think he even got that cop Leventhal on his pay."

"Leventhal, hah," Sol said, rubbing nerveless fingers over the frames of his glasses.

They tolerated silence for a while. Then Sol spoke in a hoarse parody of casualness.

"The man's name, her boss, did you happen to catch that?"

"Some guinea name. Murdio, Murlio, somethin' like that."

A cold prize of knowledge lay just within his reach, and Sol considered sickly whether or not he wished to seize it. Finally he pressed his hands hard on the counter to still a tiny flutter.

"Could it perhaps have been Murillio?" he asked in a detached voice.

"Sound like it," Ortiz answered, his head cocked curiously at the Pawnbroker's invisible twitching. "Why, you know who he is?"

"Have you ever been in a brothel?" Sol asked, toying with the gold watch, a feigned smile inviting informal conversation.

"Brothel?"

"A house of prostitution, like the one she works in."

"Oh well, couple of times when I was just a kid. But I don't have to pay for that stuff no more."

"And what is it like? Are the girls unhappy in there about what they are forced to do?" The Pawnbroker's face was lost in some nameless graveyard of thought. Yet under the placid exterior he struggled to escape burial with things he had left behind forever. He wished suddenly that he had not asked the question.

"Ain't no one *force* them," Ortiz told him, proud in an area of superior wisdom. "They get greedy for easy money an' they go to it. Oh sure, they find out it more than they bargain for. Once they in, it's not so easy to get out. Listen, they get all kinds of crazy cats in there, make them do some rough things. It's no *fun*, I can tell you that. No fun to go there as a customer either. Might as well have a vending machine." Something seemed to occur to him, and he peered at the Pawnbroker as though he distrusted the flat, white light of the fluorescents. "How come you so interested all of a sudden? Think of payin' them a visit?" he asked slyly.

"No, no," Sol answered absently, lost to the humor. For a moment his face showed a horror, as at something exhumed. His lips parted and whitened, his forehead beaded, as though sweat had been squeezed out by some terrific inner pressure. His eyes bulged helplessly behind the magnifying lenses. But inside he could recognize nothing except great shifting shapes. And soon he was able to still them, to make them lie down like placated beasts.

"You sick?" Jesus asked, disturbed by the contortions of that habitually stony face. "What's wrong with you?"

"What's wrong with me?" Sol repeated dazedly.

Then suddenly he was the Pawnbroker again, because that was what he wished to be: calm, inscrutable, giving nothing for nothing.

"Just that sometimes I become disgusted with these people, whining, begging. I become curious about what makes the creatures live like this."

His assistant looked at him with cold interest. "Why you call them creatures? Because they niggers?"

"No, no," Sol denied with a harsh chuckle. "I am nonsectarian, nondiscriminatory. Black, white, yellow are all equally abominations. Tell me, Ortiz, do you believe in God?" he asked with a vicious smile.

"You no priest, Sol. What I think is my business," the youth answered, a fitting apprentice. "I listen what my brain say to me."

"Know thyself," Sol said mockingly. "Ah, but you are all right, Jesus Ortiz. I feel you are learning faster than I did. Of course, you are lucky to have me for a teacher. Already you have learned to trust nothing."

"Like I said, you don' know what I think," Ortiz stated proudly. Then he smiled and surveyed the gray fleshy face before him. "So I got a good teacher; okay, teach. Tell me what *you* trust or don't trust."

The trace of humor on Sol's face faded almost as soon as he began talking; and was gradually replaced by a tautness, by something that reacted on his features like an astringent passion.

"I do not trust God or politics or newspapers or music or art. I do not trust smiles or clothes or buildings or scenery or smells." He reached for the light switches and flicked off the fluorescents one by one, until the store was illuminated only by the reflection of late sunlight through the doorway, and the two of them were faded, almost motionless afterimages of what they had been in the recent glare, less real than the metal instruments and the jewelry all around. "I do not trust names. I do not trust expressions or colors or the feel of texture." Outside, the early evening traffic sounds crowded the last bits of silence into the store, where it surrounded them and left them like undiscovered islands in their private dusk. "But, most of all, I do not trust people and their talk, for they have created hell with that talk, for they have proved they do not deserve to exist for what they are."

"You, too?" Ortiz asked, his voice faintly hoarse, as from too long a silence.

"I, too."

Then Ortiz umm'ed and ahh'ed and tried to make something light out of all that was ponderous and inappropriate in their wild exchange.

"Well then, Mister Pawnbroker, ain't there nothin' you *do* trust?" he asked in awkward banter, trying not to care about the answer.

"Perhaps there is something," Sol said, his eyes a cold glitter on the golden swim outside the store.

Ortiz measured his own breathing as he waited.

"Money," the Pawnbroker said suddenly, dropping the word among the golds and silvers of the quiet shop. "That might repel many people less practical than you," he said sardonically. "The old story with Jews, hah! Ah, but let me tell you, Ortiz, there is good reason for maintaining that fidelity. True, money *can* increase or decrease in value; it, too, can be somewhat risky. But at a given moment you usually have some idea of its value. You can have some basis for estimating what it can buy you; food or comfort, luxury, relief from pain, or even, sometimes . . . yes, sometimes it can buy you life itself. Next to the speed of light, which Einstein tells us is the only absolute in the universe, second only to that I would rank money. There, I have taught you the Pawnbroker's Credo, Ortiz. What else is there to know!" he cried almost gaily.

Ortiz just shook his head for a moment, an odd flicker threading through his smile as something turned over in him.

"Can't complain about that. All right, Sol, you say it all. Hey, I got to listen to my teacher, don't I! Oh, I gonna keep in mind what you tell me. What else can I do?" He held his hands out, palms upward in the pose of Semitic resignation. And yet, under the raillery and the cynicism, there was a peculiar anger, a look that inexplicably suggested regret and accusation. "After all, you the teacher. . . . "

Ortiz had left, and Sol was on the point of leaving himself when the phone rang.

"A guy name Riordan will be over," the phonographic voice said in his ear. "He'll make the delivery. Have a letter, too, some suggestions for spendin' our money. Oh, we're a great team, you and me, Uncle. I like the way you been handling things. Remind me to declare a bonus for Christmas. Oh, that's right, you don't celebrate Christmas, do you? Well, we'll make it Chanukah." The chuckle grated in the receiver like a noisemaker being swung slowly against its cogs.

"People pay well for their hungers, don't they?" Sol asked with apparent irrelevance. "For food and drink and the other pleasures of their bodies. They pay you well for these things?"

"What are you talking about? I never knew you was a drinking man."

"About all the money you make. That was what I was talking about."

"You gettin' nosy, Uncle; it ain't like you. Let's just say my investments are doin' fine, if it's any of your business. You just keep your nose clean and let me worry about the rest."

"I should not be concerned about the smell of the money then?" he asked in a detached voice, obviously just asking a normal question.

"It wouldn't be too healthy. What's with you, Uncle?" Murillio demanded. "You losing your respect for money?"

"No, no, I am just rambling. I am sorry I asked. Forget I said it."

"I'll forget. Just see you do, too, Uncle."

"Uh, Riordan, you say. What happened to Savarese?" Sol asked, the bubble indicating level again.

"He was undependable. We try the Irishman for a while."

Sol nodded as though his partner could see him.

"All right, Uncle, I'll call tomorrow or the next day. Meanwhile . . . "

"I will keep my nose clean," Sol said.

Murillio laughed so the delicate diaphragm in the earpiece rattled. "You just do that," he said, appreciative of the humor, and hung up.

Sol stood with his hand on the phone for a moment, groping for the next step in time. It was Monday; what did he plan to do on Monday? The false measure of time clicking from the many clocks offered him nothing. The hours were too slick to seize and led nowhere anyhow. His body smelled like clay, faintly damp, sunless, old.

"Tessie," he said aloud. "I told her I would come tonight."

And that was at least something to advance him to wherever he was bound for ultimately. He began locking the many accesses. When he was done, he went down the street in a hurry, like someone late for an assignation.

## ELEVEN

The old man, Mendel, sat in the kitchen staring grimly at the radio, which was blaring dance music at him so loudly that the small speaker rattled. Sol studied the four cards in his hand, trying to decide which way to build tens. Across the bridge table, Tessie chewed tensely on her cuticles. Every so often she looked at the clock, and darted a quick, furtive glance toward the door before turning an accumulated intensity on the cards. Upstairs, a Spanish program competed with the old man's dance music and a man and woman shouted in apparent argument, as though the loud Latin music were a mere accompaniment to their anger. The old pipes shuddered and whined. Someone laughed hysterically, veered dangerously toward strangulation, and subsided into coughing. A child cried. The rooms had a damp-plush smell, like a train car opened after a long sealing.

"So play already," Tessie said irritably.

"You are in a hurry?"

"But to just sit there!"

"Why are you so nervous?"

"Nervous, why should I be nervous? I am a happy, peaceful woman. Everything is wonderful for me. So why should I be nervous?" She glared guiltily at him, her yellow face scoured and worn by petty miseries to a texture that obscured the massive old deformities.

"You're upset about Goberman," he accused.

"The man drives me crazy. The other night, late, he was here, pounding on the door. He woke the old man. The things he threatens, the curses."

"There's nothing he can do to you. He is just an annoyance. I told you I would deal with him, so what are you getting excited about?"

"Where is he?" she said, looking toward the door.

"It is as though you want him to come."

"What if he comes after you have gone? What will I tell him then? He won't believe me."

"I don't understand you. How can you be so disturbed about what he says. He can't do anything to you. Just tell him to leave you alone or you'll have him arrested. There is nothing he can do to hurt you."

"Oh no! That is how blind you are. He can drive daggers in me, he can ruin my sleep, he can tear my heart out."

"That is nonsense! You have nothing to feel guilty about, neither of us do. We have been in Hell and we have escaped. We owe no one."

"Have *you* escaped?"

"You are a hysterical woman. It would be good for you to get a grip on yourself or you'll be in for a nervous breakdown. Yes, I have escaped. I am safe within myself. I have made an order for myself, and no one can disturb it. It would be good if you would try to do the same. When Goberman comes, I will straighten that out for you, and you will see how simple all these things are." With that, he laid down his ace on top of a seven and the Good Two. "Building tens," he said.

Tessie slapped her ten down on top of his "build," and her expression was wicked and vindictive as she slid the cards toward her.

Sol smiled. "See, like that," he said. "Grab what you need without mooning and sighing. Take, do, act! Life is the here and now. Focus on what is before you. Bear down, push away whoever impedes you. Take what you need; money, relief, peace."

"I had a child, I had a husband," she whispered savagely.

"What do you want from me?" he shouted. "Kill yourself then, and be done with it!" He threw his cards down and shoved the table away from him. His face was like a rock from which tiny grainings were being shaken loose under a child's weak but persistent hammering.

Tessie held up her hand fearfully, her face violet-lidded, deep-eyed, raw. "Wait, wait, sit," she cried. "I'll go make coffee, I have cake. We will eat something, Sol."

He fell back sullenly and closed his eyes in agreement.

Tessie went into the kitchen, where the dance music sounded with unmitigated violence over the old man's mutterings.

"Turn it down, Pa," she said. "I can't hear to think."

But the radio continued its assault. It was only one sound in the cacophony of the building. Tessie made more noise than necessary, to hold her own in all the din. She slammed the coffeepot onto the stove and struck the saucers with the cups. One of the pieces of china made a dull, suicidal sound.

"I broke it," she said bewilderedly.

The old man shut off the radio with a groan. "Listen to those murderers screaming the *Deutsch*," he snarled forlornly.

"That is Spanish, Pa, not German," she told him in a dull voice.

"They are all *Deutsch*," he roared, then, in a sly, vicious tone, "You are not mixing the *fleishica* dishes vit the *milchik?*"

"No, Pa, everything is kosher," she said wearily.

And then the door shook under a pounding fist.

Tessie gasped and went to the doorway of the kitchen to look at Sol. He glanced disdainfully at her before getting slowly to his feet and walking toward the front door. With his hand on the knob, he looked back at Tessie and nodded.

"Who is it?" she called in a shakily innocent tone.

"Your conscience, Goberman. Pay your debts," said the hoarse voice on the other side of the door.

Sol swung the door open suddenly. A short, thickset figure stood there, revealed like a joke in the wake of the heavy threat of the voice. Goberman had a pale face from which all the large features strained as if he were the victim of a slow garroting. The tip of his bulbous nose was snowy white in its thrust, his lips pressed forward in a grotesque kiss, his boiled-looking eyes protruded like those of birds that can move each eye independently. His chin and cheeks were mangy with patches of unshaved beard, as though he shaved with a dull kitchen knife; it lent the whole face the look of something just dug up and not yet shaken clean of the grayish poor soil of its recent burial.

"Who are you? The light is bad here," he complained in that rough voice. "Where's the woman here, that Rubin woman? Ah, but you look familiar, too. *Du bist ein Yid?* Oh yeh, aha, I see," he said triumphantly, squeezing past Sol into the lighted room, his eyes victorious on the tattooed numbers on Sol's arm. He held up a chewed-looking brief case and waved it at Sol's face. "I expect from you, too. The Jewish Appeal. Do you know how many Jews are still in Cairo? I'll tell you for enlightenment. Thirty-seven thousand six hundred and twenty-two. That's as of last week. God knows how many been killed since then. And in Syria! Twenty-nine thousand eight hundred and forty. Then we got seventeen thousand four hundred and thirty-three in Iran, thirty-six thousand and seven in Germany, nineteen thousand . . . "

"Let me see your credentials," Sol said coldly.

"Credentials, credentials," Goberman spat indignantly. "Where is she, where is that woman who would like to ease her conscience? You don't reside here. I got in my address book, lives here one woman, Tessie Rubin, aged forty-three, one man, Mendel Solowitz, aged seventy-five. You are a interloper. I will deal with the woman of the house."

"I'm here, I'm here," Tessie called fearfully. "It's all right, Goberman. This man handles my business."

The old man peered wildly over her shoulder, muttering against ancient crimes.

"Your *business,* he handles," Goberman said nastily. "I *see,* I see very well. The husband cold in the grave, so you must take care . . ."

"What right have you to come in here like this?" Sol said. "Before you say another word I must see your credentials."

"My credentials, you want to see my credentials? All right, I'll show, I'll show." He plunked down the brief case, which made a wet soft sound, like the body of an animal. Then he tore off his coat and rolled up his sleeves muttering, "Credentials, credentials, I'll show credentials." On his left arm were the familiar blue numbers framed in a border of white tape like some weird sampler on the hairless surface. "Inside my heart is more credentials, too. Go get a knife from the kitchen and open me up. I'll show you the stab wounds, the burnt pieces from the murders of my wife, my five children, my mother, my sister. Go, get the knife; I'll show you credentials, printed in red, in BLOOD! You want more? Chop open my brain, see there the pictures of the walking dead, the raped, the disemboweled." His breath came in shuddery gasps, his eyes threatened to fall out and roll down his face. He stood crouched and threatening, exuding a violence of smell and fury, his shirt pulled half out of his pants, his neck beating a wild rhythm. "Is that credentials, tell me, is that?"

"All right, Goberman, I'll give, I'll give," Tessie wailed. "Is there any need to go on like that. I try; you have no reason to curse me. I feel for the Jews, I do, I do!"

Goberman slid the coat back onto his shoulders with a smug, righteous expression. He looked at Sol. "And you, can you refuse the slaves, the suffering *Yiddlach?*"

"I have been looking at you, Goberman," Sol said in a soft, thoughtful voice. "And I have been trying to recall where I know you from. And now, suddenly, it occurs to me. You were there, yes you were. About 1941, in Dachau . . . no, no, Bergen-Belsen. Yess-ss, I remember you very well."

"What, what?" Goberman said a little nervously. "You couldn't have remembered me. I was . . ."

"Yes, yes, I'm certain now. You were even a little fatter then. You had a method for getting more food. There was some talk—I don't know for sure how true—but there was some talk of *co-operation* with a certain . . ."

"It was a lie, a complete lie!" Goberman shouted, beating on his brief case. "No one could accuse . . ."

"If I am not mistaken there was someone who claimed that you even informed on members of your own family. . . ."

"That is the greatest lie in the world, the most abominable piece of filth anyone could say about a man," Goberman screamed, his voice leaping the decibels to a sort of shattered alto.

Sol shrugged, obviously just repeating what he had heard.

"Not my own family, never my own family. What kind of a person would say a thing like that? Here, look at me, see how I collect money for the Jews, how I bleed for them all over the world. Day and night I try to get money for their salvation. I scream, I threaten, I sacrifice my self-respect to do for them. And this, this is my reward! No one can say to my face that I . . . *never* in a million years would I have done a thing like that to my *immediate* family. Do you think I could sleep at night, do you think I could sit still for a minute if . . . ? Would I run around like a madman, day and night, if I . . . ? Wouldn't I sit still and try to have some peace and quiet . . . ? How could anyone . . . ? It is beyond imagining that such a person could walk the face of the earth. . . ." His mouth sagged like a too-wet formation of clay. "I NEVER . . . SOLD . . . MY . . . OWN . . . FAMILY . . . NEVERNEVERNEVERNEVER!"

"What do you do with all the money?" Sol asked in an icy voice, his face and body motionless, remorseless. "Do you sew it into your mattress or are you enlightened enough to put it into a three-and-a-half-per-cent account? What are you saving for?"

"I save for the Jewish People," Goberman wailed, his face soaking wet and pulpy. "The Jewish People."

"You save for Goberman. You are a crook, a fake, Goberman. I could have the police on you. Or better still," he said, thinking of Murillio, "I could have you beaten to a pulp with just one phone call."

"You don't understand, you just don't understand what I have been through." Goberman was weeping like a woman by then, hugging the sloppy brief case to his chest and sobbing.

"I understand you very well, Goberman. You are a common type. A professional sufferer, a practicing refugee. You are an opportunist who can put anything to profit. But you feel guilty about some of your crimes, you cannot sleep too well. So you run around with that brief case and try to make everyone else feel as guilty as you, meantime turning a pretty penny. Now I do not judge you, understand, it does not matter to me what you do. Only you must know that you are naked to me. You do not impress me." Sol took off his glasses and began wiping them, staring meanwhile at Goberman with the flat, nearsighted gaze which looked so remote and beyond appeal.

"Are you any better than I am? Don't tell me you didn't leave your dead there and run out as fast as a rabbit, saying good riddance to all this, to all the smelly dead. Don't tell me," Goberman whined, his finger accusatorily pointed at Sol's face, his eyes like jellyfish in the welter of his teary features. "Can you stand there, Tessie Rubin, can you let him say this to a representative . . . to a rep . . . Is it human to stand there like a rock and tear a person to pieces, to throw up his griefs to a man, to a victim!"

Sol began to laugh, a harsh metal-on-metal sound which made the listeners wince. It set the teeth in Goberman's mouth in a mold of rubber. Tessie stared in horror at Sol; she had never heard him laugh before, and it was as though he revealed a monstrosity in the unprecedented sound. The old man whimpered and withdrew into the kitchen, and even the noise of the surrounding building seemed to observe a shocked silence for a few seconds.

"Oh, he is priceless, this Goberman," he said to Tessie. "Why did you not tell me he was so amusing? You have no sense of humor, Tessie. The man is rare, absolutely rare. Goberman, my friend," he said, turning suddenly, "do you realize how you are wasting your time? You should be on television or the radio. You are one of the funniest things I have ever seen. With that brief case, that face, and your dialogue . . ." He began to laugh again. Tessie covered her ears, but Goberman just stared and trembled, the fat tears running into his doughy mouth. "Talk . . . talk some more . . . Gober . . . man," Sol wheezed. "Entertain us. Laughter is said to be healthful. Make me laugh some more." And then, suddenly, he had the glasses back on, and his face turned to inhuman stone. *Make me laugh some more!* the Pawnbroker snarled.

"What do you want from me?" Goberman wailed. "I'll

go, I'll go. You are worse than all the Nazis, you are worse than my nightmares."

"Much worse," the Pawnbroker agreed from his great height. "I could break you in a million pieces."

"I never sold my family."

"You are *dreck,* Goberman; you should be washed away."

Goberman stood transfixed by the thick-lensed gaze over him, his body seeming to come apart under the sloppy clothes, so it was as though only the grip on the pulpy brief case held him in one piece.

"Now go, SHVEINHUNDT!"

Goberman leaped into the air as though the word had electrocuted him. He gave one whimper, bumped softly into the wall with a cry of pain, and then ran clumsily but very swiftly out the door. The racket of his heels on the tiles of the hallway was like a machine gun.

Tessie held her cheek. The old man moaned terribly in the kitchen. And all the noise of the building descended on them again.

Later, Sol took her on the couch with a cold fury, and she sobbed and pleaded for something she could not name. Yet in spite of her crying and her inchoate begging, it was for Sol as though he made love to a dead woman and the act was a horrid travesty. When it was over, he threw himself to his feet and stood reeling, his heart pounding the blood through the constrictions of his veins.

"What are you sniveling about? Did I eliminate him for you? Do you have what to complain about? You are a miserable creature yourself." He bent over her, still panting and furious. "What do you require of me; that I bring you the Garden of Eden, *Ganaydem*!"

She held her hands over her face, and her voice came muffled and distorted through them. "No, no, nothing. You give me nothing. Only go away now; I can take no more from you."

So he dressed and straightened himself and went out of

there without farewell; and before he closed the door, he stuck some money under the samovar, enough to last her and the old man until he came again.

His long journey by subway and car was quite uneventful. But he had this terrific ache all over his body. He decided it amused him. While he drove, he said aloud, "If I were Selig, I would think I was having a heart attack."

Otherwise, he thought of nothing.

## ✽ *TWELVE*

"Come, Solly dear," Bertha said to him affectionately. "We're just now having coffee and dessert." She waved at the man and the two women at the table with Selig. "You know Doctor Kogan, his wife, Martha. And this is *Dorothy*," she said, implying all the nice things they had said about the masculine-faced, fashionably dressed woman. "The Doctor's sister . . ."

Sol nodded and murmured a hello.

"Hello, Sol," the white-haired, sleek-faced man said. "How's the gift business?"

Sol glanced distastefully at his sister, and Bertha pleaded with her eyes for him not to expose her affectation.

"My business is fine, thank you. And yours, you have no slack seasons, do you?"

The Doctor laughed. "You know better than that," he said.

"So you are in the gift business," the unmarried sister said eagerly, not at all impressed by the big, unkempt man with the strange eyeglasses and the unhealthy, puffy face; but she responded by instinct to his eligibility. "I am in the retail business myself, Mr. Nazerman. . . ."

"Call him Sol," Bertha insisted, tilting her head mischievously.

"I am a buyer for a department store, so I guess we are colleagues," Dorothy said brightly.

Sol nodded and sat down to his coffee and chocolate cream pie. He had not eaten at Tessie's and the sweetness on his empty stomach nauseated him slightly. He poured himself another cup of coffee to wash the saccharine taste from his mouth.

"I don't know if you realize, Doc, but my brother-in-law here is a very educated man. Taught at a university in Poland at one time. Before the trouble, of course." Selig smiled over at Sol. "I've often said he should be a teacher."

"Teachers are paid poorly," Sol said. "I would have difficulty meeting my obligations on a teacher's salary," he added with a malicious twist to his mouth.

"Dorothy has an excellent job as a buyer," Bertha interceded quickly. "She even goes to Europe every year."

"Is that so." Sol nodded listlessly. "And how is Europe these days?"

"Oh I'm mad about Paris. Of course most of my business is there. But Rome and Berlin are my second loves. There is an atmosphere we don't have here, something mellow. You can almost smell the difference."

"Rather a stink, as I remember," Sol said, wanting to sever all the talk.

There was a white silence for almost a minute before Bertha leaped in like an alert lifeguard. "My brother just loves to shock people. Joanie calls him a character. You just have to understand his humor. Solly, *please,*" she chided smilingly, as for a slightly racy joke.

For a few minutes they talked carefully around him, and he sat like a stone in their chatter. The single woman glanced curiously at Sol from time to time, trying to establish her attitude. Finally she aimed her modish head at him.

"Where is your gift shop, Sol?" she asked.

"It is not a gift shop," Sol answered deliberately. Bertha turned with an expression of dismay for her relaxed vigilance. "It is a pawnshop. I am a pawnbroker." He gazed innocently at the looks of politely veneered shock. "True, some people may buy things as gifts. But mostly it is a hock shop, a place where poor people obtain ready cash on the collateral of anything and everything."

He got to his feet then and turned a pleasant smile all around. "Now if you will excuse me, I have had a hard day. It was a pleasure meeting you, Miss Kogan. . . ."

"Call her Dorothy," Bertha said weakly.

"Perhaps sometime when I am feeling better . . ."

Behind him, he heard Bertha's voice struggling to cover the unsightly hole he had left.

"Of course, Sol has had a difficult time," she said. "And then he is so bookish. But we are gradually drawing him out, getting him to join in the community a little. . . ."

Upstairs, in the darkened bedroom, he put himself to sleep by calculating the compound interest of his savings; he made ones and fives and tens go jumping like green birds, which he added and multiplied and divided until his mind seemed filled with just that feathery rustle, and he slept.

*He was flat on his back, staring at the glaring surgical lamp. Around him was the starched rustle of the surgeons' and nurses' white smocks. But he could see nothing except the purpling violence of the light. Some of them were laughing and making jokes as they worked just out of the peri-*

*phery of his vision. He felt no pain. But he heard the saw-*
*ing of bone, and he knew that it was his bone. There was*
*such a cheery exchange between the doctors, though, as be-*
*tween men enjoying a mutuality of interest. It was hard to*
*realize . . . he felt no pain. Then there came the clunking*
*sound of parts dropping into a bucket, the sounds of leak-*
*ings and drippings.*

*"WHAT ARE YOU TAKING OUT OF ME?" he screamed, see-*
*ing himself "boned" like some beast being prepared for*
*someone's meal. "STOP, STOP," he shrilled, visualizing so*
*clearly how he would be as a soft, collapsed carcass of flesh.*

*"Shut up, Jew," a blue-eyed nurse snarled into his face.*
*"Shut up or we'll take your prick, too."*

*So he lay still after that. However small a destruction*
*they aimed at, it was far larger than they knew. But at least*
*he felt no pain now and he could pretend he was dead.*

*"All done," a doctor said. "It will be interesting to see*
*how he functions now." A murmurous medley of voices*
*sounded a cold glee. "If he functions, if he functions at all,*
*if you know what I mean."*

*Someone laughed in gentle admonition.*

*"Ah, Berger, Berger, you are a terror, you are," another*
*voice said.*

*Sol howled in a fall of dizzying terror.*

He stared at the quiet, moon-made shadows on the
American wall. There was the sound of the family's minor
alarm, the footsteps of Selig and Bertha taking advantage of
their brief wakefulness to go to the bathroom. And then the
silence, which Sol wouldn't allow to claim him. He lay awake
with bulging eyes until the sun came into his room like a
trustworthy guard. And he slept a little while then.

## ✳ *THIRTEEN*

Another of the whores came in first thing in the morning. She was a tall, very dark Negress in her late thirties. Her face was welted and swollen with the marks of old and recent beatings, and her eyes sparkled like black stones. She had a gold cigarette case to pawn and she spoke with a cigarette in her mouth, her head tilted back against the smoke, one eye almost closed.

"Come on, Dad, what this worth? Got to have eatin' money. Yeah, ol' Rose fired from d'house. Got to go in business for myself. Got to have a place to park it, you know. Hey, but dis gold, Pops, worth big money, ain't it?"

She watched him examine it, muttering all the while so her cigarette rode up and down in her mouth.

"Got to pay the ol' doctuh fo' mah sickness an' get me a

pad to lay mah bones. Got to have a little somethin' for a beverage to still mah nerves. Cause mah nerves is real bad, let me tell you. So, Dad, you tell me, you tell me." She wore a red satin dress and her bare chest was turtle-skinned, her breasts stiffly delineated like those of an old woman wearing a steel-ribbed brassière.

"Ten dollars," he said, breathing through his mouth to avoid the overwhelming stench of her perfume.

"Oh, Daddy-o, Ah got to *live*," she whined, her swollen black face further contorted by the cigarette smoke.

"Why?" he muttered through his teeth.

"Make it fifteen, Dad," she said, hearing only her own plea. "Ah could make it wid fifteen."

"Ten, ten, that is all," he said, raising his voice.

"Okay, okay, Mistuh, sure, sure," she said placatingly, too marked up by men to argue. "Ah take it. Thank you, thank you, fine." And she made deep nods of agreement, like a child accepting the firmness of punishment.

A man came in with a couple of suits, and Ortiz took him upstairs to try some newer ones on.

An old, white-haired man with a snowy mustache edged into the store. He was dressed in a neat but worn-looking suit and a slightly frayed blue shirt, buttoned up to the neck but without a tie. Under his arm was a neatly wrapped package, which he clung to as he hovered near the doorway. For a few minutes he looked wistfully out at the street. Then he took a firm breath and marched over to Sol.

"I would like to raise some money on this, young man," he said, shouting a little. "A temporary loan. I want the transaction carefully recorded. I plan to return for my property in the very near future, so don't try to sell it." As he talked with his eyes admonishingly on the Pawnbroker, his arthritic fingers fumbled with the knot.

"We keep merchandise for a prescribed period; it is the law," Sol said with a tiny smile. He watched the misshapen fingers struggling with the knot for a minute.

Then he took a razor blade and slashed quickly at the cord. The old man stepped back at the pop of the severed string, dismayed at its being taken out of his hands so quickly.

"Mind you, now, I know how much this is worth," he warned weakly, glancing down at the hands that had failed him.

It was a beautifully carved chess set of rich hardwood, and a chessboard of inlaid teak and walnut. Each piece was carved in the likeness of an ancient figure; the rooks were elephants with howdahs on their backs, the pawns were foot soldiers, the knights proud horsemen, the bishops sly clerics with oriental features, the kings and queens lordly, towering majesties.

"It is a lovely set," Sol said in a musing, tender voice. His father's brother had owned a set similar to this, a million years ago. "They are obviously carved by hand." He picked up the white king gently and smiled down at the miniature sternness of the features.

"You have an eye for these things, I see," the old man said happily. "Oh yes, it's very old. My father bought it . . . oh, it must be over eighty years ago now. I've had it for over forty years myself. I wouldn't part with it for a minute only . . . temporary reverse. Act of God, so to speak. There's been some confusion about a pension check. Even at my age a man must eat." He chuckled and touched his mustache in a lordly gesture, obviously a man above haggling.

"I can only loan you fifteen dollars on it," the Pawnbroker said in a flat voice.

The old man looked up in surprise; it was as though another person had taken the place of the man who had admired the beauty of the carving. He looked at the gray, expressionless face and said to himself, no, no, this is a pawnbroker, take what you can. So he nodded without deigning to watch the formalities of the transaction, and after it was done, he went out with the money buried in his pocket, all his frayed, starched dignity intact.

And before Sol could draw a breath of quiet, two women came in with a small electric sewing machine between them. His mind recoiled in idiotic humor and he thought of Solomon offering to cut the baby in half for the two warring mothers.

"Whose is it?" he asked wearily.

The two women looked at each other speculatively, suddenly sly and greedy for ownership.

Sol looked fiercely at the tuba on the ceiling.

Ortiz was hungry. As he headed out the door, he called to the Pawnbroker, "Be back soon." But Sol maintained his heavenward stare while the two women bickered in whispers.

In the cafeteria, Ortiz took the pea soup, pork and beans, coffee, and a piece of gingerbread. Then he threaded his way among the tables, looking for one that was empty. He sat down and salted the soup.

"Hey man, sit here with us," Tangee called. Buck White and the bony-faced Robinson sat watching him sleepily.

"Maybe it better if we talk like this . . . separate," Ortiz said, turning back to his food.

"Why, what for?"

"If I think I know what you want to talk about, it might be smart to. . . ."

Tangee widened his eyes appreciatively. "Yess-s man, that's smart," he agreed. He aimed his eyes in elaborate attention on the two men he was with as he spoke. "Do I understand you interested in something then?"

"It might be," Jesus said, chewing deliberately on his gingerbread.

The Pawnbroker had said money was next to the speed of light. *The Speed-of-Light!* There was something terrible and exciting in the thought. The Pawnbroker himself had chosen, and Ortiz didn't dare examine himself to see if he regretted that conclusion. He was tiring of masturbatory dreaming.

"You know what we got in mind?" Tangee asked, his mouth wooden and stiff, trying to talk the way experienced cons talked when they wished to disguise their conversations from the guards. Robinson smiled scornfully.

"I don't need a picture."

"Okay. Now the thing is, to do it right we need you."

"I know you do." Ortiz put down his spoon and sat rigidly in his chair, staring at the center of his table. "So hear me, man. I ain't say nothing definite yet, see. I got to think it out a little more, got to plan and see if they a way to make it work."

"We know, man. It work all right, don't worry about that!"

"You don't know nothin'. You just get a good idea, guess you gonna walk into a place and that all there is to it. I don't want nothin' to do with a guy that dumb, hear!"

"Okay, okay, relax," Tangee said placatingly, forgetting to keep his lips still.

All around them was the innocent clatter of people eating in a public place; the sounds of feet on the tile floors, the clatter of dishes, the tinny jingle of cutlery, the great uneven and howling softness of conversation. Ortiz stopped eating again to stare at the big plate-glass window. People walked by, their dark skins more reflection than color in the hot light. The stores across the street were a discord of faded and garish colors, an idiotic anagram of message; Firbish, Ye Style Shoppe, 24 Hour Service, Weeny Hut, Tabernacle of Jesus Our Lord, White Rose Sal . . . Just out of sight, the three gold balls would be shining in the sulphurous sunlight. Beauty.

"*I* got to be the one that calls the moves. *If* I decides to go ahead with it," Jesus said in a burning low whisper.

"Well sure, man. We figured you for that," Tangee said with his hand over his mouth. Buck agreed with a nod, but Robinson just sat in a rigid silence.

"And if this thing goes, there be no shootin', see. You need a piece, okay, just for show."

Tangee and Buck nodded solemnly, and Robinson watched them superciliously, as though they were children involved in a nonsensical game.

"Because shootin' is trouble, it stupid. We do without, no matter what, understand!" He risked a look at them and saw Tangee and Buck still nodding agreeably. Robinson compromised with a bend of his lipless mouth. Ortiz toyed with his food, no longer hungry, his appetite not appeased but mutilated beyond recognition. "*If* I decide to go ahead with it . . . *if*. I say when and how, *if*."

Finally he stood up and lit a cigarette, staring through a cloud of smoke at the three men, making a sort of contract with his gaze but also telling them that it was not signed yet and that they must wait.

"Take it cool, man," Tangee said with a smile.

"That the only way I take it," Ortiz answered, suddenly furious before the sleepy, hidden opinion of the flashily dressed man.

In the store, Sol looked up from the throbbing, invisible rise of dirt around him. His skin felt dry and aged, his eyes burned from the poor sleep of his nights. And he beheld Marilyn Birchfield standing before him like a substantial vision of cleanliness. She had an unwrinkled paper bag in her hand and she was smiling.

"If you remember, we have a date for lunch by the river," she said.

Sol looked at her dazedly. He was astounded by her smile and her brightness and for a moment he wondered what she had to do with him.

But then Ortiz walked in and he was able to convert that daze of weariness to a sudden, sardonic humor.

"I'll be back soon," he said to the puzzled face of his assistant. "I am going on a picnic."

And he walked out of the store with the woman. He left a bewilderment behind him where Jesus Ortiz now held a brief reign.

## ❋ FOURTEEN

They sat on the low wooden beam that made a sort of curbing at the edge of the river. A few feet below was the greenish-brown water, from which the sun managed to bring shimmering sequins: out of all the muck an illusion of brightness. Sol swung his gaze along the chaos of the opposite bank. Directly across from where they sat was a coalyard with a chute that led down to the water. Boys were leaping off into the greasy river and then climbing back up to jump again. It was amazing how fresh the water looked when they splashed it up into the sunlight. There were brick buildings and corrugated metal roofs. A great, heavily laden barge moved ponderously toward them. He continued his perusal of the familiar place as though something about it might have altered in the few hours since he had last been there. The same wide derelict expanse bordering the river, a piece of desert-like sand in a huge triangle, a space of no apparent use, which had not even collected the usual junk and refuse that most emptinesses invited in that part of the city. And the usual vista of the nearer dirt-caked tenements with the unreal, towering mirages of the great office buildings far downtown.

And then—her! A bright, full-faced woman, smiling at him and talking, still remarkably fresh and clean-looking, even with the faint shine of perspiration above her lip. What was he doing there with her, this voluble American woman with her girlish face and full, womanly body?

". . . because, frankly, Mr. Nazerman, this city is still rather strange to me," she said.

He tried to focus on the context of their relationship, there in the hot sun, beside the flow of polluted water. The immense, stony growth of the city was all around, and he sat in a body he had long ago outlived, while a foreign woman spoke to him in a language he had thought he understood.

". . . then I said to myself, Marilyn, old girl, come off it. They're all people. Only they have a variety of problems I'd never come up against. And suddenly it was all much simpler for me. This place began to seem less a foreign country than a part of my own home town I'd never noticed before." She smiled her wholesome smile. "There I go talking too much again. Perhaps that's the weakness of lonely people. Either people clam up on me and I feel compelled to break through to them, or else they act friendly and I feel I owe them a lot of talk. I admit I risk my dignity sometimes, often I feel I'm an out-and-out pest. But when I get through to someone, when I do make a friend . . . well, the risks seem negligible."

"I do not wish to inflict a failure on you, Miss Birchfield, but I must be frank also. To be honest, I do not welcome your prying, your *interest*. In most times I probably would have been quite positive and brutal about discouraging you. Only lately I have been . . . not quite myself." He chuckled harshly. "Not quite myself," he repeated, deriving a perverse pleasure from the irony. Then his face clouded and he seemed to have difficulty seeing through the heavy lenses.

"I have not been well these last few weeks. Poor sleep . . . It makes me somewhat dull," he said. "Normally, I keep to myself. I do not usually let people unnerve me. It is strange, this feeling, I don't know. Perhaps I should see a doctor and be done with it. Doctors, oh yes, they have great tricks these days, they effect amazing changes. Oh, I have figured some of the reasons for the way I feel. I have many pressures on me, financial pressures. And then, my business exposes me to the poorer elements, dirty ignorant people. It is a business that has some precarious aspects. And yet I have borne up quite well with it for a number of years now. It will all pass. I am perhaps somewhat tired, tense. My age increases too; I will be forty-six in the fall."

She widened her eyes involuntarily. He looked much older. He was only ten years older than she; it jarred her idea of their relationship. Partly, she guessed, he looked so much older because of his poor color, the inexplicable thicknesses of his face. Actually, it was hardly lined and his hair was dark and free of gray. Yet there was great age in the very way he held himself, in the *mass* of his face, which made the bone structure unguessable.

"However, I am here now and perhaps it will do me no harm to sit quite idly in the sun for a short time."

"And eat these sandwiches I bought," she reminded him with a humorous raising of her eyebrows.

"And eat the sandwiches *you* bought, but which *I* paid for last week."

She laughed delightedly at that, her head back, her strong-muscled neck taut in the brilliant day. Then, still smiling, she asked him if he would like a corned-beef sandwich.

"For some reason, I cannot eat meat. It goes against me. Perhaps I did without it too long. Usually I lunch on cheese sandwiches."

She held up a wax-paper-wrapped sandwich triumphantly. "You see, I have an instinct for your likes. Cheese for you, I'll have the meat."

He smiled as he reached for the sandwich.

She sat back with an affectation of amazement.

"I saw it!" she said.

"You saw what?" he asked, the smile slowly fading.

"You were off your guard for a moment, and I saw it. You have a *charming* smile, Mr. Nazerman. I'm beginning to think you're hiding a human being under your cold manner."

"Do not bank on it, Miss Birchfield," he said, beginning to eat.

"I don't understand. Why are you so afraid of being thought human?"

He just held up his hand.

"Do not get out of your depth, please. So you are a sociologist, a modern, logical person. Of course I am human; I have no choice about that. But I am a private individual, also, and I prefer to remain so. This is pleasant," he said, taking a little deeper breath of the tarry, heated air. "I feel it rests me a little. Do not spoil it with silly analysis." His face became grave for a moment. "Besides, you might find things you could not bear at all. Let it be simple. Say I am a rather cold person, that I have had a difficult life and prefer the peace of being left alone."

She nodded respectfully. Then she squinted a little curiously at him. "Tell me this," she said, "do you have any contact with the people you deal with every day in your store? Do they make any impression on you?" She ate slowly with her attention on his face.

"Frequently they disgust me. Nothing more."

"I see," she said thoughtfully. "Now this question may be

a little offensive. Please put it down to my insatiable curiosity, and excuse it. I've always had the impression that pawnbroking was a somewhat unsavory business, that poor people are taken advantage of. Am I completely wrong?"

"Of course not," Sol said easily, gazing at the river. "First of all, because poor people are always taken advantage of, and there could be no business in our society without that being so. Yes, pawnbroking thrives on people's woes. But what of that? Undertaking thrives on people's deaths but it is not responsible for their dying. What is the difference at which point in the chain of lives a man sets himself up in business? For me, this particular trade was ideal. I am not required to solicit or cater to people, as in many forms of business. I do not have to sell. Besides, there is considerable profit in pawnbroking. I want a certain income to afford the privacy and independence I require."

"But tell me this: as a human being, don't you, like everyone else, sometimes feel a need to justify what you do? What I'm trying to say is that I feel there has to be some real importance to our work, at least occasionally. Otherwise we are like mice on a treadmill with no feeling of beginning or ending." She had stopped eating and now watched his idle study of the river.

Slowly the hard, habitual smile spread over his mouth, and his eyes glinted almost cruelly from the depths of the thick glasses.

"As a *human being* again?" he said sardonically. *"Justify,* you say. All right, I will justify. I will make it logical and laudable, for everything can be explained and defended from a certain point of view, absolutely everything. Say I am like their priest. Yes, do not be shocked, I *am.* They get as much from me as they do from their churches. They bring me their troubles in the shapes of old table radios and watches and stolen typewriters and gold-plated crucifixes and half-paid-for cameras. And I, I give them absolution in hard cash. Now what do you think of that! Oh yes, they know I only give them a small fraction of what the thing is worth. But what they get is still a prize to them. They know how difficult it is to get *anything* from me. If I were to soften up, I would devaluate their little triumphs. They would be shocked and confused; I would be like a priest giving in to temptation. Oh, their pleasure is short-lived; the little I give them must be spent in no time at all. But they walk out of my store smiling and reprieved." Suddenly, his eyes were faintly clouded. It was as though he had just discovered an amazing particle of truth in his harsh joke, and he turned to her with a hint of perplexity in his hard smile. "Tell me, Miss Birchfield, tell me this: who can give them any more than a reprieve?"

"I don't know," she answered. "I really don't know. Perhaps I *am* out of my depth. My view of life has been pretty naïve. But I'm getting older; certain horrors have gotten through to me." Dreamily, she gazed at the half-naked bodies of the boys across the river as they splashed into the water and then climbed back up the coal chute like gleaming, newly caught fish. "I was a fat and amiable kid; everyone seemed to like me. The boys thought I was a great sport. I remember some of them used to tell me solemnly that they thought of me as a sister." She laughed, quite without sadness. "Well, in that odd category I went to a lot of parties and had loads of friends. It really wasn't too bad. Oh, I had wistful moments when I imagined myself sylphlike and exotic. But my childhood wasn't traumatic, rather happy, as a matter of fact. Only one day I discovered the most excruciating malady in myself—*loneliness*. I fought it, despised it. Just self-pity, I told myself; come off it, kiddo, look around at the people who are really in trouble. But you know, when I did look around, it occurred to me that most people suffered from the same thing. And pitying myself, I began to pity them, too. Now I'm sure as heck not asking for your sympathy. I suppose my teeny sorrows must seem frivolous to you, maybe even offensive. But everybody suffers on his own. All I'm trying to say is that I made a discovery, at least for me. I figured that nobody was responsible for my sadness, so there was nobody to be bitter against." She sighed and made a wry expression, almost a smile. "Loneliness is probably the normal state of affairs for people. And any happiness you're able to get . . . well, it's contained, sort of . . . oh, you might say happiness is contained in the *context* of sadness."

Now she turned to look directly at him, her light-blue eyes almost masculine in their frankness and vigor. Her features were too strong for prettiness, and she owed her attractive appearance to her expression, which was at once compassionate and humorous, innocent and sensible.

"I know there's misery and cruelty and injustice in the world, Mr. Nazerman. I'm not quite such a dewy-eyed fool as you may think. But I have hope for everyone. Even for myself." She let her hand shape a gesture that asked for his patience—a slight curving of the fingers she held aloft, a holding of attention and a sign of beckoning. "Sometimes it's hard for me to maintain dignity. I'm a spinster—not the most attractive role to play. In my worst times I feel involved in a tasteless joke." She mitigated her statement with a smile, hopelessly sunny under all the regret, as though she knew better than to aspire to tragedy. "But mostly I have few complaints. My work gives me a great deal of pleasure; it seems important and worth doing. And most of all, *I'm not bitter.*" She faced him resolutely, her face sternly Yankee, her eyes expressing the Protestant belief in self-control. "I have some idea of what you've been through, Mr. Nazerman. I would expect a great deal of sadness and grief to be in you. But why are you *bitter?* By now you should have discovered that it's a poor shield."

Sol studied a pair of gulls gliding vigilantly over the dark water, dipping now and then as though they thought they had discovered life in that unrevealing flow, only to rise up with hardly a movement of their wings when they discovered their mistake.

"My dear Miss Birchfield, how touchingly naïve you still are," he said finally, shifting on the wooden curb of the river, his face shining with sweat, his glasses picking up flashes of sunlight and flinging them at her like tiny darts. "You discovered loneliness, you found that life was unjust and cruel. What an astounding accomplishment! And with commendable humility you say that I might despise your suffering, that it might seem less dramatic than my own. Very well—but let me try to make some sense to you." He leaned intimately toward her. "There is this, my dear *sociologist*. People who have 'suffered' in your little world may or may not become bitter, depending, perhaps, on the state of their digestive system or whether they were weaned too early in infancy. But wait, this you have not considered. There is a world so different in scale that its emotions bear no resemblance to yours; it has emotions so different in degree that they have become a different *species!*" He tilted his face up toward the sky in the pose of a sunworshiper, but his eyes were malevolently open. "I am not bitter, Miss Birchfield; *I am past that by a million years!*" After a minute he closed his eyes, less, it seemed, from the brightness of the sun than from a sudden access of irritability. "Bitter," he said scornfully. "Why should you say that? Do you hear me curse people? Have I delivered a diatribe on the evils of fascism, the infamies of Hitler? Do not be silly. I am a man with no anger and no desire for vengeance. I concentrate on what makes sense to me, that is all. I want nothing at all but peace and quiet."

She handed him a bottle of soda and watched the movement of his neck as he swallowed; when he lowered the bottle, she spoke immediately, as though she had merely been waiting for his attention.

"Tell me this, then, Mr. Nazerman. If your reasoning

about your needs is correct, why haven't you found peace? Isn't it possible your philosophy, or lack of philosophy, or whatever you live by, is in error?" she said, trying to bring the sweet smell of her own history to an ugly Jewish man on the banks of a filthy river; for she had a heritage of missionaries, and like her ancestors she was willing to brave a variety of wildernesses.

"People like you have not let me have peace, Miss Birchfield."

"Then it would follow that your philosophy is no good, because you have to live in a world just full of people like me," she said.

He smiled suddenly. "I must apologize to you, Miss Birchfield. I have underestimated you. You have the makings of a debater. But I will not debate with you. Really I am extremely tired of all this. There is no sense going on. Besides, it is much too warm here." He got to his feet slowly, unbending with such deliberation that it seemed he might never stop rising, and she looked up at him with awe. "Also, there are the vicissitudes of my business. I have a strange assistant, my Jesus Ortiz. I understand him as little as he does me. There are times when he seems quite dedicated to his job, and other times when I think he would kill me and rob my safe." He gave a little chuckle. "Who knows but I may go back now to find my store looted and empty."

"One last question," she said.

He waited as she collected the rubbish from their lunch in the paper bag. Finally she stood, too, a full-breasted woman of great warmth and perhaps wistfully unused passions.

"Are there *no* emotions left to you? I mean, don't you ever feel pity or love or . . ."

"Yes, yes," he snarled, suddenly wound tight by the feeling of impending disaster, which made his head ache. "I have some respect for fear. Love I will not talk about; it is too offensive—the obscenities committed in its name. But fear . . . If a person is capable of such fearful imagination that each time a creature is beaten he feels the pain himself, then I have reason to feel safe with that man. Your *brave* men, and your passionate *lovers,* are dangerous. No, give me the spineless, undedicated ones with the quivering, morbid imaginations, those selfish enough to constantly project themselves into any act of brutality; I can hold my own with them." He took a deep, steadying breath. Then he gestured toward the street, and they began to walk.

"For a little while it was quite relaxing, Miss Birchfield. But when you insisted on profundities, you made it tedious, you ruined it."

"I'm sorry, Mr. Nazerman. You're right," she said evenly, capable of some slyness herself. "It's that damnable compulsion to break into people. Plain nosiness, probably." She sneaked a look at him out of the corner of her eye. "But look, if I *promise* not to probe like that any more, would you consider doing this again?"

"Why, Miss Birchfield? Really, now, why?" he asked as they gained the street.

"Well, that's silly. . . . I mean because I like you. After all, there's nothing more natural. You're a man and I'm a . . ."

"Oh, Miss *Birchfield!*" he said incredulously. *"Please."*

She reddened and looked down at her feet, but went on bravely. "Well then, say there are no good reasons. It is possible that I enjoy your company, and if you thought you could enjoy . . . "

He frowned, feeling the heat weigh on him with increasing pressure as he approached the store. "It is hard to know, I cannot say. . . . " He had some difficulty seeing his feet on the glare of the pavement.

"How about taking that Hudson River excursion on Sunday?" she blurted out quickly. "It's really a lovely trip."

"You are unbecomingly forward," he said.

"I guess I am. Maybe that's why my classmates called me

a 'regular guy.' But there are some advantages to being 'forward.' For one thing, you're more apt to get direct answers," she said with a slightly mischievous smile. "Would you like to go?"

"I do not think so, Miss Birchfield. Thank you, but I am afraid not, not at this time. Sometime when I am . . ." He shrugged; there was no name for the future.

"Well, just in case you change your mind," she said, her smile intact as she handed him a little card which bore her name, the name of the Youth Center, and her home address and telephone number penciled above the name of the Center.

"Yes, yes, fine," he said, squinting ahead at the gold balls glowing in the sun.

"Good-by for now then, Mr. Nazerman," she said, watching his changing expression.

"Thank you, yes, good-by, good-by," he said impatiently. Then he put the little card in his pocket absently, hardly noticing when she walked away; his vision was darkening already in expectation of the fluorescent dimness of the pawnshop.

"I must speak to you," Sol said to the wiry voice in the phone.

"So speak. What are you being so dramatic for?" Murillio said.

"In person, I would like to speak to you in person."

Just the shade of hesitation indicated that Murillio was taken aback by the unusual request.

"What do you expect of my face? You would get no more out of me in person. I am a excellent poker player, Uncle." Murillio sighed, insincerely; he was not a man given to sad acceptances. "Ah, I hope you're not getting cute, Uncle. We got such a nice relationship. I pride myself on having one *colleague* who never gives me no trouble. You ain't going to get sly on me now, are you?"

"I am not being sly. I do not know what I expect of your face. Just that I feel I must talk to you, personally. May I come to your apartment this evening?"

"Okay, Uncle. You got such a flawless record, I suppose you deserve a few minutes of my valuable time. Up to now you ain't been a pest." He chuckled. Then he was not chuckling and his voice came like the one that gives the time and the weather. "I expect you at ten fifteen tonight, *punctual,* understand?"

And then Sol was looking at the phone humming emptily in his hand.

"I am sorry, I am sorry," he said aloud. "My health will not permit this. I am certainly not squeamish, but I must guard my health, I can depend on no one. I must draw the line someplace. . . . "

He would be trying to fool himself if he didn't recognize that his nerves were in a bad state. Never mind what physical things might be wrong. The fact was that he was shaky and, while he had small patience with analyzing himself in terms of the life he had lived, he had to accept the fact that there *were* some things able to pierce his numbness. He still reacted to certain things even while he despised the idea of memory. Something more terrible than a disease of the body faced him. For the first time, his oppression began to show the features of terror, and he was amazed and mystified because he could not think what he feared. Murillio's relationship with the brothel rode his consciousness with galling persistence. He would not strain himself with searching for the whys and wherefores of it; they would reveal their sources with painful clarity if he looked. Enough to know that he must do something about alleviating the most apparent strains.

For now his body seemed affected by his odd indisposition. There were a great number of insupportable positions for his body, positions he could not maintain without his hands or head or legs beginning to tremble a little. Fatigue pushed at him, too, even though the day had been relatively quiet. He found himself yawning frequently or taking great shuddering breaths which ended in sighs. It was all right to scorn phantoms, but to pretend they did not exist was just foolhardy. He would talk it out with Murillio, straighten out at least that one painful kink in his spirit.

He locked up the store and walked across the street toward the cafeteria. He had about an hour to use up before he took the twenty-minute subway ride to Murillio's apartment downtown. The street was lit by street lamps and neons, but, up above, the sky was still light, a cooling blue which faded to the palest denim in the west. And that delicate balance, just tipping toward night, seemed to find its horizontal somewhere around the level of Sol's head. For the few people walking by, it gave a look of uncertainty to his face, an ambiguity of color in that part of the city so stricken with the color of skins. From almost a block away, Cecil Mapp thought he recognized Sol Nazerman, and he nudged John Rider, beside him on the single step, asking if that wasn't the Pawnbroker that John worked for. But John was focused on the close-up pages of Deuteronomy and he just grunted in the pungent summer evening.

In the cafeteria, Sol stared at the array of foods on the steam table. He didn't know exactly what he wanted from Murillio, what he was going to ask for. It would be better not to try to plan now. He would only confuse himself more. Face to face: he had confidence in that magical contact of vision; he would know what he wished to say then.

"Nothin' here suit you, Mac?" the skinny Puerto Rican complained from behind the counter. "How 'bout some chili? Chili's good tonight," he said, ladling some up and dropping it with an ugly plopping sound.

"No. Eggs, two eggs, poached on toast, and coffee," Sol said. Then he stood gazing myopically at the steaming coffee urn and tapping his fork in an absent rhythm on the brown plastic tray.

Only I must do something or I will get a breakdown. Who would help me then! Oh yes, there are good reasons, I know about that; the date of all . . . all that. But there are the money pressures, the animals I have to deal with. Look, I'm getting no younger, either. It is natural. The point is that I must not let myself get into a state like that. No, it is ridiculous. I will simply say to Murillio . . .

"I said, 'You gonna want anything else?' Hey, you food gonna get cold like ice. Hey, Mista!" the food-server said, raising his voice in the bored solicitude he used for the old and the hard-of-hearing.

Sol found a table near the window. He ate with the garish perspective of the street before him but with his eyes blind to it, his attention inward on the dark, wet chewing of his mouth, the monstrous, bestial swallowing and digesting. The involuntary movements of his organs disgusted him, and he dwelt inside himself like a tiny, bodiless creature fascinated by something that lived mindlessly but persistently.

When he was through eating, he found his hands strangely in his way. A few tables away, a burly Negro in a leather stevedore cap let out a huge, pleasurable explosion of smoke from his mouth and then stared with sleepy fascination at the white cigarette in his dark fingers. Sol wondered why he had never tried smoking. How relaxed the man looked! On an impulse, he got up and walked over to the smoker.

"Pardon me, could I perhaps buy one of your cigarettes? I have forgotten to bring my own," he said, enjoying the dexterous little lie.

"Sure thing," the man said. "That's all right, man." He held up his hand to forestall payment. "On me," he said. He even lit the cigarette for Sol, but frowned at the awkward way the white man sucked on it.

"Very good," Sol said, letting the smoke seep from his lips in what he thought was a professional way as he looked at the cigarette. "Just my brand, too. I thank you."

The capped man waved away the thanks again and went back to his almost erotic delight in smoking.

For a few minutes Sol found a childish pleasure in making the big puffs of smoke that covered the little Lazy Susan in the center of the table. He enjoyed the fierce glow at the tip of the cigarette each time he drew on it, enjoyed the look of the clean, white cylinder between his cumbersome fingers. He watched himself smoking and found himself cataloging the act, listing it as a therapy that might strengthen him. Unconsciously, he began to hum, a thin, minor-keyed melody whose notes he shaped with the single-syllabled *"Dy, dy, dy, dydydy, dy, dy . . ."*

Suddenly the sound caught like a hook in his heart. A wisp of smoke went down with his disturbed respiration, and he began to cough violently. When he recovered from the fit of coughing, he had a strange, cold hurt in his chest, and the pleasure of smoking was gone as though it had never been. The thought of Murillio tightened his stomach once more.

He got up with a sigh and went out into the street. And it was now unquestionably a nighttime street, with darkness above and the stars lost to the people for all the harsh artificial lights they lived by.

He went down the gum-and-spittle-scarred steps of the subway and stood in the dirty light of the platform, where everything had the color of grime and everything was defaced or mutilated—signs, walls, trash cans, everything.

I will just say to him, Look Murillio, I am not being fussy but I am just not a well man. No, that is not good. I will say, for reasons of my own . . .

The yellow eye of the train advanced through the tunnel, coming from a hundred filthy platforms like the one he was on, heading for a hundred more. The whole city was cancered with these dim tunnels, whose filth spread to the streets above with the people, spread to the whole world. Murillios behind him, ahead of him. Yesterday and tomorrow, all the same. A constant assault, which he strained against, awake and asleep. What was the point? Just to maintain life? He was too weary. There was this pressure in him, a feeling of something underneath, which caused the growing tremors on the surface of him, perhaps heralding some great and awful thrust which would rend him, destroy him. And what was it? he wondered as the train rocked and screamed through the tunnel like a projectile toward him. Was it terror? Of what—death? Ridiculous that he should fear *that!* No, he didn't—perhaps, even . . . He leaned over the platform edge. The wind of the train fanned his face, the light blinded him. The train multiplied its speed, rushed to swallow him up.

And then he was standing back, watching the windows flash by like a streak of light which gradually, as the train slowed, separated into rectangles framing human heads. He watched the doors open, standing and rocking a little, his heart pounding, his brain refusing the immediate past.

For most of the ride he just slumped in an access of exhaustion. His mind seemed empty. He sat, his mouth slightly ajar, staring at the rushing darkness of the tunnel; the roar of the train flushed his brain of the gathering crystals of memory as soon as they began to form. At about the halfway point in the ride, he experienced a sour burning in his throat; it tasted faintly of egg.

"Now even eggs," he said disgustedly, before going back to his cataleptic repose, his head rocking with the sway of the train, his eyes indifferent to the faces of many shapes, the newspapers of many tongues.

The apartment was of white brick, some twenty-five stories high. There was a huge, glass-enclosed lobby, through which Sol could see an elegant, too-orderly garden with white stone benches and floodlit shrubs. A doorman appeared. He raised his eyebrows suspiciously at the bulky, heat-rumpled man who looked to him like a seedy salesman desperate for business. But he had no case of any kind, so the doorman considered the possibility of a crackpot fanatic of even more devious purpose.

"Can I help you there, Mac?" he asked, ready at the least sign to turn the fringe politeness into bullying. "Someone here you want to see?"

"Mr. Albert Murillio," Sol answered, staring dully at the doorman's stagy white uniform.

"Well suppose I just give him a little ring for you," the man said uncertainly, reshuffling his stack of attitudes at the familiar name. "Make sure he's up there. Save you a trip." He went to the wall phone and pressed one of a long column of buttons. "Just check and make sure he's . . . Oh, hello, Mr. Murillio? Oh hi, Joe, this is Sweeny, downstairs. Got a fellow down here says he wants to see your boss. What? Oh, wait, I'll ask. . . . " He covered the phone with one hand, and quizzed Sol with his eyes. "Your name, your name," he finally said impatiently.

"Sol Nazerman. He is expecting me," the Pawnbroker said, staring out indifferently at the floodlit garden. He wondered if the vegetation were real.

Only in the almost silent ascent of the elevator did his exhaustion recede enough for him to feel apprehension again. When he stepped out at Murillio's floor, words were tumbling uselessly through his head. Which of them could he use? What did he want of the man? If *he* didn't know, how could he expect . . .

"Come in, Uncle," Murillio called from beyond the man in the linen jacket of a servant. "Sit down, sit down," he said as Sol came down the two steps to the sunken living room. "This is a rare honor, partner. You might have something there, putting us on a personal basis. Want a drink? Name it, I got it; Scotch, rye, bourbon, gin. Hey, you ever try this coffee-flavor brandy? I got it in Haiti. Expensive stuff."

"No thank you. I do not drink. I have a delicate stomach."

"Well, sit down, anyhow," Murillio said, wearing expansiveness like something he knew the look of but not the feeling; and, as the Pawnbroker unbent that much, he smiled energetically. "I tell you, Uncle, I often think I like to get together with you. People I come in contact with are a bunch of dumbheads. I know you're a intelligent guy, been a teacher in the old country and all. Well, I ain't had the regular education, you know, but I got a taste for the finer things. Listen, I know the real-big operators all had a feel for the big things. I read a whole bunch of books, history, art, the whole bit. I get a big kick out of it. It's the only thing that really interest me. I got dough, all the gash I want. It gets boring, you know?"

Sol studied him as he talked, amazed that the voice benefited not the least from being heard in person. It wasn't just the remoteness of the telephone conversations; the man's voice seemed to have nothing to do with his face. Murillio had powdery-white skin and the sleek blue shadow of carefully shaved, very dense beard. You were aware of how perfectly all his hair was groomed; the beard shaved fantastically close at least twice a day, the hair trimmed to perfection, the hands peculiarly hairless, as though they, too, were shaved or denuded by some strong depilatory, although the wrists erupted a few strong hairs from under the starched white cuffs, the eyebrows faultlessly curbed, the nostrils neat. Sol had the feeling that only the most careful attention kept Murillio from a hairy collapse into apishness. The shadow of beard came up to within an inch of his eyes. But there the simian quality ended. For his eyes were the pale-gray color of slush, the mixture of rain and snow before the snow has been soiled, a translucent, light-conducting texture rather than a color.

" . . . but sometimes all that stuff seems just a hair beyond me. Like I read a thing . . . Some college kid touted me on this *Crime and Punishment*. So I read it and I understand it —it's a good story, you know, with the kid murdering the old woman. I finish it. I could tell you the thing from beginning to end. But I got this feeling, kind of irritated, like there's something I missed. The same thing happens with music. I like good music, opera particular. I got a good ear, too. But I get that same feeling like it's leaving me out of something. I get mad really."

Suddenly he was aware of the Pawnbroker staring flatly at him.

"Well, it takes a lot of thinking," he said sullenly. "Hey, if you wanted to come here to just stare at me, I could of send you a picture. Okay, what's the beef, Uncle?"

"There is something on my mind. It has been bothering me. You will find it strange but please be patient," Sol said, staring down at his hands. "It is just that . . . " He looked up to engage the slushy eyes. "Tell me, *do* you own the brothel down the street from me? You do, don't you?"

"Now wait a minute, what is this?"

"The house of prostitution behind the massage place, it is yours, isn't it?"

"Just a second, let's get straight before we go any farther. Are you just trying to get your nose where it don't belong or have you got something special you want to say?"

"Yes, something special," Sol said. "I will try to be clear . . . even though it is perhaps not too clear to me myself. You see I have not been too well lately, tension, what have you," he said with a shrug, as though it were really of no importance. "The point is that I would try to cut down my tensions, regardless how foolish they seem even to me. They exist, they burden me. There are things in my past, never mind what, I prefer to forget about them. But they make certain things difficult for . . . " Some vacillation in him seemed to firm then. His face got cold and strong. "I do not want your money if it comes from the whorehouse," he said in a matter-of-fact voice.

"What's that? You got me . . . what?" Murillio leaned forward, his fearsome face momentarily comical. He had the slanted expression of a half-deaf man; you would almost have expected him to cup his hand to his ear.

"We can make some other arrangement . . . I do not know exactly what. Maybe I will buy you out or you will buy me out. Any way. Only *I do not want the money from the whorehouse.*"

Murillio regained his hearing, and he began to laugh, although his mouth was shaped to just a mild smile. It was as if the laughter were something from earlier in the evening and Murillio played it over now for Sol to hear, gave vent to it from behind his stiff smile.

"Oh, you're a hot one, Uncle, I got to say that. There's nothing typical about you. It's all right, it's all right, I get a kick out of it. No, really. All these other assholes I deal with—Christ, I can tell when they're gonna fart, when they're gonna smile, when they're gonna moan. They get on my nerves. I get sluggish, you know. I mean with you I keep my wits active, like in training. I can never anticipate." He was still smiling, and now his humor seemed quite real. The expression of his cold eyes was different enough from the usual to indicate some emotion approaching affection. "Okay, I'll bite; why don't you want the money from the cathouse—assuming if I *did* own a cathouse?" he asked good-naturedly.

"What difference does it make why?" Sol asked wearily.

The smile drifted off Murillio's purplish lips as easily as a casually wiped food stain. His eyes darkened, and the irritated cougar showed from under the neat, human face.

"I like you, Uncle, otherwise I would of lost patience with you long time already. But now it's getting past a joke. I'm getting a little bored. It makes a difference when you come up here and waste my time. You drop a nutty statement like that on top of my lap and I'm suppose to say, fine, fine, write the whole thing off. Don't tell me, 'What difference does it make?' It makes a difference!"

"It is personal, an idiosyncrasy, if you will. Call it an allergy, say I am allergic to brothels. Say what you want. Only I say this—I insist, I insist . . . something must be done. I will sell out to you or you will sell out to me. It has been bothering me, and now I must do something about it."

Sol took a deep breath in the silence he had invoked. He exhaled it slowly, imagining he felt relief now, that he had gotten something accomplished. He made himself ignore the black-and-white beast planted motionlessly in the far corner of his eye. Slowly, casually, he scanned the soft buff walls. You must make no sudden moves with certain wild things; sharks were said to strike if you made a commotion in the water. He looked intently at the several oil paintings. They were of some insignificantly saccharine school of Italian painting; late nineteenth or early twentieth century. Girls with pitchers on their heads, homely street scenes; one was labeled "The Barber" and showed a rosy-cheeked man cutting a small boy's hair while a doting mother stood watching, the inevitable pitcher on her head. Each painting had a little lamp over it, such as are found in certain academic galleries. It suggested that the air in the room, for all its air conditioning, was dry and dusty and unlived in.

"I see you admiring my art collection. You like it?" Murillio asked in a soft, speculative voice. "Cost me a small fortune, believe me. But I like to surround myself with beauty. Maybe sometime I become a patron, hah! Sometime maybe . . . " He turned an enameled smile on, and his face seemed to become depthless; you imagined the mouth opened to no more than a fraction of an inch of polished granite, that the eyes began in the rounded surface. Like some half-convincing bas-relief, he aimed himself at Sol. *"But not yet, Uncle.* Okay, let's make ourselfs clear, hah. For some reason you got it in your head, or your conscience or something, that you don't want to be connect with money from a whorehouse. You got a *allergy*. Okay! So set your mind at ease, Uncle. See how patient I am. You can tell I'm a reasonable man, can't you?" He waited for Sol's stiff, wary nod. "All right, from now on I'm gonna make a special arrangement just for you."

Sol listened intently, eagerly, for a moment imagining that some incomprehensible ray of salvation might come from the lips of this man.

"From now on I'm gonna send you *different* money, see! The dough from the cathouse I'm gonna send to another associate. You I'll send only *clean* money, money from legitimate, blue-chip investments. How's that, fair or not?"

Sol's face registered the slow descent from bewilderment to anger. He opened and closed his mouth on his indignation a few times like a fish not sure of its atmosphere.

Murillio howled with laughter. It was a terrifying thing to see that barely amused face and realize that the monstrous noise of glee came from it. Sol turned his head from one side to another, as though trying to figure out where the sound *really* came from. He saw the linen-jacketed servant standing in the doorway, expressionless and vigilant, his swarthy, crushed fighter's face like the surface of a mirror aimed at the fog.

"You think I am a fool?" Sol cried out furiously. "I will not have this. No more, I say. I want to terminate our agreement. There will be no further association between us. Do not toy with me!"

The laughter stopped abruptly.

"Shut up, Uncle," Murillio said with a softness that struck the ear like a shot. He walked over to stand above Sol. His lids were lowered so his eyes seemed heavy and toxic. "Yes, I do think you're a fool. Who you think you're dealing with, Uncle, some little Jew merchant, some half-ass little 'businessman' with a vest full of pencils and scraps of paper in every pocket to write down the *big deals*?" Though he was a much shorter man than Sol, he now seemed very big, hung over the Pawnbroker like some dangerous weight. His eyes were so close that Sol could see the icy lacing of his irises.

"What you *want* don't interest me one bit. I am a little concern about what you say and do though. So listen to me, Uncle, listen careful because it is very important to you." Now he leaned over and rested his hands on his knees as though he were talking to a child. "You can't get out on your terms. I want things just like they are. The very best you could hope for is that I let you out without a penny, with nothing to show for your work there except a few wrinkles. My money start you in that store; you're a partner only because it's convenient for me to have your name on the papers. Now you want to be smart, keep going like before, okay. You draw yourself a nice buck over the years, save enough for your old age maybe."

"You have no right to . . . "

"Let's not talk silly, hah, Uncle? I just told you the *best* you could do if you upset me. You know what else could happen?" He studied Sol's face with inhuman curiosity, like a great cat watching with unblinking interest the reactions of its prey when it cuffs with covered claws.

Sol just sat there, ignorant for the moment of both his expression and his feelings. Only it seemed this had happened before, or almost happened or been dreamed of. He tried to focus on his needs, on the tangibles he was risking, the money, the privacy it bought him. But the colorless gray eyes demanded more from him.

"Well I'll tell you in plain words, Uncle. I could kill you." He nodded slowly to the gray face below him. "Kill you dead. Uh huh, that's what I said. It's no big thing to me. You don't want to live no more, Uncle?"

Suddenly he patted Sol on the shoulder, and the touch made the Pawnbroker flinch. Murillio laughed merrily.

"Hey, your nerves *are* really bad, Uncle. Well that puts a different light on it. Whyn't you take yourself a nice weekend vacation, hah? We could let that kid handle things for a day or two. I'd have someone keep an eye. I tell you what.

You're tense? You could knock off a piece of ass at the 'house.' Anytime you want. No charge—I give you a credit card. Hah, how's that, Joe?" he said, turning swiftly toward the man in the doorway. "A *credit card!*" Joe obliged with a weary grin. Murillio turned back to Sol and aimed an affectionate punch at his jaw, just brushed it humorously. "Sure, it's just your nerves talking. I won't talk no more about it. Forgive and forget. You get the idea, hah?"

"I am not a child, Murillio. This is no way to treat me. No, I am not satisfied. You threaten me but I am not . . . Something must be done. Something. . . ." He had been subtly made to feel like a dirty piece of flotsam in that vulgarly rich apartment. "You cannot shut me off like that. I am not . . . " He stood up, half maddened.

And suddenly Murillio nodded, his eyes looking over Sol's shoulder. Sol felt the cold touch of metal against his cheek. When he swung his head to see what it was, something unbelievably hard crashed against his teeth; opening his mouth at the pain, he felt the cold metal thrust between his teeth and he tasted the bitterness of steel.

"Now don't move, Uncle," Murillio said, his eyes on the man behind Sol. "Stand absolutely still and lick on that gun barrel for a while. That old Joe would pull the trigger if I just winked at him. He don't give a shit, do you, Joe? Nah, not Joe, he's a son of a bitch. Yeah, you just stand there like that a while, taste the bit. See, you're just like a horse. Get a little balky and we pull the reins. Get real wild . . . well, you know what they do to horses. Just stand there and think things over, see things like they are, no bull shit, no nice talk, just that. . . . "

And Sol stood there gagging on the horrible curb in his mouth, his gaze swinging wildly over the trappings of the hideously sumptuous room: the oil paintings, the brocaded chairs, the polished hardwoods. It had been so long, so long since his nightmares were as real as taste and touch, since they came to him in waking hours. He should have remembered more faithfully that this was the real taste of life, that it was not confined to dreams.

He sweated in spite of the air conditioning. He fluttered like a half-crushed bird, his heart pounding doom into him like a long iron nail. His stomach sickened, and he wondered what his fate would be if he vomited on the expensive, wine-colored carpeting. Downstairs, the gardens would be shining gorgeously in the floodlights and the white-uniformed doorman would be rocking contentedly on his heels, admiring his bailiwick. The city was dozing in hot weariness, and quiet got its brief handhold over the immense growth of stone. And Sol Nazerman stood in the center of an air-conditioned nightmare, wondering whether he might not be wiser, after all, to suck death from the gun in his mouth, to have done with all of it.

But inexplicably, when Murillio said, "Then you will be a good boy, Uncle, you will keep your nose clean and not bother me with this foolishness no more?" Sol just nodded and looked at the gun as it came out of his mouth, all wet with his saliva. "Because I don't want to have no aggravation. We had a nice relationship, you know. Let's see if you can't get back in good standing in my books, hah?"

And Sol just stood there nodding. After a while, he began edging toward the door, his head still going up and down.

"So we all straightened out now, right, Uncle? Everything in good shape?" Murillio followed him to the foyer, and the linen-jacketed Joe stood attentively by the door. "You gonna go home and forget this all came up."

"Yes . . . all right . . . I will . . . try," Sol said, each word having to vault some hurdle in his throat. "I do not know what it is . . . I mean I did not want trouble. . . . "

"Yeah, I know, Uncle," Murillio said solicitously as he gently pushed Sol out the door.

"Only, you see, I have felt myself to be in a great deal of pain . . . nerves . . . Some things bother me. . . . But I want only to be left in peace, to make the money I need and be left alone. I do not wish to lose the little I have, you understand, the store, the privacy. It was just that certain things have happened to me. . . . "

The sleek, carefully groomed head nodded understandingly. But the murderous eyes fixed on the Pawnbroker's mouth, growing a little bored even in menace. And then that womanly attention to his mouth made it appear like some stare of twisted love to Sol, and he was terrified more than before.

"Good-by, Uncle, I will call you. Keep your nose clean, now. . . . "

Then Sol was out in the hallway and walking toward the elevator, moving stiffly, as though his partner's eyes were still on him. He was dreadfully tired. He had to think each forward attempt of his legs and direct his finger to the elevator button and command himself to step into the elevator when it came. In that paralyzing tiredness, the thought of his bed in the quiet of distant Mount Vernon seemed fantastically appealing.

In the kitchen, he ate standing up, a clumsy, indefinably mutilated giant. He leaned against the counter chewing on a soapy piece of American cheese and sipping root beer from one of the old *Yortzeit* glasses. Bertha hustled around him with affected timidity, and Selig slipped in for an unreturned pleasantry. Their voices bounced off the hunched rebuttal of him.

"You're not still angry about our little differences Sunday, are you, Solly?" Selig asked. "We're a family; these things . . ."

"I am still here, am I not?" Sol answered. He stared out the kitchen window at the blackness and he tried to decide whether the mysterious assault came from within or from outside himself. Then he wondered if it might not be a two-pronged drive, and shuddered visibly.

"What's wrong you're shaking?" his sister asked, her small eyes suddenly calculating behind his back. "Sit down so the food will do you some good, Solly. I always tell Morton he shouldn't wolf . . ."

Sol just shoved the plate away and threw the remains of the cheese onto it.

"Give me some coffee. I will take it up to my room and drink it in peace." He stood waiting impatiently, a gray, alien figure in all the gleaming chrome and formica, while Bertha poured his coffee. She slid a piece of coffeecake onto his saucer with elaborate coyness. Sol just shrugged and took the cup without the saucer.

On the upstairs landing, he met his nephew. Morton had a large pad under his arm, and his untidy, vulpine face was smudged with charcoal.

"Uncle Sol," he said.

"Hello, Morton." Sol frowned for a grip on amenity. "What are you drawing? Show me. After all, I have an investment," he said with a little twist to his lips.

Morton held up a charcoal sketch of the back yard. The scene sparkled, seemed to be in a crisp twilight, and the roofs and branches were sure, steady shapes in a subtle pattern that hid under the obvious one. In one corner of the picture was a shapeless figure in a garden chair, and all the twilight led to it, so there was a brightness of sky and a brightness around the man and great darkness between.

"Could that be me?" Sol asked, pointing to the figure on the paper.

Morton nodded, cautious of opinion.

"I see. Well it seems to me to be very well drawn. What you have done with the light . . . Good, good, my money is apparently not wasted." He gave as much smile as he had. Then he touched his nephew's shoulder. And though it was just a nudge to clear his way up the stairs, his nephew took it for a touch of acknowledgment and drew the warmth he desired from it. And when Sol brushed past, Morton stood on the landing for a moment, watching the huge waistless figure ascending, and there was a cherishing look on his face.

Sol drank his coffee slowly, his head resting on the wooden headboard, the lights off so he could see the faint light from the moon casting a diluted illumination that resembled twilight. There were the roofs and the branches as Morton had drawn them, the angle only slightly lower than that observed from the boy's room upstairs. He finished the coffee and leaned over the window sill to look down at the yard. Looking for the shapeless figure of a man as his nephew had drawn it? But that man was himself and there was only one of him. Or was there? God forbid there should be ghosts! He would not have been able to bear that. If there were ghosts, he would be destroyed, or *had* been destroyed long ago and was now a ghost himself. But he felt pain, deep inside him, a growth slowly extending to pierce him, to meet the stabs from people outside himself, people who would raise their hands to him. So he couldn't be a ghost . . . could a ghost suffer? Ah, leave me my brain at least, do not let me go mad. Like a litany, he enforced the rules of life on himself: You live, you eat, you rest, you protect yourself.

He took a burning-hot shower, followed it with shocking cold. Then in the surface peace of his numbed body, he lay on his bed and read from *Anna Karenina* in Russian, relaxing in the familiar words he had read several times since his youth.

The crickets came and went; the darkness was very old when he finally put the book down and closed his eyes with the light still on.

Through his opened window he heard the harsh, demanding whispers of his sister and brother-in-law in the next room. "If you're not too tired, honey . . ."

Love.

Sol thought even sleep would be better. His body relented, went limp. The room faded toward black.

"I will sleep like the dead tonight," he said longingly.

But he slept like the living.

*The guard wouldn't let him turn his head from the window, knocked with menacing playfulness on the side of his jaw every time he tried. So he looked into the vast room which was broken into many cubicles. There were women in each one, some standing at the open ends with weary expressions, some seated listlessly on their beds gazing at the floor. Wild laughter echoed from various parts of the great subdivided room and, like the perverted echo of the laughter, the low crushed sound of moaning.*

*But for all the rest of the calibrations of the compass, the needle of his attention had only a disinterested hovering movement. His eyes swung back and forth in ever-lessening arcs until they settled with trembling force on the one cubicle. His wife, Ruth, sat on her bed with a sheet up over her nakedness and she didn't see him looking in, for her own attention was riveted on the entrance of her cubicle with terrified anticipation.*

*"Let me go from here," he begged the guard.*

*"You bothered and bothered. 'What's happened to my wife? What exactly is she doing?' you asked. 'Why did they take her from the Woman's Section?' You wouldn't be satisfied with half-truths, would you? 'I must know exactly,' you said. All right, I got fed up with you. So here we are. I'm being generous, I'm taking you to see for yourself," the guard said, giving another of those little nudges to the side of Sol's jaw. "So look, keep looking, that's what you're here for. After this you won't ask me any more, you'll know."*

*"I know now, I understand. It is enough. Please, I couldn't stand to see any more," he whimpered, dry spasms shaking his body like chastising hands.*

*"You'll stay and you'll look, once and for all,"* the guard said, pressing his short truncheon into Sol's neck.

*So he turned back for what he deserved.*

*A black-uniformed man entered Ruth's cubicle. He took off his clothes and for a few minutes just displayed his exposed body to the terrified woman on the bed. Finally he pulled the sheet from her nakedness. He seemed to be speaking to her, but only silence reached Sol outside the glass. Ruth began shuddering. Her face turned the color of calcimine, the texture of some powdery substance that could crumble at a touch.*

*For a minute or two the SS man handled her breasts and her loins vengefully. Her mouth stretched in soundless agony. As though he had been waiting for that, the SS man pulled her to her knees and forced her head down against his body.*

*Sol began to moan. But just before tears could bring mercy to his eyes, he saw her recognize him. And from that hideously obscene position, pierced so vilely, she endured the zenith of her agony and was able to pass through it. Until finally she was able to award him the tears of forgiveness. But he was not worthy of her award and took the infinitely meaner triumph of blindness, and though he was reamed by cancerous, fiery torments, he was no longer subject to the horrid view, no longer had to share the obscene experience with her. For a while, he could see nothing, could only feel the air moving around him, hear the familiar sounds of the camp, which now had a homely, familiar note and which made the blood beats of pain in his joints almost bearable. And then he went a step further toward the empty blackness of animal relief; he fainted and felt nothing for a long time.*

He woke palpitating and drenched in sweat, wondering where he was. For a minute or two, he stared full at the lamp bulb. Then he turned his violet-starred vision on the rest of the room, on the window from which a tender breeze came, filtered through the heavy foliage, and then, finally, on the length of his own body, shining with sweat.

"Good God, how can I stand this?" he said.

With the answer, that somehow he would have to, vibrating in his brain, he got up and went into the bathroom. He stripped the wet underclothes off and took another shower. When he was dried, he went back into the bedroom. He propped his pillows so he was sitting up, took his book, and began to read. Outside, there was the near-silence of the night, and only his own breathing made the slightest distraction. He read without stopping until morning.

Marilyn Birchfield woke up behind the walls of her apartment and saw morning with the familiar sensation of hollowness. She swallowed against it as though it were hunger for food.

There was a delicacy of taste evident all around her room; handsome modern prints, white walls, a nakedly structural bookcase copied from a prominent designer's work and filled with good books, the speaker connected to a high-fidelity phonograph in the living room. There was a Japanese lantern hanging over some austerely simple chests of drawers and a comfortable chair upholstered in brown corduroy upon which lay a bright-orange pillow.

Only her own body suggested grossness and superfluity.

"A lot of woman for so little living" was her own self-effacing joke. It convinced her family and her friends that she was well-adjusted and wholesome. Well, she supposed she was, really, in spite of the guilty images to which she was susceptible in the early morning or late at night, at those times when her body betrayed her because of its idleness. She felt the heavy swing of her breasts and thought of all the babies she could have nourished, moved the wide strength of her hips and felt furtiveness like a pain at the thought of the man they could have brought joy and comfort to.

But only the vulnerability of her first waking defended those thoughts. She threw her powerful legs over the edge of the bed and so flung herself bravely into the day. Smiling dignity, that was one of her poses; there were worse ones. Just as long as her eyes were open, as long as she continued to laugh at herself whenever her poses began to impress her as truth, she would not become grotesque or pitiable. Having hungers, she must admit them to herself and not dress them in some other guise, like those childless spinsters who dressed their dogs in sweaters and caps and talked to them in baby talk.

She washed thoroughly in the shower, brushed her teeth for a full five minutes, brushed her shiny brown hair a hundred counted strokes. And then, mildly Spartan, stared square into the mirror at the round, immaculate face, the clear eyes with the beginnings of age mapped in the little intersections around them. It was like morning calisthenics of the spirit, that gazing unflinchingly at her plain, plumply healthy face and, as with calisthenics, she was invigorated by facing clearly who and what she was.

Not that she was completely tranquilized by that, only that she took the weights of unhappiness from a firmer footing. As she dressed, she noted again her firm, rather gross body and she felt a touch of regret. Now, it was not self-pity, though, but a form of disapproval—she had been brought up to abhor waste in any form. And this somehow recalled the face of Sol Nazerman to her, because she sensed a vast waste of spirit in him. In her pity for him, she exposed herself to an old hurt, too, for she felt hope throb in her where she had thought there was only scar.

"Oh that poor man," she said aloud as she sipped coffee and stared from her kitchen window toward the distant glint of the river, with its bridges like a child's erector-toy in the morning haze. But she didn't like the patronizing sound of that. Where did she get the idea that he required her pity? She had no idea what went on behind that puffy, alien face. "If he could only be brought out of himself a little . . ." But then she warned herself against self-deception. Now, now, Marilyn old girl, let's be clear about our motives. Let's not pretend altruism when there is even a suspicion that the return is the most important factor. Yes, Sol Nazerman was a man. But he seemed so full of suffering that she guessed he was not so vulnerable to a woman, after all. Besides, she was rather protected against coveting him as a man, for he was unattractive physically, indeed, seemed old and remote and out of the context of man-woman relationships. But if she had no personal profit in mind, was she perhaps a professional do-gooder?

Somehow she thought that she was innocent of that, at least as far as he was concerned. There was a profounder disturbance evoked in her than she experienced among the impoverished children she worked with. Something vast and nameless seemed to drag at her spirit when she looked at him or even thought about him. It was as though a great, distant wailing came to her ears, and she felt she could not live in the same world with that sound without trying to do something about it.

She washed out her cup and saucer and set them in the drainer. Then she closed a drawer, shut a cupboard door, and straightened the slightly biased plant next to the phonograph. Finally she gathered herself for the day at the Youth Center; she loaded her brief case with notebooks and pencils and pads and smiled at the ineffectual aspect of the tools of her trade.

When she was in the doorway of the apartment, half out in the hallway already, she turned to gaze back inside a little absently, as though she might have left something behind. And in that pose of musing, her finger resting beside her mouth, the brief case weighting one side of her, she spoke aloud to the empty rooms.

"I will just have to be a pest with him. I'll keep after him. He has too much pain for one person. I can tell by his eyes. . . ."

## SEVENTEEN

He was busy from the hour of opening. People drifted in quietly, one after another, as though some momentous message had reached them, as though each of them came in answer to a great, silent call. They milled around expectantly with their mobile lips, their ill-shaped teeth and stained, veinous eyes, waiting their turn with ponderous patience. And Sol looked up at each succeeding face with a sort of horror for the appallingly long gauntlet before him.

Over the heads of the nearest, he saw others still outside, looking in at the display of the windows or just staring at the hot light of the street in an indecisive way as they jingled their tiny treasures, uncertain about what they could gain inside.

"What do they think it is—Bargain Day?" Sol muttered.

Over at the other counter, Jesus Ortiz handled his share of the traffic calmly and efficiently. Occasionally he called out some question to his employer, and Sol answered vaguely or agreed with some likely guess. But mostly Ortiz operated with complete self-confidence. There was something reminiscent of Sol in his mannerisms, in the way in which he busied himself with things out of his customers' view when he wished to show disdain for a request, in his habit of returning the object of pawn to reject a demand, in the silent shake of his head, which left no doubt about his firmness, and in the single spasmodic nod that signified agreement. And all of it might have been some unconscious evidence of respect for his teacher as well as pride in a thing well learned.

In contrast, Sol seemed dazed by the great volume of customers. He looked up frequently to peer out at the street, and felt the weariness from the start; he had a strange feeling that all the city's millions waited in line outside, that he might be there behind the counter for eternity, dealing with succeeding generations, endlessly bargaining, arguing, and struggling against the ugly, benighted faces.

The objects that people handed over and for which they showed expressions of loss, or regret, or anger at him for taking, all turned cheap and valueless in his hands. He became filled with the idea that he was building a tower of junk, struggling and draining himself to amass nothing. Sometimes he looked up for the face of his assistant as though trying to find sanity in what he was doing. But there would be Ortiz, slim and calm in his vitality and offering no reassurances at all. So he tried to let his mind range out beyond the quietly murmurous crowd, to think wildly of the size of the world, to try to picture other remote ends and strivings, only to finally be forced back into what *he* was doing. For him, then, the core of life was there in all its reality; brutal, wretched, and grasping. This was what he was down to; below this, there was nothing. So he clung to that harsh actuality as to an abrasive, whirling rock, terrified, furious, and hopeless.

A coffee-colored man in a black Loden coat, and goateed and horn-rimmed, took a loan on a shiny trumpet. A tall effeminate youth pawned a woman's watch and argued about the price in a high, strained lisp. A chunky Negress wearing fancy harlequin glasses, taking her perpetually pawned heating pad out of hock, spoke in the minimum of monosyllables. An athlete with a closely shaved dense beard that made a shadow on his very dark skin took a loan on a bag of golf clubs and a pair of hockey skates, and his expression said with dismal common sense that he was too old for that stuff anyhow. Puerto Rican women in two stages of life (the disastrous beauty they are prone to and the sudden ruin that follows so early) came and went like a repetitious parody. A man with a brown, Lincolnesque face and wearing an orange shirt pawned his wife's wedding ring. A trio of boys with hollow warrior faces made loans on identical navy-blue suits. A sleepily majestic Negro, who looked like a Swedish king, offered an elaborate truss for money as solemnly as if it were his own insides being proffered. A Chinese-eyed mulatto who wheeled a television set in on a dolly stood bored and tough, and took the first offer with such odd softness of speech that it seemed the words barely made the trip to his lips. A fat, sad white made a hopeless request on his pocket watch, then took Sol's offer with only the slight lengthening of breath that might have been a sigh. A boy no more than fourteen who claimed to be twenty, and tried to raise money on a cigarette case made of tin, cursed professionally when Sol refused him, and threatened malevolence from his vicious turkey-chick's face. From all walks, runs, and stumblings of life they came, and their supply never was exhausted.

Sol's head began to come apart by the middle of the

afternoon. It was as though a crack, begun at the base of his skull in the morning, had now widened to the point where his brains could spill through at any moment. He felt driven to scream, and even opened his mouth; but suddenly he found quiet and emptiness. One late beam of sunshine cut through the dust of the recent stampede. He looked at it for a long, numbed minute. Then he slowly raised his harrowed face like a very old man.

Jesus Ortiz smiled at him and nodded confirmation that they had been through that assault and were there to tell the story.

"What are you smiling at?" Sol asked in a croaking voice. He felt that tremulous irritation the old feel at the sight of something young and fresh looking.

"I guess I like my work," Ortiz answered.

"Aha. And perhaps you would like to have a shop of your own?" Sol asked with deceptive blandness. "One like this—perhaps this very one?"

"I wouldn't mind it." Ortiz looked around slowly. "I would make systems and all. And I would put my name on the door in gold letters—Proprietor, J. Ortiz. Yeah, I comin' to think this a good business for me. Like the surprises—you get a lot of surprises in a business like this. You never know when a special item gonna come you way here. A great diamond, a old, old piece of gold jewelry, *valuable* things . . ."

Sol began to laugh, a harsh, devilish sound in the quiet.

Ortiz looked at him curiously, his face tight and wary.

"Why you laugh, Sol? Is it so funny what I say?"

"Oh no, no, it is really not funny at all. And you want this so badly that you would do almost anything to get it?"

Ortiz didn't answer. He stared guardedly at the Pawnbroker, wondering what the Jew knew or thought he knew.

"Yes, of course you would," Sol said in a distantly musing voice. It was as though he felt a perverse pleasure at recognizing the shape of the walls that closed on him.

"It's a way to make money, ain't it? You say makin' money is the big thing youself. Ain't nothin' else matter much, do it?" He spoke from where he stood, still behind the other counter, and there was something oddly formal in their conversing across the store like this: the quality of a debate or a trial in which the issues were mercurial and ever-changing.

"No, that is right, nothing," Sol answered. He stared at the empty floor where lately so many customers had been. "And even that, sometimes . . . it, too, can turn to dust. No matter, though . . ."

"Yahh."

"Is it not funny how they pile in here like that for hours on end, and suddenly—no one."

"It funny," Ortiz agreed.

They spent some time contemplating nothing, while outside the store the street unrolled its seamless, unexciting tableau whose background changed color subtly with the waning daylight.

Finally Ortiz asked in a sleepy voice, "What was that you was startin' to tell about them real-good diamonds?"

"You won't see any of those in here," Sol said.

"Maybe not, but I want to know, just in case. . . ."

"Well, what is the difference." He sighed and then replenished the exhaled breath. "The very best, of course, are the rare fancies. They come in all kinds of strange colors, like bronze and canary and even black. But aside from those, which are very, very rare, the best of the others are the jagers, which are a sort of brilliant sky blue inside, like a burning core of daylight. Then you have the wesseltons, which are a harder, more metallic blue. After that you have the river diamonds and the crystals. . . ."

And, hardly conscious of what he was saying, almost soothed by the litany of his own voice, Sol unfolded more of his peculiar craft, and Jesus Ortiz drank it in thirstily, sensing without knowledge that a deep hollow in him filled with the Pawnbroker's voice. Sol ran his fingers over the dusty oratorical award under the counter as he talked; Ortiz toyed absently with the small silver medal on his chest. But both of them seemed to listen to some third person as their eyes gazed vaguely at the street.

Until suddenly the Pawnbroker seemed aware of the remarkable lapse of time. He frowned and took off his glasses to clean them.

"Enough already, Ortiz. Straighten up around here a little," he said coldly.

"Sure thing," Ortiz said. "Class dismiss, huh?"

Sol scowled questioningly.

"You know, you my teacher. I'm the student to you," Ortiz said with a grin on his fine, dark face.

"You are nothing to me," Sol said savagely as the phantom pain suddenly shot through him.

Ortiz shrugged, but his face turned to a starched mask and the soft ease of daydream in his eyes was blown away like clouds before a wind. And after that there was no more between them until he left for the night.

When he was gone, Sol moved around the store carefully, to favor the great split in his skull. He straightened, he brushed, he picked up pieces of paper and squinted at them, unable to derive any meaning from them. Every so often he stopped, with his hand up to his mouth, imitating someone who is so busy he has to decide which of his pressing chores to do next. And then, faithful to his small impersonation, he went on doing nothing in particular. He adjusted the position of an old dueling pistol in the glass case, picked up one of the cheap, imitation Black Forest hunting knives and held it point up in front of his face before putting it down in a slightly altered position beside the dueling pistols.

He picked up Mrs. Harmon's silver-plated candlesticks. Something nipped at the edges of his mind, so he stood there with the candlesticks in his hands like a great votive statue, trying to chase away the flickers of feeling.

Mabel Wheatly came in with a swish of blue satin and strong scent. She stopped suddenly in the middle of the store, staring at the Pawnbroker, who stood with the empty candlesticks formalizing him. And she had a momentary impulse to perform some sort of obeisance; he looked holy.

## EIGHTEEN

"Candlesticks," Sol said to her, nodding in a dazed way at his hands.

Mabel looked back over her shoulder uneasily, considering retreat from that strangeness. The fluorescents hummed softly, and one faulty tube flickered every so often; it gave the scene the quality of an old, much-used movie.

Sol twisted his face spasmodically, looked in disgust at the candlesticks, and put them down on the counter.

"All right, what can I do for you?" he asked, going behind the part of the counter where the barred wicket was. He felt sure of himself there. It relieved Mabel to see him there, too; he was the Pawnbroker again and nothing confusing or disturbing. You could always do some kind of business with the Pawnbroker.

She smiled and moved to the counter with her hip-grinding, professional walk.

"Where Ortiz gone to?" she asked, bending her head to her pocketbook and looking up at him from the corners of her eyes.

"He has gone already for the night."

"Oh?" She looked around nervously, then leaned against the counter in a manner calculated to display the bare tops of her breasts. "Well I just out for a walk—killin' time like."

He stared blankly, no haven for the restless.

"You know . . ." She smiled slightly and gazed at the wall with conversational ease. "I been tryin' to raise money. Seem like I got this idea to go into business."

"I had thought you already *were* in business," he said sourly.

"Aw no, not like that," she said with a little giggle. "I mean legitimate, real business."

"You, too?"

"Well, a acquaintance of mine has got this idea for a business. . . ."

"I have a good idea who your acquaintance is."

"The whole thing is, you need cash."

"What are you telling this to me for? I am going to close the store. Do you have something to show me? Otherwise, please, I am tired, it is late. . . ."

"Well-l," she said with uncertain coyness, her eyes everyplace but on him. "I gonna have a nice piece of jewelry later in the week. . . ."

"Suppose we talk about it then." He turned away from her and went back to that aimless straightening of stock.

"Maybe I got *somethin'* right now," she said in a loud half-whisper. She flicked a glance toward the doorway before turning back to him. The thing was, she had to get some money quickly; she felt that Jesus was considering some plans that excluded her. Suddenly she had conceived the wild idea of selling her body around the clock, day and night without letup.

Sol turned back to wait for what she had to say.

"Uh, you live around here, Pawnbroker?" she asked, sensing dimly a need to slow down her importunities with this man. But he certainly didn't look as if he got what he needed from women; he should be eager to accept her kind of offer.

"What is this? I have no time for visiting. Come to the point. Do you want something or are you just passing the time of day?"

"Well I tol' you I need to get some money. . . ." Suddenly she saw her simple plan fading in the cold glare of the Pawnbroker's stare. Desperately, she threw her dog-eared cards on the table. "I'm *good,* Mister, real good. You know what I mean. I know tricks you never even dream of. Anythin' go with me, Pawnbroker. You give Mabel twenny dollars an' I make you so happy. . . ."

She leaned toward him as much as the counter permitted, and Sol stared speechlessly at her soft, swelling flesh, not sure for the moment which dimension this was happening in.

"You got a back room here someplace, a couch like? Oh man, I can give you such a time. We could make it together like this. . . ." And she proceeded to catalogue in explicit detail all she could offer; the obscene words came from her lips quite dryly and unshockingly.

After a few minutes of the Pawnbroker's stunned silence, she walked to the little gate and came around behind the counter, hesitatingly at first and then more confidently, until she was close to him. Then she cupped her breasts in her hands and asked him to lock the door so they could get on with it.

If he had suddenly shouted at her, or even struck at her, she would not have been so startled. But he spoke in a quiet, ancient voice that chilled her through and through.

"You do not have to do this. Your body does not interest me," he said. And it was true; the slow, heavy thudding he felt in his groin betokened pain rather than pleasure. "Take your pitiful flesh away from me. Here, here is money," he said, reaching into his pocket and pulling out a crumpling of dollar bills, which he shoved at her hands. "You have nothing worth buying, you see. So just take the money; it is charity. Take it and go very quickly. Get out of here. You sicken me. I am sick enough already. Go on, go . . . GET OUT OF HERE!" And though by contrast the last few words seemed like a shout, all of it was really soft and icy and inflectionless.

And it seemed to Mabel Wheatly that suddenly a power out of her childhood condemned her again. She tasted again the verminous shame of her first sins, and quivered as she had then. She ran out from behind the counter crying, "Aw no, I sorry, I sorry . . ." and her apology followed her out of the store at some small distance.

"How do you like that!" Sol said aloud to the stillness. "Was ever a man visited with such insanity, with such creatures!" He began to chuckle mirthlessly as he started locking up. But the chuckle was so brittle and unreal that it degenerated to an indescribable shuddering. He stood with his head bent, one hand on the switches that had darkened all the lights but the one small incandescent night light in the office, the other hand on his head to hold it steady in the harsh, dry spasms that hammered at him. The spasms stopped, as quickly as they had come. He walked, with that careful head-favoring gait, out of the store and into the warm evening of the street.

He moved lumberingly, a great accumulation of strange severances, of poorly connected cogs and gears and ratchets, off balance, the imbalance overcompensated for, and so balanced again. His every motion was the result of some precise plan. His memory was screened off, his hopes had long ago been amputated. Each sense was allowed only a moment's play as he walked down the motley avenue, past a church that looked like an old theater and promised Redemption in hand lettering, past a butcher shop whose sign was in Spanish and whose screen door was blanketed with meat-hungry flies, past a dazzling dental office that looked like a big store and advertised a dozen dentists (No Waiting). And he was filled with a garish complexity of vigilance, every part of him wired and patched ingeniously; he saw, he moved in a chosen direction, he got through the days, earned money, held things at bay. Who could tell that inside, his spirit was like an old and shoddy carnival ground, threadbare, precariously tied and repaired, and with those parts that were too mangled and atrocious to look at discreetly covered with worn canvas and shoved into the dark and littered corners of his soul? Let him just continue like this, let all the wiring hold, let the screened-off parts stay covered, the creaking, squeaking machinery keep going, until death could come and eradicate the whole laboring thing all at once. Just don't let it come undone now, he asked in what would have been a prayer had it been addressed to anyone outside himself. Just let it hold until I'm dead; don't let it happen while I'm alive, or I will be forced to live in the chaos.

He crossed the street, looking carefully in both directions first, like someone whose safety really concerned him. The asphalt was still soft from the day's heat, and the cars moved over it with a faint sucking sound. He came to the cafeteria and looked in the window as he passed.

Halfway back, Jesus Ortiz sat talking to three men. Sol couldn't be sure of one of them at that distance; the black suit might or might not be Tangee's. But the ash-gray suit was as forbiddingly unique as a granite boulder in a field of flowers. For a moment or two, he stood swaying in front of the window like a plaintiff at the Wailing Wall, his mouth twisted bitterly, the sound of his laboring breath filling his ears.

"Yes, yes, Jesus Ortiz, I should have known . . . all of you, all of you . . . "

He began to walk again; one foot forward, then the other. Swing the pelvis, lean the heavy mass, thrust, push, operate the body by memory. Past the Army-Navy store, and the open-air clothing mart, its bins filled with color, its pipe racks decked with house dresses, and the dark women moving chatteringly around and about the clothing like eager birds; past a fried-chicken and fish-and-chips restaurant redolent of frying fat and saloons sending out gusts of beer smell and coarse laughter.

Across the street, a policeman stood swinging his club for amusement. He stopped suddenly to stand motionless and watchful, in a manner that made the hairs stand up on Sol's neck. The shabby street compressed the air around him. He began to walk a little faster, stumbled, and righted himself with a sense of panic. Now he set one foot before the other with even greater concentration; it looked as if he were walking through mud and it was a terrific effort; his breath struggled through an elaborate series of barricades and torturous turnings. He began to feel nauseated, and in his attempt to control the nausea, he clenched his steel teeth. It only made his breathing more difficult.

Then he came to the river. The air was slightly cooler there, no fresher or sweeter smelling, but full of a small and steady movement. He stopped at the edge to let his shuddering breath slow down.

A dark barge moved at a funeral pace, and he stood watching it pass under one bridge after another, heading for the invisible sea. A sudden yearning raked him, and he imagined himself lying flat on his back on a barge as somber and silent as that one, moving toward the sea, seeing one bridge after another obscure the sky briefly, feeling the water grow bigger beneath him, spread to the endlessness of open ocean, with stars over him so distant there was no way to judge movement by them, and all quiet except for the murmurous, tending sea and him lying there with folded hands, floating in eternal peace. . . .

After a while, he began to walk again in the direction of the garage. He went under the railroad bridge, under the almost constant roaring of the trains pulling into or out of the 125th Street station. Bits of soot dropped on him. The din comforted him, deafening him even to his thoughts. People were like shadows, their voices were part of the one huge clatter of trains and cars. Almost by instinct, he turned at 125th Street.

There was always a gathering of people there, clustered around the magazine stand, going into or out of the station.

A man was standing and arguing with the news dealer.

"You try to humiliate me, right in public. You accuse me of stealing—what, your cheap pornography, your stupid . . ."

"Let's just see in your bag there then, if you're so innocent," the news dealer, a gray-stubbled man with a face like a collapsed balloon, said in a tired, ruthless voice.

"This, this," shrieked the man, whose back was to Sol, as he held up a swollen brief case. "I have only important business papers in here. Lifes and deaths is in here!"

"I seen you reading that Yiddish paper and now it's gone. I only had the one," the news dealer said, leaning over the counter as though to be ready to grab the accused.

"Ah, so there's no end to the persecution, is there?" the accused man said with a quivering, hoarse voice. "All right, I am used to torture—twenty-four hours a day I have it. Look," he said, opening the brief case. "I have just this one *Forward* I purchased this morning in the Bronx," he said slyly, holding the paper up in triumph.

"That's the paper, you tricky bastard. The *Forward* don't come out until two. Pay me for that paper or I call a cop."

"No end, no end," the man with the brief case cried out in ridiculous yet strangely convincing agony.

He turned around with his hands out in a beseeching

shrug for the world to witness. And Sol saw it was Goberman.

With his arms still out, the heavy, open brief case dangling from one hand, he recognized Sol. For several seconds they stared at each other without movement. Even the news dealer seemed puzzled by the sudden paralysis of his opponent. The uncertain light caught glints in Goberman's protruding eyes, hard little brilliants, at once false and tragic, like diamond-studded tears in some odd commemorative statue. Then Goberman's arms sagged, his eyes ran down Sol's figure like two timid mice, and he was a rag figure, teetering on the edge of his own abyss.

Sol began to walk past him, and Goberman turned back to the news dealer.

"How much, then; I haven't the strength," he said.

Sol hurried a little now. His back held the force of something following but he didn't dare turn to find out what it was. Somehow he knew he would not see what it was even if he turned.

When he got into his car, he raced the motor. Then he jammed his foot on the accelerator viciously, so that he skidded out into the street like someone escaping from a crime.

It had been cloudy and hot all day Thursday. But at seven thirty in the evening, as Sol walked down the battered causeway of Bathgate Avenue toward Tessie's house, the sun came out with a cruel brilliance that seemed to curl up the bits of rubbish in the streets. This satire on sunsets struck like flame against the weary old people sitting on steps and goaded the children to excesses of noise and violence. Two boys bounced against him and kept going, oblivious of his absent curses. A block away a woman screamed at someone who didn't answer her. He almost slipped and fell on a moldering lettuce leaf as he turned into the hallway.

"The doctor is here," Tessie whispered when she opened the door. "The old man is bad. He urinated blood yesterday, and today he couldn't go at all. He is in such pain he couldn't get up. I called a different doctor, a *Shwartsa* who has an office next door."

Sol walked past her into the living room. The place smelled of alchohol; it was a relief from all the other odors. He sat down and looked at her without expression. She had just a black slip on, and her hair hung loose and wild and dark. She was like one of those perpetually mourning Italian women; her skin was white and as translucent as quartz against the black slip.

She looked at him for a while and then, unable to bear his bland, indifferent gaze, lowered her eyes to her hands.

"You have eaten yet?"

"I came right here."

"I have eggs, fish. . . . "

"Make some coffee. I will have a little something with it."

They were eating silently in the kitchen when the doctor appeared in the doorway, wiping his hands on a towel. He was a rather stout Negro with the heavy shoulders of a former athlete. His eyes were slanted down at the outside corners and gave him a melancholy expression. Though he appeared to be in his middle thirties, his hair was quite gray and already receding from the top of his head.

"He's very bad, your father," he said cheerily, as though in contrast with his naturally gloomy face. "I hardly know . . . " He suddenly noticed Sol and smiled shyly.

"This is a friend, Sol Nazerman," Tessie said.

"Hello, Doctor," Sol said. "What is the diagnosis?"

"That's a good one, Mr. Nazerman." He sat down at the table and nodded his thanks for the coffee Tessie poured. "The diagnosis? Only that the man's body is a crime. A man shouldn't be like that if he lived a thousand years. Oh, kidneys, lungs, heart, anus, intestines. How did he get like that? Some bad accident or what?"

"A very bad accident," Sol said dryly. "Of birth. He was in the Camps."

The doctor looked puzzled for a moment, and his heavy face, with its down-slanted eyes, resembled a bloodhound's face. Then his eyebrows raised in understanding. "Oh yes, of course. I noticed the tattoos." His eyes checked Sol's arm and then Tessie's, and he grimaced in a way that shaped his face in the lines of his smile. "I'm sorry. Some world we live in, isn't it? Well, then, I can eliminate my bedside diplomacy. Mrs. Rubin, your father is dying."

"Who isn't, Doctor?" Sol said. "The question is, how close is he to death?"

The doctor sighed heavily; it appeared his great weight oppressed him. "I could be very professional and evade by saying this many hours or this many days," he said. "The truth is, I don't know how in hell he ever lived through whatever smashed him up like that. My medical training gives every evidence that he had to be killed long ago. But the human organism defies evidence. Whatever has kept him alive up till now may still hold onto him stubbornly. Lord, I don't know, I just don't know. He could go anytime. A lot of help that is. In all honesty, that's the best I can do."

"Is there anything I can do for him?" Tessie asked without intonation.

"I've shot him full of dope. I don't think he will be in too much pain."

Tessie grunted and filled Sol's cup again.

"Feel free to call me anytime," the doctor said.

"How much do I owe you, Doctor?" Tessie asked, looking at Sol.

"Oh well, look; my office is just two houses down. It wasn't even out of my way home. Suppose you give me the dollar for the shot I gave him. Call it an introductory offer —maybe you'll be a regular customer, Mrs. Rubin."

When the doctor was gone, they sat in the living room listening to the drug-dimmed moans of the old man in the bedroom.

After a while, Tessie got up and came over to sit next to

Sol on the sofa. She looked at him for a few minutes. Then she slipped the straps of her slip from her shoulders, exposing her big, white breasts. Sol sat there stonily. She took his hand timidly and lifted it to her nipples, rubbed it against the warm softness of flesh.

He jerked his hand away. "No, no, forget it," he said.

She shrugged and returned her breasts to the slip. Then she laid her head back on the couch and stared at the ceiling with a bitter smile.

"How is the *business?*" she asked finally.

"Marvelous. Ah, I have trouble with Murillio. I want to get out of being his partner. It is impossible. Then I have a funny feeling about the *Shwartsa* who works for me. He is a strange kid. Sometimes I think he . . . Anyhow, I have this suspicion that he has something up his sleeve. He hangs around with these criminal types. I do not know but what they may be thinking of robbing me somehow."

"And your family, do they still bother you?"

"Some more animals. What is there to say! The whole world is a big zoo. Maybe I will go to Alaska, to the North Pole," he said with glassy humor. "The polar bears should be amusing company."

"They are said to be vicious animals, the polar bears," Tessie said seriously.

Sol began to laugh harshly. She shushed him, reminding him of the old man. Later on, she lit a memorial candle for one or another of her dead. Then she began to cry, and Sol had to make love to her after all. When he got home, he fell into his bed like a piece of butchered meat. He didn't even consider the risk of dreaming. But he did dream.

*He was standing with his hands up to his cheeks, staring at the child's dead body twisted on a monstrous hook which pierced it from behind and came out the breast. He began screaming, the screams of such unbearable size that the sensation was that of vomiting or giving birth. His grief forced all his blood out of his pores. He could not contain it; soon his body would fly into pieces.*

*"Naomi, Naomi* kinder, *my baby, my baby . . ."*

*And then, suddenly, there on the same childish body appeared another face. It was a grotesque face for that delicate, childish body, a young man's thin, sallow face—Morton! And then there appeared the lined, pathetically depraved face of George Smith. And then the face was that of Jesus Ortiz. Each face appeared on the frail baby body with the cruel hook pointing up toward the head. They were like slides projected there. Yet in spite of the unreality, the succession of faces brought him no relief, indeed, made his pain grow worse, become cumulative, and each moment he thought to be the ultimate agony was exposed by the next moment's increased intensity. And the faces kept changing over the body of his child impaled on the hook, on and on, a descent into Hell that had no ending. Mabel Wheatly took her place on the hook, Tessie, Cecil Mapp, Mendel, Buck White, Mrs. Harmon, Goberman, one after the other without end. . . .*

He woke up so drained by poor sleep that it seemed he was more exhausted than he had been the night before. His limbs could have been just old weathered bones, riddled with porousness, as remote from life as anything on earth.

But in his head and his breast there was a crush of anguish, and he gasped in the morning light, "Perhaps I will die soon. All right. But what is all *this* about then?"

## TWENTY

Selig caught him in the living room and asked for two hundred dollars for a hernia operation, speaking out of the corner of his mouth as though the intended surgery were some illicit entertainment. After Sol nodded and mumbled something about arranging it, he was waylaid by his sister, who warned that the house would be flooded if plumbing repairs weren't forthcoming. In the yard, his niece, Joan, asked for " . . . a loan, Uncle Sol, strictly a loan. Until I get caught up with my vacation savings. I insist you charge me the regular rate of interest."

And Saturday had been a bedlam in the store, so that by the time he reached his quiet bedroom and fell on the bed with a book tented over his chest, his nephew's knock on the door was like a physical blow on his body.

"What do *you* want, Morton?" he asked, barely masking his irritation.

"Well, I have to get next semester's art supplies, and I was wondering if . . . "

"Money, you want money, too? I am made of money for all of you. There is nothing else, just a man made of dollar bills. Someday you will peel all the money off and there will be nothing underneath, just air. What will you do then?"

"I don't know. . . . I just . . . " And then Morton's face found a dignity in anger, too. "If you don't want to give me the money . . . "

"Oh, I will give it. Don't I always? What else is there for a money man to do? Nothing else. Make money, give it away, make some more, on and on." He got up and went to the bureau. He took a checkbook and a fountain pen from the drawer and stood there, looming huge and shapeless over the youth. Morton looked away from his uncle with a bitter expression on his face. "All right, Morton, how much shall I make the check out for? Or perhaps I should just sign it and let you fill out the amount? You could make it a thousand, a hundred thousand, even a million. There is no limit."

"I need twenty-four dollars," Morton said in a flat voice, his eyes on the dusk in the yard.

For some reason, that figure pierced Sol, and he closed his lips against his own words. He wrote out the check for the amount and handed it to his nephew. Morton went out of the room without thanking him, hunched and self-protecting, like someone with a severe pain in his middle.

"If I do not want to give you the money, hah!" Sol said to the closed door. "What would you do if I did not want to give you the money? As though you would go someplace else for it, as though you had other alternatives, Morton, you miserable creature. Do not make me laugh with your offended dignity, do not make me laugh. . . . " And then he stood there before the open checkbook, pen still in hand,

and nowhere near laughing. He was filled with cruel vibration, like a savagely plucked violin string, sick and dying and yet nowhere near the ease of physical death.

Outside, the hot summer evening soaked in itself with all its soft sounds. It surrounded the house, and finally the room in which hc stood, a teeming, slowly exploding hulk with only the pen and the checkbook to hold on to.

He had no strength for a shower, could just about make it to the bed. He fell slantwise across it and lay without moving, feeling the dirt of the day's dried sweat, his hands coated by all the old, soiled objects he had handled that day.

After a while, he twitched slowly toward sleep.

*A mountain of emaciated bodies, hands, and legs tossed in nightmare abandon, as though each victim had died in the midst of a frantic dance, the hollow eyes and gaping mouths expressing what could have been a demented and perverse ecstasy. Sol felt an instant's envy for the dream they might have reached in the last popping of their brains as the noxious air had soaked them in death. Certainly he envied what they had now—a blindness to scenes like this. The great pile seemed to creak slightly, could be heard in spite of the shouts of the guards, because its phantom softness was an immense thing.*

*All right, he would obey them, the men in the uniforms; he still, unreasonably, feared the death they could award. He helped throw the bodies onto the growing pile of the crematorium, full of shame, and praying that a familiar face wouldn't be revealed, that dead eyes wouldn't fall on him with terrible, accidental wrath. He kept his glance away from the heads, just seized the dry, bone-filled limbs and heaved. His mind fastened on the idea of work.*

*The sky was veiled over him, cloudy with a suggestion of blackness behind the pale gray. The guards' shouts fell short and shallow under that sky, and the soft, subtle creaking*

*seemed to rise and lose itself in the high, colorless ceiling.*
*All the more-distant bodies were a blur; he couldn't see as*
*far as the barbed-wire fence. It was better that way. Just*
*reach and lift and stretch and throw. The bodies were really*
*quite light, even for one as ill fed as he was. He still had his*
*bulk, was stronger than most of the prisoners. It was as*
*though he had begun with so much more strength that he*
*would always have more, no matter how much he failed.*

*As he tugged at a corpse, something bright and delicate*
*tumbled at his feet. He bent down quickly. It was a pair of*
*spectacles, remarkably unbroken. He put them on, and the*
*whole vast spectacle leapt into horrid clarity. He clenched*
*his jaw as though to break the bone there and went back to*
*his work, inflicting the cleared vision on himself. It was the*
*very least he could do.*

*But oh, the smell, the smell—it turned him inside out. His*
*eyes strayed to the heads with that new-found clarity of*
*vision. God help him if he should see Ruth's face, the chil-*
*dren's faces! God help him for having to see all the stran-*
*gers' faces, for seeing at all.*

*He continued working with the round, old-fashioned*
*spectacles on. They made everything savagely clear, but he*
*kept them on. That was the least he could do.*

"No, no, I don't think I'll lead right off with talking about
Spinoza," George Smith said aloud, lowering the library book
he had been reading. "I will mention some of the Spaniards
casually, Baroja, Iglesias, Unamuno, Gasset. And then, in the
course . . . " He circled cleverly, planned his benevolent assault
on the Pawnbroker from his sway-backed bed. The scabrous
walls almost disappeared at the ceiling; his gooseneck lamp
was turned shade down for reading. There was an orange
crate painted black and covered with a flowered curtain. Inside, he kept his toilet articles. He had an old end table he
had bought in the Goodwill Store, and he ate his meals on
it. There was a two-burner hot plate on which he cooked

Japanese style, right at the table. Between his bed and the wall was the bookcase he had built himself. It was filled with a number of paperback books and three with hard covers: the Bible, Shakespeare's complete works in one volume, and a wildly obscene anthology of pornography. This last one he kept way in back and covered in a wrapping-paper dust jacket, as though secreting it from himself. But his secretiveness did no good at all; he knew the book was there, always.

Now, George Smith was safely occupied and he gave no thought to the book or the sounds of the families in the other rooms of the apartment. He smiled at the thought of Spinoza and the Pawnbroker. One of these days soon he would have to work up the nerve to invite Sol Nazerman to spend a whole evening in peaceful, unhurried talk. Maybe they could just take cans of beer and sit for hours at the edge of the river. Talk and talk and talk—all the great things would be in their conversations. Oh, he would have to broach it carefully, tactfully, make it casual and attractive sounding. He couldn't completely forget the Pawnbroker was a white man. Not that there was any question of his being an ordinary *ofay*. No, not at all. The Pawnbroker was a man of great learning and understanding, to whom color was less than nothing, a man who had suffered himself and so could be sympathetic to others' failings, a man who . . .

George moved his slight, hairless body on the bed, smiling, thinking of the great subtleties of philosophy and literature, of all the avenues for exploring them, opened to the Pawnbroker and himself.

Unconsciously, his hand crept down his body to his groin and moved lightly over that part of him while his eyes stared musingly at the dim ceiling. But then the excitement of sensation confused the excitement in his head. The terrible, beautiful images began to make him tremble as he caressed himself. A child laughed in another room, and he closed his eyes in a sick ecstasy. His body began to writhe as he sank into his lust and began drowning in it.

The book fell to the floor, and he opened his eyes, startled. He reached down to the floor and seized the book with both hands. The Pawnbroker's face appeared in his mind, quiet and wise behind the thick glasses, but also sorrowful, as though pained at the filthy habits of his friend and intellectual companion, George Smith.

"No. No more. Can't think about those things. Ruin everything. And what would *he* think if he heard I got in some kind of trouble again? Oh, he wouldn't condemn, too big for that. But still, it would ruin everything."

He raised himself up on the pillow and began thumbing through the pages of the book. Finally something caught his attention and he started to read. Gradually he relaxed and after a while he felt drowsy. He slid lower down on the pillow, careful not to disturb the pleasant torpor.

He was almost asleep when he heard the child's voice again and the torturous desire hit him like a charge of electricity. His body arched on the bed and he gasped aloud. His hand started its sly, evil descent down his leg again. He whimpered a little. But then his fingers touched the crisp vellum of the book. He clasped it to his chest and held it there rigidly, beseeching peace and safety from it, like a child with a Teddy bear.

Robinson took off his ash-gray jacket and hung it carefully on the one wooden hanger. His room was narrow and small as a cell, and a window at the end took up almost half of one tiny wall. A dull neon glow flickered slowly on and off against the thin shade.

He took off his clean, starched shirt and hung it neatly over the jacket. He folded his pants and caught them by the cuffs in the top drawer of the bureau. Then he slipped his shoes off, brushed them briefly, and lined them in perfect parallel with the hanging jacket above. At the sink, a tiny, doll-like bowl in a slight alcove to the left of the door, he turned the water on and looked into the small mirror above it. He contemplated the death's-head without expression. The strange blue eyes made it like a view into nothingness. He lived almost entirely in moments. What had ground him down to that skull-like appearance was not just buried, but burned out beyond resurrection. Vaguely, he knew it was a fortunate thing that this was so; he would have gone howling through the streets otherwise. He remembered the physical facts of a horrible life but had no sense of his past feelings. He knew the names and dates of the times of beatings and humiliations, of betrayals and obscene violations; he could recall every day he had spent in prisons and hospitals. Yet he had no emotional recall of any of it. This moment, this need.

He was dirty now. So he soaped the stiff scrub brush and began to scour all his upper body, which was bone-thin and resembled a washboard or some odd drying-rack. He did the same thing to his face and, later, after removing his undershorts, to his legs and genitals. And when he burned like fire all over his body, he dried himself and put on clean underwear.

Then he went to his bureau drawer and took a small hypodermic out. He filled it from one of the boxes of ampules kept in the tiny icebox in the corner, and injected himself in the arm, which was stippled with many tiny marks. He smiled his bleak smile as he contemplated the latest needle hole.

"My kicks," he said sardonically. He was a diabetic and the ampules contained insulin.

He took a small, inexpensive harmonica from the drawer. Then he sat on the edge of the bed and began to play a medley of waltzes. The thin music wailed through the room, seemed to ricochet from one wall to another so there was an eerie and confusing echo which confounded the familiar tunes. After a while, his face sagged and became weary; it had seemed of indeterminate age, but now it began to appear quite old. And then the shocking gleam of tears appeared in the corners of his eyes. His face twisted fiercely, as though at the poor quality of tone from the cheap harmonica. He thought of the wonderful instrument he had hocked to the Pawnbroker.

Suddenly he stood up and heaved the harmonica against the wall, his face writhing. He went to the drawer again and took a blunt-barreled revolver out. He carried it back to the bed with him. He propped the pillow and settled himself comfortably on it. Then he rested the hand with the gun on one bent knee and began pulling the trigger on the empty chamber. He sighted it on the colorless wall, which pulsed softly with the diffused reflections of the neons outside.

*Click, click, click.*

It was amazing how loud that hammer was in the tiny room.

Jesus Ortiz was apparently talking to his mother. But he expected no answers from her, used her instead as a sounding board, because he would have been repelled by the idea of talking to himself.

"I mean who I learn better from than a Jew? Besides, there one thing about him—he no bull-shitter. He don't jangle my nerves like, you know. Like I *rest* there in the store. Oh, not that he don't work my *cojones*. You know Jews, they get full value. But it like I feel . . . I don't know . . . *easy.* I got the feelin' he ain't never gonna do me no evil like. . . . "

There was a brighter dart of light against the windows of the Ortiz apartment. A faint, distant rumble sounded above the low din of the nighttime traffic.

"But I don't owe that Sheeny nothin' really. What is he to me?"

Marilyn Birchfield saw lightning from her apartment window. She looked up to a sky that reflected the city's lights but showed nothing of itself, and she wondered if it would rain.

Sol Nazerman came out of his early sleep all drenched with sweat and dry mouthed from gasping in dreams. He saw the sudden flash and heard the rumble of thunder and he yearned for the cooling sound and feel of rain. But he had no hope for it. He lay for many hours without hearing any more thunder, and he was still awake when daylight came, clear and hot and dry.

# *T W E N T Y - O N E*

Sol got out of the house without waking any of his sister's family. He was so intent on eluding them all in the Sunday quiet that he let the car roll down the driveway to the street before he started the motor. Then he was off with a roar.

Mount Vernon was peaceful in the heat of early morning. The bundles of Sunday newspapers were still tied and waiting before the closed stores. The houses slept behind their wide, awninged porches, and here and there were children's tricycles and toy trucks, abandoned suddenly the day before, as though because of a play air raid or some other child-sized disaster. The wires and tracks and signal towers of the railroad glinted in the sunshine. Already the cicadas had set up an intense and threatening buzz, which reached up to the hot blue sky.

He drove with both hands tight on the wheel, as though he had just learned to drive. All the bright light threatened him like a single massive flame. And he was filled with mysterious dread for the unusual emotion he now seemed to recognize—a sudden and unbearable loneliness. He saw himself as the last living creature on a burning orb. He had known many solitudes before, but the sense of isolation he had now made all that had come before seem only like a bad dream there had been hope of waking from.

The car motor hummed, the uncared-for body of the vehicle creaked and squeaked over each bump. He yearned to cry but knew he was not capable of crying. He pulled off the road near the entrance to the highway and sat with his mouth open. The heat collected around him as he stared at the parched grass that edged the road. Nothing, nothing. His hands fluttered over his body. He adjusted his spectacles. He put his hands on the dashboard, on the windows, into the glove compartment. There was a flashlight in there. He took it out and flicked the switch on; he could just about see the pallid glow of the tiny bulb's filament. Then he aimed that infinitesimal illumination at the immense cauldron of white sunlight; it made him shake his head, and once he had begun it, he found he could not stop. The heat rose to the temperature of an oven, and he sat breathing heavily through his mouth, a gray figure in the motionless car, on the desolate landscape.

Idly, his hands began to rifle his pockets, played with tiny crumbs of lint, with keys and coins. His fingers pondered the thin, dog-eared edge of a card. He took it out and held it before his eyes for several minutes before he was able to read it. "Marilyn Birchfield, 210 West 75th Street, New York City, PLaza 6-3109."

For a few minutes more he moved his eyes from the card to the brilliant landscape. He was parked on a mild slope, facing the highway and the sky. Off to one side, where there was a widening of the road's shoulder, an aluminum phone booth was silhouetted against the blue.

He got out of the car and trudged up the slope over the dry, crackly August grass. The smell of the baking concrete road came to him. There was a humid sweetness from the ground. He went into the booth and, leaving the folding doors open, dialed the number on the card.

"Hello?" She appeared to be startled and drowsy. Her voice sounded rich and lovely to him.

"This is Sol Nazerman, the Pawnbroker," he said.

She was silent, breathed surprise.

"Oh yes, hello," she said finally. "Hello there," she emphasized in welcome. "I'm very glad you called. How are you, Mr. Nazerman? Is there anything wrong?"

"It is so very early," he said apologetically.

"Oh, I don't sleep late anyhow." Then she allowed a pause again, uncertain of his intentions and afraid to frighten him away.

"About your suggestion of the other day—the boat excursion. If you could still see your way clear?"

"Ohh, oh my, Mr. Nazerman, yes, yes certainly," she said, with an excessive enthusiasm that she knew sounded false.

Sol began to see how ridiculous his call was. "It was really presumptuous to call you like this. I am very sorry. Forgive me. I just happened on your card and it occurred to me that the boat excursion . . . Ah, but to call you like this. Accept my apology. I am perhaps not quite awake myself. Perhaps another time . . . "

"No, no, really! I am delighted you called. I'd love to go. It's going to be a scorcher today. It will be ever so much cooler on the boat. Oh, I really am glad you called. I had no idea what to do with myself today. Do you think you can find your way here? Are you driving?"

"Yes I am driving. I believe I can find this address," Sol said, nodding as though she could see him, his glasses

steamed in the heat of the booth; his smile twitched in relief. "I am near the highway now. I could be there in less
than an hour."

"Oh, I'd better get busy then. I'll make some sandwiches
and dress. I'll be ready by the time you get here. And, by
the way, I have plenty of cheese," she said.

"Yes, good, good—our little joke, is it?" he said, taking
off his glasses and wiping his eyes with his arm. "This is
very good of you."

"Nonsense, Mr. Nazerman, I was hoping you'd call. It
will be my pleasure, too."

He nodded, appreciative yet impatient of her kindness;
he knew the truth of it. "Nevertheless, it is good of you."

She was silent for a moment. Then she spoke brightly.
"You just get in your car and hurry along. The boat leaves
at nine. I'll see you soon. . . ."

This river was so different from the one he saw every day
on his way to and from work. It was wide and generous,
bordered by green hills and full of great sweeping turns. The
steady hum and vibration of the boat filled him with a restful feeling, and he dared deep breaths of the persistent
breeze.

"I guess you're glad you decided to come, after all,
aren't you, Sol?" Marilyn said from the chair next to him.
She was smiling, and her face seemed appropriate to the
wide, sun-filled vista. She wore a yellow dress which cast
up a buttery glow under her chin, and her eyes were soft
with contentment or some other odd joy. "I know I am."
She sighed peacefully. "I like my work and I'm glad I do
what I do. But, well, I was brought up in a different kind of
place, a happier place. There are times when that city makes
me sad and tired. I find myself just yearning for a day like
this." She tilted her head back and smiled softly. "How
many times our family used to have picnics on a lake, spend
the whole day in the sun and the air. People's voices sound

so different in the country, happier, easier. My father used to say that people had to get off the concrete of sidewalks sometimes just to remember what the earth is like underneath. He liked to sound like a homespun, country philosopher. Of course, he was born in the heart of Boston, but he was a big weekend nature-lover. He'd take us for long walks, identifying birds and trees. 'Breathe deeply,' he'd say. 'Smell the air the way it's supposed to be, untarnished by soot and smoke and carbon monoxide.' " She laughed wistfully. "Untarnished, oh dear! As though our town were another Pittsburgh!"

And Sol, caught by the mood of the place and her voice, responded in kind.

"I seem to remember once," he said, waving his finger pedagogically, his eyes up in a dreaming corner, "that I also took a river trip. On the Vistula, it was. Now whether it was when I was very small and we went by river boat to see some relatives in another town . . . Wyzgorod was their name. . . . But then it seems to me that I went with some students when I was at the university. There must have been two different times. There was much singing and playing of concertinas. . . . I confuse the two trips. Oh, but yes, the time with my mother was a longer trip. We had a stateroom, and I woke in the morning filled with delight and amazement to see the world moving by the tiny porthole. Fantastic how that little detail comes to mind. It must be forty years ago. But I recall so clearly the sight of the river and the banks moving by and knowing that I had traveled all that way while I was sleeping. . . ."

The boat chugged softly along, past the neat Hudson River towns. The burble of people's voices all along the deck was like part of the sound of their passage. Marilyn sat without moving, her lips slightly parted, her eyes bright and tender on the Pawnbroker's strangely softened face; she maintained her stillness as though she feared to puncture the delicate surface of his reminiscence.

"We took our food then, too," he went on. "Of course my mother would not have us eat the food that was not kosher. We sat on the deck, just as we are doing now, and we ate and watched the farms and the woods going by." He took off his glasses to blind himself to the present, and his fingers traced the shape of them around his eyes. "The types you saw then! Peasants like animals, a few crazy Russians bellowing songs . . . It was a beautiful country, a beautiful river. . . ."

When he put back the glasses with a stern expression, she began unpacking the lunch.

"I don't know about you, but I'm getting hungry," she said. "Not that it takes much for me to get hungry. My appetite is my ruination. Someday I'll just blow up like a balloon and burst."

"You are not too fat," he said politely. "It is becoming for a woman to be, to be . . ."

"Fat," she said humorously.

"No, no," he protested, his hand up in objection as he smiled. "You are a healthy, attractive woman."

For a minute there was an awkward silence between them; something obviously impossible had been touched upon. She busied herself with the sandwiches and the thermos bottle while he frowned unseeingly at the approaching Tappan Zee Bridge.

They ate in silence for a while. They passed under the great span and left it behind. Then, after Sol had eaten one of the sandwiches, he sat back with the other one, still wrapped, in his hand.

"One forgets how attractive America must be," he said. "Most of my time has been spent in the city. Of course, I live in Mount Vernon, which I suppose is an attractive-enough town. But I derive no pleasure from it. There must be thousands of miles of lovely countryside, and I have heard that some of the mountains are very impressive. Often I have thought I would like to go up some very high mountain. I have the idea it would be very beautiful and peaceful. The world might look quite worth while from those heights. You would not see people or dirt or . . ." He waved his hands at those things he did not wish to mention.

"And yet," she said, "nowadays Americans all want to go to Europe. They go by the hundreds of thousands. People save for years just to have a few weeks there."

"Why is this so?"

"Oh, I guess people are impressed with the history and the sophistication, the culture."

"They are fools. Europe is a graveyard," he said harshly.

"You have seen it at its worst," she reminded him.

"Not at its worst—as it really is!"

"Would you judge all people by the very worst you have seen?"

"I do," he said coldly. "But this is an unpleasant turning our conversation has taken. Please, I am finding the day very restful. Let us not examine, you promised not."

"Yes, of course. I'm sorry." She sighed and let her head fall back on the chair. "Wouldn't it be wonderful," she said, "if this trip could last for a long, long time? To think of nothing except what pretty scene might appear around the next turning. To talk and eat when we were hungry and sleep when we were drowsy. And then to wake, as you did when you were a child, to see the woods and fields going by and know how much went by while you slept."

"That would be nice—if it were possible."

"For now, we can pretend it is."

"I am not very good at pretending."

"But you will try, just for today," she begged with a smile.

"I will try," he agreed gently.

The country grew wilder and greener, and the houses were farther and farther apart. Occasionally, a swift cruiser passed them; sometimes they passed a tiny rowboat with people fishing. Hills scalloped the sky, and the sun covered the water with a multitude of tiny brilliants, which flashed in their faces and made them close their eyes and talk sleepily of small, almost intimate things.

"It's hard for me to realize that I usually have to read to get myself to sleep," she said. "Right now, I feel I could sleep without the slightest effort."

"I have the habit of reading before bed, too," he said.

"I read mostly novels, the old ones: Thackeray, Dickens, stories of a simple world. Sometimes I read Chekhov's short stories. They're gentle and funny and sad."

"I am fond of Chekhov, too. To me, his writing is as unreal as a child's story. Yet it is lifelike for all that. Perhaps because there is no affectation in him."

"*A Day in the Country,*" she said musingly.

"Ah yes, that is a lovely one."

And then, for some time, both of them dozed. Sol seemed to hear and feel the throbbing, comforting vibrations of the boat even in sleep, and he forgot his age and his life for a while. Once, he woke with a smile and looked over at the woman beside him. She was breathing deeply, her full bosom rising and falling. A tiny pulse in her strong neck throbbed faintly, as though an invisible moth fluttered its wings against her flesh. A tendril of her shiny, dark blond hair swung gently against her cheek. He let his eyes grow heavy again as he faced her and he carried the sight of her into his light sleep.

Later, she woke for a minute or two and stared at his gray face, all slack with sleep. She looked at the blue numbers on his arm and she became sad. But then she convinced herself that the numbers looked fainter, that they might disappear altogether in time. She dozed again.

Late in the afternoon, they walked around the decks, exchanging little nods and smiles of amusement over the various passengers. They went inside, where there was a lunch counter. Sol bought some packages of poundcake and two containers of coffee, and they took the food out to the chairs, where they ate and talked a little and looked at the ever-changing shore.

On the return trip, their chairs faced the sunset. The water was a pink-gold, the sky washed with vermilion and purple and orange. Each cloud was outlined with fire, and the hills of the earth were deep in shadow; it was as if the passengers floated on the edge of day and night and had the choice of either.

"I've never seen a sunset like that," she said in a half-whisper.

"It is very beautiful," he said. "But somehow I do not trust its beauty, it is too blatant, too obvious."

"Sometimes the obvious can be trusted. All appearances aren't deceiving," she reprimanded gently.

"Perhaps not, but it is safer to follow the old Roman law—guilty until proved innocent," he said.

There was a low hot moon and full dark had come when he saw the lights of the city on the horizon. A massive weight settled on him.

"I fear we must stop with the make-believe," he said, gesturing toward the approaching lights. "We are approaching the hard facts."

He seemed to hear the millions of voices like the shrilling of countless animals, to smell the dirt and age and sin of the teeming city. And his sense of doom came up over him like some dark, damning clothes he had put off for the while.

"But we can do this again," she said plaintively. "There's no reason why not."

"Agh, how many times can you use a dream? It wears out so quickly against life. Never mind, it has been a pleasant, restful day. Perhaps I have regained some energy. I thank you very much," he said with cool courtesy.

She just nodded, her lips tight in the dark. She wondered if he would be able to see if she cried. It was dark enough. And he made her feel like crying. Oh, how she felt like crying!

On Monday, the day after the excursion, Sol had experienced a curious feeling of lightness, a sense of remoteness which had been quite pleasant and had coerced him to a brief idea of ease and peace.

But today, Tuesday, August 26, he recognized the limitations of reprieve. Now the past two days took on the quality of a crueler deception, and he realized he had only been made more susceptible to the formless, thrusting virulence in him.

Each dark face he encountered in the store tore at him; at times he seemed barely able to function.

His vision played tricks on him. A customer would come up to the counter and it would seem the customer's face zoomed so close that Sol could no longer see the features, was blinded by the magnified surface of human skin. A tide of succeeding skins. The brown, the tan, the red-veined, the large-pored, pimpled, and scarred world of flesh. He spoke to great walls of skin, to cracked lips, to hairy nostrils, to veinous, crusty eyes. And he tried to endure in the sounds of voices, to make understandable what he must, to compensate, like any afflicted person, by developing another sense, by decoding the scattered, at least recognizable words. And the people who had never expected anything but strangeness from him were further bewildered by his singular habit of closing his eyes and repeating, over and over, his wildly illogical offers.

"Two dollars, two dollars," he said, with his eyes shut.

"You crazy!" a voice said indignantly. "Two dollars for a Leica camera! What the hell you sayin'?"

"Two dollars."

"You flippin' you wig, Uncle, you out of your mind for sure," the voice said. And Sol never knew when the customer, whoever he was, had taken his camera and walked out of the store.

"Two dollars," he said from that self-imposed blindness.

And the woman with the pawn ticket looked at him in amazement. She had gotten a loan of fifteen dollars for gold earrings two months before and knew from experience that she should have to pay at least twenty to get them out of hock. But who was she to question a mad bargain? "Well *okay!* Here the two bucks, let's have them earrings," she said.

But Jesus Ortiz had a peculiar vested interest; for some reason beyond him, there were certain inequities he would not tolerate.

"You owe us twenty-two bucks and fifty cents, lady," he interrupted, taking the ticket from Sol as though from a sleeping man.

Sometimes, as though by lucky coincidence, the Pawnbroker made sense in his transactions. By keeping his eyes on the counter and off the faces, he was somehow able to conduct his business with a semblance of normality. Money rustled through his fingers; his hands were dulled with the handling of metal and glass and wood and cloth. But even in those times when he imitated proficiently the hard-eyed, cool appraiser, he made bad bargains.

He ran his fingers searchingly, professionally over the seams of suits and then accepted mildewed, moth-eaten garments, so it was as though his examination were merely something to satisfy some scientific curiosity, had nothing to do with gain. He posed as a crafty metallurgist, scratched and tested brass only to end up paying for gold. He knocked authoritatively at the body of a fine, handmade Italian violin and offered a minute loan on it. Then, a half hour later, he ran a bow over a cheaply made, child's practice fiddle, frowned knowingly over its shallow whine, and offered more in loan than the instrument had cost new.

And all the while, Jesus Ortiz worked at the counter near him, handling part of the traffic expertly yet always having time to look over at Sol with a strange, almost regretful calculation. His employer was going to pieces for reasons far beyond his knowledge; that was clear to him. He supposed he should take the Pawnbroker's look of impending collapse as a portent. There seemed no sense in his waiting for intangible things to decide him. He would make his move soon now. It occurred to him consciously, for the first time, that opportunity could reside in other people's destruction. And yet he wondered why he felt no promise of triumph, felt oppressed, rather, in direct proportion to his resolution. He grew impatient with himself, irritated with all the wasteful conjecture, and concentrated on eliminating nonfunctional thoughts.

He continued his dealings with the stream of supplicants, humorous with this one, brusque with another, harsh, seductive, sympathetic with others. He was facile and cool and clever, able to deal well enough with both his own customers and those the Pawnbroker almost made disastrous deals with, jumped back and forth with a dead-pan alacrity, like a man playing all the instruments in an orchestra peopled with lifelike dummies. And still, even in the presumptuousness of taking things out of his employer's hands from time to time, he managed to defend the Pawnbroker from ridiculousness, to preserve his dignity by some innate sense of diplomacy as delicate and touching as that of a son who contrives a semblance of usefulness for an aged and ineffectual father.

Under his almost instinctive protectiveness, though, his mind worked its way down a smoothly direct corridor. I will talk to Tangee tomorrow, he told himself. Now or never.

"No, *no,* Sol, that there is junk," he pointed out with impunity to the dazed Pawnbroker, who was just then pondering a cheap, toylike camera. And with that strangely gentle condescension, he nudged Sol to one side and gave the tiny loan it called for.

And Sol, lost in a world of ugly, pitiful skin, nodded at the smooth coffee-colored hide Ortiz was to him, and began occupying himself by turning the pages of the big ledger, as though searching for a route through the confounding maze.

Suddenly, in the afternoon, his vision became normal. But then it was the sound of people's voices. This was somewhat easier for him to handle. At least he was able to assay the merchandise with something like his usual expertness, to offer prices commensurate with value, and to turn down what was unreasonably demanded. There was still considerable pain in it for him, though. The voices rang in his head like gigantic bells, and he had to squint and lean forward as though to make out each tiny note in the great volume of a carillon. His expression became querulous, and his face held the lines of his straining to make sense of the crashing vibrations. He heard agonized cries in the most uninflected phrases, thunderous bellows in the tiredest sighs of acceptance.

By midafternoon he stood in the lull of an empty store, his eyes and mouth sagging, his head turning from side to side as though he were looking to see if there were any survivors besides himself.

Jesus thought the Pawnbroker would die where he stood, and he felt a sense of panic at the idea; he realized that all his own plans would collapse with him.

Without a word, he ran out of the store and came back with a paper container of strong, black coffee, which he put down against the Pawnbroker's hand.

"I brung some coffee," he said, studying the gray, staring face, which seemed somehow smaller and less puffy. "Go ahead, drink it while it's hot, Sol. You don't look too good; better drink it."

Sol looked down at the coffee, then back up at his enigmatic rescuer. He nodded stiffly. He picked it up, put it to his lips, and grunted as his mouth sent a message of pain to him. "It is hot . . . good. . . ." He passed his hand over his eyes, then covered them with the same hand as he began to sip. It was as though he thought the coffee might expose his eyes to an unbearable light.

For a couple of minutes, Jesus watched him drink. Then an odd rage hit him, and he curved his lips savagely and turned away. He would earn what he got from the Jew. All this crap got to end, he snarled silently, I had enough of him. Filled with a melancholy fury, he applied himself to writing up the transactions he had undertaken in the past hour.

When the phone rang, Sol caught it on the first ring.

"Yes?" he said.

"Sol, this is Marilyn Birchfield. How are you?"

"I am fine," he said from memory.

"I hope you're still feeling rested from Sunday. I can tell you it did *me* a world of good."

"I see," he said. Then, after a moment's silence, "What was it you wanted?"

The icy sound of termination in his voice chilled her, and she felt all her overhearty friendliness fall back on her like water thrown into the wind.

"Well now, that's fine . . . I'm glad . . . why I called was . . ."

His silence indicated indifference as to why she had called, and she forced herself to go on speaking.

"I just thought you might want to have dinner at my apartment," she said in a rush of words. "I think I'm a good cook, although mostly I just cook for myself and . . . and *all* food tastes just marvelous to me." She waited again, listened for breathing or the dial tone; hearing neither, she realized she would have to say something that demanded answer. "Will you come to dinner, Sol?"

"No-thank-you," he said, like someone who knew just those three words of a foreign language.

And she, incurable good sport, perennial pitier who was renewed by the abuse that kept her from enjoying her pity, made something bearably courteous from his indifferent rudeness.

"Oh, you're busy then. Well, perhaps later in the week, maybe Friday? How would that suit you?"

"There is no point to it."

"I don't understand."

"You don't understand," he echoed. "Let me be clearer then. There is no point to any relationship between us, *no point at all.*"

"I see," she said, her voice soft and admitting of the fact that she had understood right from the first word. "I don't know just what is troubling you, Sol. I wish I did; I wish I could help you. Apparently I can't. So I won't pester you. I realize how pushy and tiresome I can be sometimes. But I believe there *could* be a point to our relationship, at least for me. I like you and I enjoy being with you and talking with you. I enjoyed our excursion Sunday more than I can tell you."

"Look," he said in a dry, aching voice, "how can I say . . . You try, yes. You are goodhearted. Only do not think of becoming intimate with me. For your own good I say this." He paused for a moment, and then his voice became brutal. "You would be guilty of necrophilia—it is obscene to love the dead."

Marilyn made a funny little choking sound, like someone whose nostrils are filled with water.

"All right, Sol, all right. Call me when you think you can. If there is ever anything . . ."

For a minute or two, he stood fussing with the telephone dial, putting his forefinger into each of the little holes.

If there is ever anything! It was growing, spreading. The surface of him was filling with a sharp-angled network of cracks. He felt his body to be a dry, deteriorating husk flooded with a malignant life that could dwarf all his past suffering.

He began to move around the store more quickly, performing little chores with a jerky speed that made it appear he had to accomplish as much of even that pitiful and shabby work before he was destroyed. He rushed about, he shouted at Jesus, he wrote up tickets in a frenzy and wriggled his fingers at slow-moving customers. His ponderous body moved swiftly as a penned elephant behind the counter. And as he charged on a deserted battlefield, everyone saw his dementia with a curiosity bordering on envy; they looked at him and it was as though they speculated on the terrible, private visions of an opium eater.

Ortiz just stepped back nimbly from his employer's mad

rushes, flattening himself against the shelves like a matador while his cool, lovely eyes filled with the matador's same murderous pity.

He going, he going fast, Jesus mused. Soon he going to fly in a thousand pieces and there be nothing left. Crazy, he going crazy. But even as he phrased that scornful thought, he knew it was more than that; the Pawnbroker was headed for something stranger and more terrible. And since he could fathom nothing worse than death, he thought, That man going to die! And he closed himself to the thought of his own implication in the Pawnbroker's destiny.

At five o'clock, George Smith came in with money and a fistful of pawn tickets. His face was as gay and expansive as a drunkard's when he steps into a cozy barroom filled with convivial-looking people.

"Hel-lo there, Sol," he called out in a voice edged with laughter. "Got a handful of business here." He held up the pawn tickets as he walked confidently over to the counter. He leaned on it and settled himself comfortably for a long stay. It was quiet in the store, perfect. He had gauged the hour after a long study of the pattern of the store's business. Hardly anyone came in between five and six-thirty. With a little luck, he might have a full hour. He might even broach his idea of their spending a few hours together some evening. Well, he'd see how things developed; discretion was important. If not this time, then another time.

"You remember I mentioned I was reading the Spanish writers," he said, handing the tickets, one at a time, to Sol. "Well, I read Baroja and then Iglesias. You familiar with them, Sol?" The Pawnbroker seemed a little too concerned with the pawn tickets, and George frowned uneasily at how quickly Sol seemed to add up the figures. "Or Unamuno or Gasset?"

"Forty-three dollars," Sol said, fluttering his fingers impatiently.

"Oh, yes, certainly," George answered, maintaining a

smile. Probably tonight wasn't the ideal time to bring up the evening together. The Pawnbroker seemed nervous, distracted. He counted out the money and gave it to Sol with a conspiratorial wink; it was a secret between them; they both knew the real purpose of his frequent visits.

"And then I got to Spinoza. Not that he can be categorized with the others. He is strictly a philosopher, not a literary figure."

"What are you saying?" Sol asked. He had all the items George Smith had pawned during the past several weeks arrayed on the counter and he waited for the little man to take them up. There was the hurricane lamp, the gold money clip, a silver railroad watch, a cigarette lighter faced with mother-of-pearl.

"Here are your things," Sol said. "What else do you want?" He held the money in his hand, and his vision was once more afflicted, so he saw only the bone-tight surface of George's skin, the myriad fine lines around the eyes, the parched scoring of the lips which trembled in time with his strange rhythm of breathing.

"Spinoza," George said weakly, his smile only a monument to the pleasure he had felt a few minutes before. "I was talking about Spinoza. I was going to say . . ."

"Spinoza, Spinoza," Sol said dazedly. "But you *have* your things here."

"Where he proves the existence of God by saying . . ."

"Why are you banging my head with your talk?"

"No, no, I wanted to say that . . . that . . ."

"Go, go away. Come on, come on now. This is a place of business; I cannot be bothered with all you crazy . . . Go, go peddle it someplace else. All you animals with your insane talk, your filth. Go on, I have no time." And he stood there, squinting and swaying with impatience to get on with all the invisible chores that needed attending to.

George Smith gathered up the items. He put the small things in his pockets and took the hurricane lamp in his hand. His smile vibrated as he turned it slowly around the store, as he took in all the wild variety of things on the shelves and in the cases, the distant, serene face of the Negro youth behind the other counter. And it was as though he took an agonized farewell of something he had struggled hard to deserve.

"Yes, certainly, very well," he said. He walked out of the store with a furtive air, as though he had been surprised in a place where he had no right to be.

Sol continued with his great rush at nothing. No one else came in, and Jesus allowed himself to lounge in a corner of the store, watching with a sort of morbid fascination as his employer rampaged blindly in the narrow confines of the space behind the counter.

But about an hour after George Smith had gone, the Pawnbroker suddenly stopped in the midst of mauling the pages of his ledger. He stood perfectly still for the first time in hours and, as he peered at the doorway with a puzzled frown, he asked in a clear, calm voice, "Who was that in here?"

"No one in here for almost an hour," Jesus answered.

"Who was the last one?"

"That George Smith always come in here talking about books he read."

"Oh yes, him," Sol said, his face suddenly twisted in profound distaste.

When the long shadows of evening led or trailed all the passers-by at a great distance, Sol called, "Ortiz?"

But there was no answer; his voice sounded abandoned as an echo.

"He must have gone," he said aloud. He felt he moved at the bottom of an infinitely deep well and his hands groped for the dark sides. He reached for the phone and dialed the familiar number.

"Murillo," he said as he heard the phone picked up at the other end. Then, without waiting for confirmation that he was being heard, "It is no use. I do not care . . . regardless. I cannot take any more. I am a very sick man. I have a legal right. Just give me some reasonable sum of money, some arrangement. Even if I must go to a lawyer, I have a legal right . . ."

"Wait a minute, calm down, Uncle. You're all excited. Something in particular got you upset? Okay, let's see we can't straighten it out. I'm getting very disappointed with you lately, running off half-cocked every few days, gassing to me all your crazy complaints. I'm a patient man, but the truth is, Uncle, you're trying my patience too far," the wiry voice said softly.

"It is no use talking. No more," Sol went on, staring out at the shadowy traffic of the street. "I have a legal right to do what I want. This cannot go on."

There was a moment's silence in the receiver. When the voice came again it was soft and full of insidious humor.

"Legal, hah. Don't be so silly, Uncle," Murillio said. "You got a legal right to your body but I'll burn it for you. *Legal!* Don't make me laugh. Hey, listen to me, Uncle. You want to be legal, better start making funeral arrangements. I'm tired talking to you. You startin' to give me a bad headache. I give you two days to call me back and say you're joking with all this. . . ." There was silence for almost a minute, then, "After that, you're dead, Uncle—asleep with the worms."

The phone clicked in Sol's ear, and for a moment it seemed to him his consciousness might have been turned off, too.

But almost immediately his body revealed itself again. He felt the persistent sense of strain, of imminent eruption. His mind began conjuring movement out of every shadow. Suddenly he felt a terrific desire to get out of the store. It was as though he expected his mysterious fate to call on him very soon, and he did not wish it to find him there in all the shabbiness of old clothes and battered metal.

He flipped off the light switches, locked the windows and the door. But once outside, he looked back in and realized he had forgotten to leave the night light on. He groaned in frustration as he unlocked the door and went back inside. The darkness made the store seem like a vault. He sighed over and over again as he fumbled for the switch. Finally he turned it on and hurried frantically to escape once more. He stumbled over a corner of the case and moaned in terror. Then he was outside, and the strange store was locked and bolted. He stood on the sidewalk trying to breathe, and his face was covered with a chilly sweat.

When he got home, he went straight up to his room without eating, without even answering his relatives' greetings.

He half lay on his bed, one leg dangling toward the floor, as though to be ready to spring to his feet at some signal. Finally he picked up a book and read for a long time without really knowing what the book was about, examining the individual words and phrases. He took a long time over each page, because his mind continued to meander into formless places. Then his eyes got tired. He was afraid to sleep, though, so he moved himself higher until he was actually sitting upright against the head of the bed. For two hours he sat like that, the book down on his lap, his eyes desperately open as he listened to the smallest sounds of the universe.

Then, in spite of every effort, he began to doze.

*Her naked, emaciated body, with the same frightful grin of all the other bodies. How ugly, what a mockery of their love! Why did she do this to him? He felt like tearing at her horrid nakedness.* His eyes ripped themselves open to stare at the moonlight on his bedroom wall. The trees whispered outside. A distant car motor receded still farther, drew its sound out finer and fainter, so he couldn't say when he ceased to hear it. *The booted feet moved up and down the row of bunks. He lay very still, his eyes squeezed shut. The boots stopped very close. He stopped breathing. They*

*moved on. "This one," the voice said. Gerstein sobbed, "I
don't want to, I don't want to . . . please, Momma, Momma
. . ." Feet danced wildly between the steady tread of boot
steps. "Momma, Momma . . ."* He pressed his face painfully against the wooden headboard. Upstairs, Morton
moaned in his sleep. The sound of a back door closing was
deafening in the quiet of the night. Some birds twittered
bewilderedly as though they thought it a black morning.
*The smell of burning flesh entered him, and it was as though
he ate the most forbidden food. A great and eternal sickness
began in him.* He sat up like a jack-in-the-box. The air was
sweet and grassy and faintly cool. His eyeballs felt peeled
and raw, and he stared very hard, as though to penetrate
the darkness. *The smoke of their bodies was blowing north
when this hideous hunger hit him. He lusted for rich meats
and heavy pastries, had an insane yearning for wine and
coffee. He dug his clawlike fingernails into his thighs to
punish himself for not praying to that fleeting, greasy smoke.
But all he felt was this great desire for food. And then this
lust turned to a hunger of the loins, and he wondered at the
monster he was, and pulled some of his hair out. None of it
brought a tear to his eyes, and his eyes became burning hot
balls in the flesh of his face.* "Oy, oy, oy, oy," he said in a
parched voice to the leaf shadows on his wall.

And it went on like that all night long. He fought sleep,
dozed into those horrid fragments, bolted awake again, over
and over and over.

Until suddenly, one time, it was morning. But it was a
morning with none of the quality of newness mornings can
have. He sat on the edge of the bed and stared at the light
through the trees, wincing every so often, as though his skin
had been removed during the night. The bright, pink light
of the sun looked like the reflection of some monstrous fire
burning a hideous fuel.

The heat was terrific by the time he got to Manhattan. As he walked down 125th Street, he looked upward; the sky was burned to the pallid blue of scorched metal. The heat seemed to soften the very stone and brick of the buildings. All the repulsive faces appeared to melt before his eyes, and Sol imagined them dissolving to dark smudges on the pavement. Metal burned to the touch, and there was a constant density to the air that made him feel he moved through an infinite number of transparent woolen curtains.

The door handle of the store scorched his fingers, and when he went inside there was only the different, older heat of a closed dead place.

When Jesus Ortiz came in, he had nothing to say. The two of them moved silently around the store as though each would deny the other's existence by his own aloofness. When customers came in, they spoke to them; but alone, they maintained their silence.

Sol moved in a leathern chamber, and to him, Ortiz was little more than another shadow in the heat, an oddly haunting movement, like that caused by a breeze whose possible coolness was out of his reach. But Jesus stole glances at Sol from time to time, for *his* isolation was grimmer and more premeditated. And in spite of his rage, which was compounded of dedication and fear and voluntary solitude, he almost gasped in pain at the face of his employer each time he looked at him.

The Pawnbroker's face seemed to have undergone an immense change since the day before. The puffiness appeared reduced, and another face was emerging; a strange, high-cheekboned, Slavic face. And the eyes behind the weird glasses were larger and darker, brooding and full of a melancholy so profound that it almost seemed to emit a sound, a strange alto resonance like that given off by a crystal glass long after it has been struck.

Later, when Jesus had become starved by the silence and would have spoken, he realized there was too much between them for talk. The tremendous heat and the layers of silence built up during the day seemed like a great din which would prevent his being heard.

When the phone rang late in the afternoon, he froze in amazement at the volume as he watched the Pawnbroker move like a sleepwalker to answer it.

"Sol," Tessie said, "please come over. He is very low. The doctor said he can't last the night. Please, please, I am all alone."

"All right, I will come as soon as I can."

"Please, please, please . . ."

He hung up and went to the ledger to finish what he had been doing. Without looking up, he spoke to Jesus.

"You can go home now. I am closing early."

"What's the celebration—Jewish holiday or something?" Ortiz said as scornfully as he could.

Sol looked up with a cold, heedless expression.

"There are times when you annoy me more than other times," he said.

"You bother my ass almost all the time," Jesus retorted, his body tensed as for a physical encounter.

"You are free to leave my employ any time it becomes unbearable."

"And you can fire me any time you want to."

Sol closed his eyes and removed his glasses. Jesus could see the shape of the Pawnbroker's skull for the first time and he had an urge to scream at the peculiar agony that gave him.

"Just go home now," Sol said gently.

And Jesus swung away with a muffled sound he couldn't identify himself. Then he hurried out of the store and was gone.

When Sol got to Tessie's apartment, his head was light with weakness from the heat. He went inside and sat down for a few minutes while Tessie paced back and forth before him, her slip thinned by the wetness of perspiration so it clung to her body like new pink skin.

"Go in and see him, look at what I have," she said over the raging sound of the old man's breathing, which filled the apartment.

Sol shrugged and did as she asked.

The bedroom was odorous with the decaying life, and the sound of the rattling breath was unbelievably loud. Mendel lay with his mouth open, his eyes bulging as though trying to see up through the floors of the building to the sky. He was made particularly hideous by the black *Yalmalka* on his head and the dark straps of the phylacteries across his brow and arm like a harness on his battered body.

*"Shmai Yisroel . . . selotka . . . cum tansen mit meir . . .* dy, dy, dy, diddle dum dum . . ."

"He is singing," Tessie moaned in horror.

Sol just watched the wretched, dented head, the yawning mouth which amazingly had the strength to speak and sing even while it made those superhuman efforts to breathe.

"A long . . . time ago vhen I vas . . . a *klayna kinder* . . . ve had . . . volves in duh snow . . . la, la, la. . . . Oy *tata, tata* . . . God in Heaven!" His eyes stretched wider, and for several seconds the breathing stopped. Sol made a move toward the bed but the sound began again, louder than ever.

"There is no point to staying in here," Sol said tonelessly. "Come in the kitchen. I could have something to drink."

Tessie moved out ahead of him, her hand up to her mouth, her eyes huge and dazed.

In the kitchen, she poured out two glasses of orange juice and then sat down to stare at the doorway in the direction of her father's rattling breath.

"I feel like a monster," she said in a half-whisper. "I find myself wishing for him to be dead already. Sometimes I have all I can do to keep myself from putting a pillow . . . Oh my God, but he is my father. When I was a child, I loved him—what, what!"

"Listen to me," Sol said loudly over the harsh rattle that filled the rooms. "Forget all that. Don't think, don't feel. Get through things—it is the only sense. Imagine yourself a cow in a fenced place with a million other cows. Don't suffer, don't fear. Soon enough will come the ax. Meanwhile, eat and rest. Don't pay attention, don't cry!" And suddenly they both realized he was talking with unnecessary loudness. His voice echoed in a silence.

They got up and went into the bedroom and they found Mendel dead, still staring upward. Sol went over and closed the dead eyes. Tessie hunched herself in a corner of the room and began to cry.

For some time he stood there with her, under the obligation to make something significant of a death. Tessie sobbed with a steady grunting sound, which was broken from time to time by her discordant straining for breath. After a while, she settled into a low humming, like someone trying to imitate the sound of a slow-moving bee. Sol looked from her to the grotesque body on the bed and a queer yearning anger came over him. Tessie and even the corpse of Mendel seemed possessed of something vital and living while he himself stood without pain or grief, like a creature imbedded in a plastic block. Finally he could no longer stand his own stillness and he went out of the bedroom, leaving the two of them.

He called the undertaker and told him everything that was required. In a few minutes Tessie came out with her hands groping in the air. Sol shoved her into a chair and handed her a half-dozen checks.

"Here are checks which I have already signed. Fill out whatever amounts you will need. The undertaker will be over very soon. He knows what to do. You must get a grip on yourself. There is no sense to your going on like this. It is over. Both you and the old man are better off. You said so yourself before. There is nothing to cry about."

She looked up at him with an expression of near-horror on her face.

"Sometimes I do not think you are human at all," she said.

"What would you have me say or do?" he asked indifferently.

"I don't know . . . cry with me perhaps. . . ."

"To hell with your crying," he snarled savagely. He felt himself trembling with anger and it seemed if he didn't get away from her, he would do something violent. "I am going now. I have a long way to go and I must get some sleep or I will not be able to work tomorrow."

"Won't you even come to the . . . the funeral?"

"How can I do that? I cannot leave the store with him."

"The store," she said bitterly. "The important, marvelous store."

"Be still, you fool!" he shouted. "Where do you think those checks come from? They would not put your father's corpse in the ground without the money from the store." He stood over her, swaying, his fists clenched, his breathing hoarse and wild.

She just covered her face with her hands and rocked back and forth without a sound. After a few minutes she murmured, "Go then, leave me. I can mourn alone."

When he got out into the dimly lit oven of the street, he saw Goberman standing uncertainly before the doorway, the ever-present brief case hanging from his arm like a curse.

"Is it the old man? Has he . . ."

"Mendel is dead," Sol cried out with a brutal gaiety. "And the funeral is tomorrow morning. You are another great celebrator of funerals, so go in my place."

"I will go, I will go," Goberman said in an odd, musing voice.

"Good, very good, Goberman. Who knows? Perhaps the rabbi will be willing to offer you a contribution," Sol said. Then he turned away from Goberman and the house and walked with his ponderous speed toward the subway. The horizon flickered menacingly all the time he rode under the street, and as he drove home in his car, he heard the very distant mumbling of thunder. He began to laugh, and stopped only when the sound of his laughter seemed to deafen and blind him.

## ✣ TWENTY-FOUR

It was starless and close; the air was filled with humidity. Seated as they were by the river, it was as though they were submerged in its vaporous overflow. Robinson sat very straight, his face illuminated periodically by the glow of his cigarette; a child-scaring figure with deeply carved features. His eyes were so light they were invisible in the darkness, and Jesus felt little reverberations of emptiness each time the cigarette's fire revealed the apparently empty whites. Buck White reclined easily on the narrow wooden curb right over the water and he seemed to be paying no attention to the talk of the two standing figures of Tangee and Jesus.

"Tomorrow night," Jesus said. "That's the time."

Tangee whistled softly. Suddenly it seemed closer than he wanted it.

"Why specially tomorrow night?" he asked.

"Because I say. Tomorrow got to be the time," Jesus said.

"Okay, okay, but jus' why tomorrow? I mean, you got a special reason for tomorrow?"

"Somethin' wrong with tomorrow? You ain't chickenin', are you?"

"Aw *man!* This all my idea originally, you know. I ain't gonna chicken out. You don' have to be so touchy. I jus' thought you have a *particular* reason it got to be *tomorrow*."

"Yeah, he jus' askin'," Buck said absently, staring at the dim shape of a barge moving past them under the tiny points of its running lights.

"Well, if you guys objectin' to my plans . . ."

"No one objecting," Robinson said in a voice of command.

"I'll tell you why tomorrow," Jesus said, slightly mollified. "Every Thursday he gets this bundle of cash from his partner. About eight o'clock he take that money and a bundle from the safe and he take it down to the night deposit of the bank. Now he use to have the cop walk him down. But he got sore at this cop Leventhal, so he don't use no cop lately. Still, it no good tryin' to get him in the street, an' if you try it too soon, he gonna have the dough still locked up in the safe. So it got to be *timed,* see. There only one way to do it." He looked from one to another, judging his power over them. He felt himself to be advancing toward a strange and icy outpost, more remote than anything he had experienced before. It seemed to have something to do with the identity of his victim. He was irritated at the haziness of his motives. He wanted to see this as a pure venture for gain, and chafed under the perplexing oppression he felt, an oppression that had nothing to do with the natural nervousness and fear he would have expected in a thing like this.

"How we suppose to know the *exac'* minute?" Tangee asked indignantly.

"From me," Jesus said.

"Well how you gonna tell us if we not there an' you gonna be with us, er if not, how is you gonna know . . ."

"Shut up, Buck," Tangee said. "Okay, Ortiz, say it."

Robinson lit another cigarette from the stub of the first. Tangee faced him, Buck faced the river, Jesus faced the city, each of them aimed in a different direction and all the directions of equal darkness.

"Usually I go home about seven thirty. He don't tell me, I jus' go. Lately he don't even know when I leave. So I'm gonna stay upstairs in the loft where the clothin' is. They's a spot where I can see down to him. When he go to the safe, I get to the window of the secon' floor and signal. Then you get in fast an' get out fast."

"An' we jus' waitin' over there?"

"It's the dress store, closed for a long time by then. You stand deep in the entrance, no one notice you. You get yourself a bunch of them Halloween masks an' flip them up over you face when you start over."

"Man, you figure everything," Tangee said admiringly. "That a cool plan, right down to the details."

"Hey, but how 'bout one thing! I mean what if, you know, the guy he goin' to act up, the Pawnbroker. I mean, what he goin' to do if, he don't let, I mean make a fuss like," Buck said, struggling with the great complexity of his question.

"He make no fuss," Robinson said. "He make no fuss at all."

Jesus waited for the glow of Robinson's cigarette to reveal his face. "Hear me, Robinson, hear what I say. No shootin', see, no shootin'."

"You worry 'bout the Jew?" Robinson said.

"I'm worryin' 'bout Jesus Ortiz. You burn the man an' we got too much trouble. Now hear me, man, I shit you not; you don't shoot that man; you do what I say." He turned to the dark shrouded faces of the other two. "This *my* plan, *my* plan. We do it *my* way. No one shoot no one, hear! I say it clear to you all, right now. Anyone shoot in that store, and it go bad, it go very bad." His voice was both fierce and plaintive in the muffling night air, and none of them answered him. They stood in just the sound of their breathing while the tiny running lights of the great barges suggested the massive movements on the river, and the time of their silence was punctuated by the little mocking glows of Robinson's cigarette. "No killin', no killin'," he said, his words a sad little condition in the choking blackness surrounding them. *"My* way, you hear, *my* way."

Buck White sighed as he reclined again on the wooden curb; all of it was unfathomable to him, and he focused on his dream of enhancing affluence.

"How much you figure he gonna have, Ortiz?" Tangee asked wistfully.

"I don't know, could be as much as eight thousand dollars."

Tangee whistled in wonder.

"How much that be for each of all of us, you know, divvied up like between of us all?" Buck asked.

"Two thousand dollars apiece," Tangee said.

"Aw hcy, I'm ona get me a Cadillac Fleetwood, black with white sidewalls," Buck said.

"I got some plans," Tangee said dreamily.

"We all got plans," Jesus said harshly.

Robinson just began playing his tinny mouth organ, a dinky scornful voice in the darkness.

"No shootin', I say," Jesus rasped furiously.

The white, momentary daylight of lightening suddenly exposed them all, and Buck White moaned nervously.

"It goin' to rain," Tangee said. "We got the message, Ortiz. Let's break up before it rain now." And each of them moved off through the light-torn darkness, in his own direction.

Jesus walked slowly away from the river. Suddenly the

night seemed to stretch fatiguingly long ahead of him. Yet he wasn't tired enough to sleep. I feel . . . I feel . . . He had a craving for something sharp and powerful and exalting. Well, he could always pick up a couple of sticks of tea. But no, he was too icy-headed for that. Marijuana was a big nothing, and only the kooks were able to let themselves get happy with that. It was like drinking; you had to be in the mood to get drunk. He could play some pool for a while and then maybe . . . Ah, all of it was so ordinary and shabby.

Mabel Wheatly was waiting for him in front of his house, pretending to be engrossed in conversation with the girl who lived across the hall from him. She looked up with poorly assumed surprise; it was obvious she had been staring over the other girl's shoulder all the time.

"Well, hi, Jesus," she said. "I was jus' on my way home. How you doin', honey?" Her smile was white and doting in the darkness. People all around were picking up the newspapers they had sat on and preparing to go inside, glancing apprehensively at the occasional flashes of lightning which made the sky line appear to be a stage setting for a familiar drama of violence. "You feel like buyin' me a beer?"

"I don't feel like doin' nothin' at all," he said grimly.

Mabel's smile died painfully, and the other girl raised her eyebrows in spiteful amusement.

"Oh, I bet you tired, hon. You want me to come up an' make you a pot of coffee or somethin'?" she said, drawing on the smile again for the other girl.

"I got things on my mind," he said, starting up the steps. "I see you around another time."

He couldn't see Mabel's pain, wouldn't have seen it even if he had been looking in her direction, even if it had been as bright as day. For she wore her pain, by old habit, inside, under her glossy lewdness. And she walked off, swinging her hips, wondering if perhaps, at that early age, all hope was gone for her.

Upstairs, his mother had her black straw hat on, ready

to go out. Suddenly he didn't want to stay in the house alone.

"Where you goin', Ma?" he asked, running his eyes over the familiar objects of the room for something to hold him.

"I thought I'd go over to the church for a while. Some of the ladies meeting over there with the priest." She picked maternally at the seams of his shirt, brushed invisible bits of lint.

He had to smile a little; she reminded him of one of those clowns in the circus, all dressed in rags yet getting very fussy about one microscopic bit of fluff on their clothes.

"Maybe I go along with you," he said.

She peered at him curiously. It occurred to her that she really knew very little of her aristocratic-looking, confident son. In many ways he reminded her of his father, that almost white vagabond who had walked out on her when the boy was only two years old. In her own dark skin and simple ways, she had felt she perhaps hadn't deserved that handsome, facile man. He had been too *white!* The boy was dark enough to reassure her, but he had the fine Caucasian features, the quick, knowledgeable ways of her husband. She was filled with humble pride at the look of him. And yet he had that restlessness about him, too. Oh, Mother of God, it was no easy thing to be the mother of a son!

"Yes, come along. It's a long time since you went," she said shyly.

They walked through the humid streets to the church, side by side yet never quite touching. She wished it were daylight so people could see them together, could be reminded what she was capable of. Once inside, they separated, the mother going into the meeting room just off the nave of the church, tossing him a little wave which he acknowledged with an unsmiling nod.

He crossed himself as he kneeled, then got to his feet and passed all the saints until he got to the altar where the crucified figure hung patiently in the dimness. He kneeled again at the low rail and rested his chin on his arms to stare at his namesake. The thought crossed his mind that the figure of Christ should have been that of a Negro. He smiled faintly. As though it made any difference. It was a fairy tale; he wondered why he allowed himself obeisance to it. Santa Claus hadn't survived his fourth year. Still, it was quiet here; the candles and the faint smell of incense eased his restlessness. Would he have dared to come if he believed? "Bless me in my plans," he said sardonically. The blood hung in the wooden wounds. And a white Jesus Christ at that! "Oh man, you don't know the half of it," he said silently to the statue above him; "it too complicated for you." And He was a Jew, too, just like the Pawnbroker; there's a laugh for you. He tried to imagine the Pawnbroker in a position like that, nailed up on a cross, the heavy, graceless body broken and naked, the great puffy face bent to one side . . . with the glasses on! He began to chuckle, harshly. Wouldn't everybody be shocked to see Sol Nazerman up there, his arm with the blue numbers stretched out to the transfixed hand? Suddenly he was aware of an ugly, echoing sound, and he turned around to see a woman staring at him with a shocked and angry face. He had been laughing aloud. He shrugged a mild apology to the woman, then turned back to the rail and rested his head on his hands. Why the hell had he come here? Why did he stay? Oh, who knows? Just . . . Oh shit man, there times when you completely alone by yourself and *nothin'* in this world make sense. It was quiet here . . . he could rest a little, even on his knees, with his head on his hands. That man up on the cross weren't gonna do him no harm, at least that for sure.

Later, he went by himself to a movie. He sat through the familiar violence of a Western, numb with boredom. But they showed a newsreel of an atom-bomb test, and he sat forward on his seat, his eyes shining morbidly at the immense flood of light and the climbing, spreading growth of thick smoke. "Nothin' bigger than that," he said to himself.

"A person like a little bitty ant to that thing!" And he felt a feverish exultation at the thought, as though it vindicated anything he wanted to do.

But when he stepped out of the theater, the air was filled with rain. It came down so hard that there seemed to be a sheet of water about a foot over the pavement, suspended there like a great piece of material, because the drops bounced that high before settling down to flood the gutters. The fiery exultation drained out of him then, and he walked home, all hunched over, nailed heavily to the earth by the torrential downpour.

Sol left the small lamp on the dresser lit as he closed his eyes for sleep. With the steady thrumming of the rain on the roof and the thunder receding to a safe distance, becoming more and more infrequent, and with the dim light of the night light making his eyelids a comforting earth brown, he felt an ancient incarnation of his childhood. They had stayed with some relatives in Prostki, near Sniardwy Lake, and he had been afraid of the unfamiliar surroundings (as though darkness, which is only a void, is different in one time or place from what it is in another), so his mother had put a kerosene lamp in one corner of the strange bedroom and had gone out with a gentle, chiding laugh for his fears, and he had lain with that same brown glow on his lids, listening to the rain in the willows.

*He walked up the gentle slope with the jar of milk and the bottle of white wine cold and wet from the brook where he had cooled them. Butterflies anticipated his route, swirling up from the high grass in palpitating clouds of color; there was the hot, peaceful din of insects all around, a drowsy twittering of sun-weakened birds. The smell of the ground made him breathe heavily, as from an intoxicant, humid and sweet. He held the wine bottle to his head and sighed at the coldness. And then he was on the summit of the insignificant hillock. Down in the hollow, between him and the woods, his family lolled among the clover and the dandelions. His father sat against a stone in his inappropriate black suit and Yalmalka, lost in his study of a book. The children, who were trying to strip the meadow of wild flowers, paid him no attention as they crawled purposefully on their knees, the baby, Naomi, holding only a few tattered flowers, while David held his riches of yellow and pink in a thick clump. Ruth and his mother turned to him, and Ruth raised her hand in greeting. "Here, Sol dear," she called. Then she smiled, her teeth showing white in her dark face. She tilted her head as he approached, her smile reminding him of some private joke between them. Her hair was a black shine of curls, and as he got closer, he saw she had put some dandelions in it, little yellow suns in the night of her hair. He held the two bottles up triumphantly. "Beverages for all," he cried out laughingly. The children looked up, then began hurrying through the grass toward him, David with his huge clump of flowers, Naomi stumbling on her baby legs, the flowers cast down and forgotten. His father looked up and smiled absently, a little embarrassed at his idyllic setting, a white-faced, withdrawn man whose natural habitat was the easily regulated climate of the printed page. Ruth got up to take the milk and the wine from him. All of them approached him with their eager smiles; his mother, his father, Ruth, the children. The humming of the bees and the flies drove happiness ever deeper*

*into him. Their faces all came closer; he would have liked
to gather them all into him, to drink them, to breathe them.
And then they stopped, every blade of grass froze, each of
them was arrested in motion: David balanced impossibly on
one short, sturdy leg, Ruth maintained her pose of reaching.
All was silence; it was like a movie which has suddenly
stopped while its projecting illumination continued. And he
was paralyzed, too, forever out of reach of the dear faces,
frozen a few feet short of all he had loved. And then it all
began dimming; each face receded, the sunny afternoon
turned to eternal twilight, dusk, evening, darkness.*

And the rain drummed outside his lighted room as though
on his coffin. He opened his mouth on the bitter taste of
agony and he wondered if the heedless calm he felt was a
foretaste of death, really didn't think he cared one way or
another. "Let it come already; enough of this . . . *too much*
of this." He lay listening to the rain again, but this time
there was no reminiscence in the sound; he kept his eyes
wide open and the scale of notes the dripping made was an
American dirge rather than a lullaby.

drring

drring

drrong

Mabel held the red negligee around her as she stared at
the dark gleam of the street. She could hear the receding
footsteps of her last client down the hallway, the laugh of
one of the girls downstairs, and the music of the radio from
the "Reception Room." She had a vision of herself in a
long white bride's gown and Jesus beside her in striped pants
and a tail coat. An organ played, and there was the murmur
of admiring people as she moved virginally down the aisle,
suffocated by the smell of a thousand flowers. Suddenly she
smiled a hard, destructive smile. Oh honey, you really flippin',

yes you is. You can't even *remember* bein' a virgin; you was laid before you *born*. She conjured up his delicate, handsome face over the rainy night scene, made a background of her mother's dimly recalled Alabama yard with its magnolia tree and its merrily boiling washtubs. Then she tried to hold on to that vision as she turned around with a mechanically lewd smile for the stranger who approached the door of her tiny, perfume-drenched room, with its basin in the corner, its Hell-fire red sheets and pillowcase on the bed.

"Oh my, sweety," she gasped in pneumatic passion. "You a terrible fierce lover," she assured the sweating, middle-aged man who struggled all by himself on top of her. And all the time she listened to the sound of the rain and watched furtively the occasional silent flickers of celestial light.

George Smith cringed at the lightning from where he stood under the awning, sick and spitefully predatory. He wished for a small, tender girl to appear so he could hurl himself on her as on a terribly beautiful stake. How would he like to talk about the Marquis De Sade, that Pawnbroker? Oh, there's a lot of things I could tell him about the "Flowers of Evil" and "The Season in Hell." But there really was no one to talk to, was there? You are alone, George Smith, so find your own road to Hell. No Heaven, but perhaps there is a Hell. It would be a relief; he would find company there, too. Oh, the exquisite terror of a small, soft body. Like the release of a fall after a long time of balancing. Such a small thing he had tried to pin hope on; one weary, harsh, impatient white man. What was that! Footsteps, light, frail. A child out at this hour? His heartbeat filled his whole body. He peered carefully out into the rain-clouded street. He hoped the end was near.

The rain spattered in little gusts on the window while behind him the marvelous voice transcended the ancient record, conquered even time. Murillio stood looking out at the blurry flowers of light below him as he swished the liquor around in his glass and the ice cubes plinked cosily.

*"Una furtiva lagrima . . ."*

He hummed along with the cello-like voice and the dim, lost orchestral accompaniment, which sounded like one feeble harmonica. Idly, he exulted in the fact of his high, rich tower, the sumptuousness of everything that touched him. It had been so long since he had had time to gloat. Besides, he usually never even thought about his success because he had always known it would happen this way, barring some accident. But there were times like now, when he enjoyed dipping into his treasure chest, savoring what he had by contrasting it unsentimentally with what he had had in the beginning. His father and mother, two people bent earthward by their work on the two acres of stony soil outside Palermo; himself, young and ragged and sullen under the yoke of poverty, maddened by the mistrals blowing up out of Africa. He wondered if either of his parents might still be alive. He had never felt obliged to get in touch with them in all the years; they had given him nothing except life, and that without premeditation. He had never had any need to placate his spirit, to propitiate his conscience. What was a conscience? There was no such organ, and if there was such a thing as a soul or a God, well that was just too bad. He would never twist himself into shapes he didn't fit. Life was a battle, and he was a battler. He enjoyed beauty, to a certain point. At least for him, beauty ran to the edge of a sheer cliff; beyond that edge was a peculiar emptiness, which sometimes echoed with dim and lovely voices. Perhaps he occasionally felt a little wistful that there were those things beyond his appreciation; it was no more than an infrequent puff of air, a frail scent—he could live without it.

Only now the thought of the Pawnbroker intruded on his idyl. That situation was no good, no good at all. He starts up trouble, makes some kind of stink, and before you know it, I got the Revenue Department on me, investigating committees. Well, no sense making a big thing out of that Yid. He would get one more warning and then . . . Too bad. I got an idea he's got a brain in his head. It might have been a pleasure to talk things over with a guy with brains. Too bad, he's just falling apart. Ah, besides, what the hell would we have talked about; politics, the opera, history? I bet he knows a little something about them things, too. Eh, you can't have everything, intellectual talkin' and efficiency both. Too bad, too bad. He began humming again as he sipped at the drink, and the rain tried to interfere, with its spitefully uneven rhythm.

*"Cielo e mar,"* he sang softly with the dead man.

He shook his head scornfully at the thought of the poor Sicilian earth; he remembered how it looked, beaten by the rain.

Upstairs, above Sol's room, Morton sat drawing at his table. He was drawing his Uncle Sol from a tiny snapshot. The paper was a blue-gray charcoal paper, and he filled in heavy darks around the large, puffy head of the Pawnbroker so that it seemed to lean out of the flat dimension of the surface. He made the round, old-fashioned spectacles reflect the light so that only a suggestion of the eyes could be seen. But in the cast of the head, the line of mouth, the weary shine of high light, he imbued the subject with a look of gentleness and infinite patience. It was *his,* Morton Kantor's picture; he could have it the way he wanted it.

His sallow, unhealthy face was streaked with charcoal, and his shirt was stained with sweat. Finally he reached a point where his charcoal stick wandered uncertainly over the paper without making contact, and he realized he must be finished. He took the jar of fixative and blew through the atomizer to spray the portrait. Then he tacked it up on the opened closet door.

He realized how hot he was and saw that the window was closed. He opened it and stood for a minute looking out at the invisible, heavily dripping darkness, the occasional shine of black leaves from unidentifiable light sources. The air felt cool and soothing on him. For a moment he contemplated the new collection of pornographic pictures he had bought with the remainder of his tuition money. Then he thought he felt too tired even for that. He wondered what his uncle would say if he knew what some of his money went for. Well, he thinks I'm milking him anyhow, he thought with painful bitterness. So I am. He lay back on his bed and lit a cigarette, drew in the smoke with all his might and slowly exhaled it as he looked at the brooding, gentle figure on the blue-gray paper. Suddenly Morton began to cry. It lasted only a few minutes, and then he went back to his cigarette. But through his opened window, above the sound of the rain, he thought he heard, from the floor below, an echo of his crying.

Jesus Ortiz suddenly sat up out of sleep with a freezing sensation all over his body. What the hell am I thinkin'? I suppose to be smart? They just gonna go in that store, take his money, and walk out with him standin' there, wavin' good-by, sayin', "Come again, have some more money for you." What was I thinkin' about? And them three niggers never even think to ask how we get out of there quiet. No getaway car. Oh, but that Robinson maybe figure he fix it with his piece. Oh no. What come over me? What I want to do, commit suicide or something? Well . . . maybe we just tie him up, gag him, and push him in the back room. Then I close up the store and . . . yeah, that's it, no need to worry. But how the hell could I go ahead and not think about them things till now. Man . . . He wiped at the sweat of his near-miss. Then he got up and went to the window to smoke a cigarette and watch the rain trying to wash the old filth from the streets. He felt calm again, quite able to ignore the icy dart of disaster he only half sensed deep inside.

Either in the hallucinatory foyer before sleep or already in dreams, he glimpsed again, briefly, the figure of a heavy man, awkwardly transfixed on a cross, a man with blue, cryptic numbers on his arm.

## ❋  TWENTY-SIX

There was a shine to even the grimy landscape of the city, and the air was possessed of the clarity that frequently follows heavy rain. Nothing looked any newer or less ruined by age and filth, and yet there was a quality of richness, as with old bronzes in sunlight. Sol gazed at the familiar store fronts, the ugly façades, and suddenly, quite strangely, he felt a nostalgia for them, as though they had been the scenes of precious life for him.

A covey of women mounted the steps to the railroad platform, servants for the wealthy of Westchester and Fairfield. His sister, Bertha, had been lobbying for a *Shwartsa* to help her with her housework, and as he thought of that and watched the Negro women going up the steps, he imagined his sister at a slave auction, walking among the dark women, pinching, checking the condition of their teeth.

He was visited once more by that sharp and bewildering poignance, and he peered intensely at the dirt-wedged bricks of buildings, the grime insinuated like the grain in wood in every painted surface, the filth-encrusted sidewalks and gutters, wondering what there was in this pesthole of a city, among these blighted, ugly people, that made him suddenly yearn and remember the mood of sadness. And he felt a rare calm that lasted only as long as it would have taken a huge, slow-moving pendulum to make its arc.

And then he was before the store and that tautness, that distended surface of his spirit made itself known to him again. He went inside, cut off the burglar alarm, switched on the lights, and began taking the wire screens from the windows; it was as though he exposed himself again to the mysterious onslaught that would destroy him. One tiny thing, he didn't know yet what it would be, would break him apart that day, and all the dark force of the growth in him would burst out for him to recognize before it consumed him.

"Today is the twenty-eighth . . . my anniversary, my anniversary," he said, standing behind the counter and gripping its edge as though for support against a vast wave. Fifteen years ago today his heart had atrophied; like the mammoth, he had been preserved in ice. What did he fear then? If the ice finally melts, the meat of the great entombed creature merely rots. One could only die once. He had been extinct for a long time, and only the carcass remained to be disposed of. Why, then, did he seize on the edge of the counter and tremble as he stared in terror at the sunlit doorway?

Jesus Ortiz came in at nine thirty, walking with an odd stiffness, as though something in the night had robbed him of his natural grace. His face was drawn, his eyes were feverishly bright, and he kept brushing tentatively at his long, straight hair, which was impeccably combed. He muttered something to Sol and then, when he got no answer, turned nervously toward the Pawnbroker and said, "Huh? What you say?"

Sol just shook his head, his eyes piercing and curious.

"I'll go upstairs, work with the clothes. You call me if you want me." Jesus looked at Sol as if there were something strange in that, as if he did not trust what he heard, even his own voice.

Jesus questioned that, too, with his eyes.

"All right, go upstairs," Sol said gently.

"Oh . . . yeah. I be upstairs. You jus' call then . . ."

The Pawnbroker nodded reassuringly, as though to a child. While he watched the slender figure of the youth slowly ascend the stairs, he continued to grip the edge of the counter.

Leopold S. Schneider came in with the same greasy bag under his arm. His hair was wild and soft, and it made a dull halo around his bony head. "Do you remember me? Schneider? The oratory award?"

"Yes, I remember," Sol answered, taking his hands cautiously away from the counter.

"You still have my award, you haven't sold it?"

"I have turned down some fine offers for it."

"Well, I'll be in for it in about a week. I have something pending. Meanwhile, just to carry me over until I finish this play I'm working on . . . I have this for you. How much can you loan me on it? It hurts me to let it out of my hands for even a week but, well . . ." Carefully, he skinned back the bag to reveal a pair of bronzed baby shoes. "My mother would turn in her grave . . . but it's only for a little while," he said tremulously, holding them out delicately for the Pawnbroker to admire.

Sol sighed heavily, lidded his eyes, and slowly shook his head.

"They're mine . . . when I was a baby," Leopold said tenderly, appreciating how touched the Pawnbroker seemed.

"How much do you want?"

"Ten dollars?"

"Five."

"All right, I'll take it. Just put them next to the award. Careful, don't scratch them," Leopold warned, his hands darting out in a flutter of apprehension. "Schneider, Leopold S. Schneider . . ."

The anniversary of Sol's death was beginning.

A tall marionette carved from some black wood, his limbs controlled erratically, approached Sol on a bias, his trunk aimed for the corner of the store as his legs twitched him to the counter. Sol waited, a little nerve in his own temple taking up the rhythm of the spastic walk, until the man was holding on to the counter with one struggling hand, his head beckoning constantly. Sol held on to his side of the counter with equal intensity, so it was as though each tugged against the other. He felt himself sweating as he tried to find the least tortured part of the man at which to look. Finally he discovered the eyes, which were black and solemnly lovely, like those of a deer, and which maintained a gloomy calm in the midst of the writhing surface of his face.

"I want to borrow ten dollars on this," he said, bringing up a large, flat, rectangular package like a silent tambourine. He settled it on the counter as one flattens a spinning coin and began trying to untie the knotted cord. But the string was a live thing in his hands; he raised his wild fingers and gave Sol a pulsing, twisting smile. "You better . . ."

And it seemed as great an effort for Sol to undo the knot. In the end, he cut the cord with a razor blade, and the spastic gave a little sigh as the string popped. Inside was a framed glass of brilliantly colored butterflies.

"What's this?" Sol said.

"Butterflies."

Sol looked at the man scornfully.

"I collect them. I have a lot more at home. For years I went into the country with a net, all the equipment. . . . I don't know, lately I have lost interest." But then, noticing a look of rejection on the Pawnbroker's face, he hastened to reassure. "Oh, but I definitely will redeem it; don't worry on that score."

"What would I do with it if you didn't?" Sol shook his head. "I'll let you have five dollars. I couldn't even sell them for that."

"Oh, you'd be surprised how many people nowadays use them for decoration. And then there's lots of collectors like me. I got some very good ones there." He leaned over the glass, his ambling fingers striving to point to the brilliant bow-tie shapes. "That there, for instance, is a monarch, and that one is a great spangled fritillary. Oh, and see this here beauty, that's a mourning cloak and that one with the eye design, that's called a buckeye. And there's a tiger swallow-tail, and a question-sign anglewing . . ."

"All that double talk means nothing to me. All right, all right, I'll give you eight dollars on it."

"That is not double talk," the spastic said, trying to compose his face for dignity. "Those are the real names of those butterflies. At one time I would have starved rather than let them out of my hands, even for a minute. But lately it doesn't seem to matter to me. All right, I'll take the eight dollars."

And Sol wrote up the transaction while the black lepidopterist danced his grotesquely patient dance; it seemed Sol could see it even through his lowered eyelids.

The next customer came in out of a flash of briefly reflected sunlight, so all Sol could see at first was the unmemorable shape of his head and shoulders and the two boxlike things he carried, one in each hand. And then he was in the undisputed domain of the fluorescents and his deformed face was like a stunning noise in the quiet store.

He had no lower jaw, only a gaping, wet redness and a restless tongue. Sol felt like screaming in rage and revulsion. What was the idea of letting such a creature out in the open?

"Yes," Sol said, fixing his attention on the two boxes and following them up when the man lifted them to the counter.

"Ah ant oo ah . . . ehee, ehee." He held up all ten fingers twice, held them so high that Sol had to see his face again through them.

"Twenty, you want twenty," Sol translated through clenched teeth, feeling nausea rise in his throat. He heard the sound that must have been confirmation and he pulled the two wooden boxes toward him. The larger one was a well-equipped oil-painting box with several palettes, many new tubes of paint, brushes, and palette knives. The smaller box contained a fine set of wood-carving knives of Swiss manufacture. "All right, twenty," Sol agreed, just wanting to get the man out. "What is your name?"

The man just waved in furious disgust.

"You mean you won't want to take them out again?"

"Aghh, aghh," the jawless man gurgled, making violent signs of rejection. Then he waved his hands in a horizontal gesture like an umpire calling a ballplayer out, indicating final and definite termination to his relationship with the paints and the knives. He took the money and walked back out toward the street. From behind, the sickened Pawn-broker noticed how shapely his head was, how broad his shoulders above the tapering, graceful torso. For a moment he felt like bursting out in laughter, but held it back for fear of what it might turn into.

A young white woman came in. She was bone-thin in her cheap housedress, breastless and stooped; really it was only that Sol sensed her to be young, for nothing in her appearance gave evidence of it. Her face was cadaverous, as from some serious wasting disease. She brought a hand mirror and a box of baby clothes in excellent condition, almost new.

"Whatever you want to give," she answered dispiritedly to his query, her voice apparently a great and extravagant expenditure for her. "I've got no use for them any more."

"Well, look here, lady, I'm in business to make money. I would like to give as little as possible. Tell me what you want to borrow, and if it's reasonable . . ."

She looked at him with weary disgust, lidded her large, doomed eyes, and shrugged. "Ohh . . . I don't know."

"The clothes are in good condition, the mirror. . . . How about eight dollars?"

She nodded.

"What is your name?"

"Rosemary O'Conner," she said in a musing, wondering way, as though surprised that she still bore that name. Then she frowned angrily and watched him set her property to one side and bring up the pawn ticket.

She ran her eyes briefly over the fine print on the back. She appeared clean and neat, but there was a faint disagreeable odor to her body, the smell of the chronically sick: sour, fetid, and dying. "And if someone else was to come in someday in my place with this ticket, could they get the things?"

Sol nodded, dumb in the ruined smell of her.

"Because God knows I sure as hell won't be back."

Where did they come from? The devil, my anniversary will be a great day! "No more, for God's sake, no more," he said silently at the sight of another customer.

But then he let his breath out in minute relief; it was Marilyn Birchfield. She seemed so astoundingly clean and lovely to him. He nodded weakly at her.

"Hello, Sol," she said softly. "See, I can't be avoided." She smiled at him, and he felt his heart lurch wistfully. To rest with her, to spend quiet, endless hours in the sunlight in her presence. Ah, an old dream, as foolish and unreal as the case of butterflies, the carving knives, the hand mirror that revealed no beauty.

"I am sorry if I seemed rude when I spoke to you last. You must forgive me."

"No, don't even speak of it. You have some private troubles and I should know better than to intrude. Only I want you to know again that I'm your friend, that I'll always be available to you." She fixed him with a serious gaze. "Go through what you must go through, but remember to call me when you're ready for friendship again." She seemed to offer something distant and bright, which he recognized as a drowning man might recognize a life ring, a means of rescue that is either too distant or that he is too tired to try for.

"Thank you; you are a fine, generous woman. If all this —" he moved his eyes over the litter of the shop in a gesture of description—"lets up, if I can see my way clear . . ."

She just touched his wrist briefly, nodded, and went out. Sol watched the life preserver disappear, leaving him in the empty, silent sea.

And then, as though that respite were something he had to pay for with usurious interest, the traffic came worse than ever before.

A stuttering deviate with the body of a dancer pressed his soft courtship for a few dollars on a silver bracelet, his ancient hunter's nostrils sniffing fastidiously in a world of close and ugly scents. And right behind him, patient for her turn, a stone-faced, masculine-looking woman stood holding her pudgy Mongoloid son's hand, paying the child no attention, but, rather, welded to him in the clasped flesh. She brought a child's sterling cup and spoon with no regret, because she had nothing she wished to commemorate. A smiling postman pawned a dazzling pair of shoes, and his smile was flat and shallow, because he appeared to live in a pocket of time only five minutes wide. An old, filthy pilgrim presented himself like an apparition, with a battered flashlight for pawn, and at the Pawnbroker's snarl of dismissal he went out of the store with the dead flashlight like some hopeless Diogenes moving under old momentum. A blind fat woman, with her hair cut in that short, institutional bob, offered up a concertina with a dull forgotten smile; her tiny, empty eyes fixed mercilessly on Sol's face, and she waited through his mutters of exasperation and disgust until he paid her. She was replaced by the filthy young Negro in the Ivy League cap with the addict's eyes and the terrified jackal's face. "I brung you dat radio couple weeks back. Come on, come on, I got to have it back. My mothuh say I don' get it back she gonna send me to the hospital to go *col' turkey*. I got to have it now, man." And when Sol demanded his ticket, he howled. "I don' know nothin' 'bout no ticket. I want dat radio, dad, you gimme dat radio." He took out a knife and began waving it at random. "I'm nobody to mess wif, man; gimme dat radio . . . come on, she gonna turn my ass in I don' bring dat radio. . . ." And Sol had to grab his surprisingly thin and feeble body and rush him out of the store, murmuring threats about calling the police on him, saying that then he would be *cold turkey* indeed. And he saw him go brokenly down the street before he returned to the store with the feel of the creature's sour body on his hands. Then he faced the tall old whore with the swollen, depraved face and the morocco-textured skin on her exposed chest. She talked with smoke from the ever-present cigarette half blinding her, and she was humble and grotesque with her false, frightened smile as she took a two-dollar loan on an alligator pocketbook that was topped with the dried body of a baby alligator and still bore the price tag of the store it had been lifted from.

On and on they came, shy, sullen, sweating, guilty, paying in fear for tiny crimes they had done and were doomed to do, striking out with furtiveness and harshness, sickened with their hereditary curse, weary and ashamed of their small dreams and abandoning the cheap devices they had dreamed with. They brought in suits of green to try to change their luck with garments of blue or cautious gray. They packed in one kind of glitter for another, haggled in soft, furtive voices, each ashamed and desperate and hungry, each filling the Pawnbroker's spirit with rage and disgust as he smelled and saw their ugliness.

He stretched on the rack of his sight and smell and hearing, saw all the naked souls ready to spill blood over him. And it began to seem to him that they all were making a profit on him, that they found ease from their individual pains at the sight of his great aggregate of pains, that they looked around at the stock of the store and saw it all as a tremendous weight on him. And that seemed to awe them, too, for as they added their own small item it was as though they piled on weight to prove his immense power, so that some of them even went out laughing, having left him a piece of their pain.

Sometimes he was aware of his assistant, down from the loft to help. He looked toward him and, if he found no relief at the sight of the clear, spare beauty in Jesus' face, he must have at least gained some minimal handhold of endurance, because he continued to exist as the Pawnbroker, was still able to appraise and declare, accept and condemn. Sometimes their eyes met to make an instant of acutely profound silence in all the sounds of voices and feet.

Jesus became blinded to all the faces except Sol's. He felt anguish and identified it as fear, and so trampled on his feeling with silent chastisement. Don't think about it, don't think about it, you got to do this, it's the only way. Then he was able to go on with what he was doing for a while with only the gloomy thought that perhaps he might always be blinded to faces after the Pawnbroker's was gone. And once it even occurred to him that this was the price he must pay to enter into the Pawnbroker's secret, that this was the price for those mysterious riches that had always been beyond him. Details of Sol's figure obsessed him; the glasses, the secret structure of his face and body, the numbers etched on his arm, all elements of something majestic and tragic, something he had to possess. Yet for all this he had only the simple words for material things: money, a business, a name.

He was even able to feel twinges of petulant greed. The Pawnbroker was loaning out a lot of money, was passing out a lot of cash; he, Ortiz, would not be around to collect its interest. And where was the messenger with the regular weekly payment of cash to be dispersed by the Pawnbroker, the money that was the incentive for all his plans? Here it was three o'clock and to his knowledge the money from the invisible partner had not come in yet. Unless it had come while he was upstairs. But no, he had been aware of almost every customer from his peek-hole upstairs, had seen the spastic, the jawless man, the *ofay* with the baby shoes, the fat white woman from the Youth Center. He strained to watch each transaction Sol made while he attended to his own, and wondered if he would recognize the messenger if he saw him: they changed so often. The last one he remembered was that white-haired Italian.

Occasionally, he was faced with a piece of jewelry whose worth he didn't feel confident to judge. He would send the customer over to Sol, wait for his recognition, and then share with him once more that silence-invoking gaze wherein they found themselves bound in a dark-lit chamber of spirit; until each of them turned back to his own tumultuous commerce, a little more dazed and stricken with the strangeness of his direction.

On and on they came, without letup, without mercy. What sense was there in all their humble, hideous vitality? Why did they exist? Sol had thought all human life had long ago been gassed and cremated. Out of what graves had all these remnants crept? Black scourged faces, white, all the shades between and beyond. Hoarse voices, whines, demanding, begging, accepting. Cells multiplying and decaying, strange mutations, smells, ugliness. All the excuses for life had been gone for a long time. What was this whole ghastly parade about? And why was he forced to endure it?

"Five dollars."

"But it's *gold*."

"Plate. Five dollars."

"Genuine."

"Genuine junk. Two dollars."

"This here brand new."

"Come on, grandpa, that suit was old for your confirmation."

"Valuable."

"Worthless."

"Hey, dad, I sell myself body an' soul for dat horn."

"Ten dollars for your body and soul."

"How much?"

"How much?"

"How much?"

At five o'clock he reeled, thought he would faint from exhaustion.

"Ortiz," he called over the heads of the people.

Jesus looked up.

"We forgot to eat lunch. I'm falling off my feet. Go out and get me some coffee, a sandwich."

For a moment Jesus was tempted to refuse. He might miss seeing if the messenger came. All of it would be worthless then. And yet he didn't dare refuse, because that, too, might upset his plan in some way. Besides, the messenger had never failed to show up on Thursday; that mysterious partner seemed to be a model of precision and efficiency. He slid quickly from behind the counter and hurried out of the store.

And suddenly it was that hour in which all the business seemed to stop as though by regulation. Sol was alone in the settling dust. He let his head fall onto his hands. The glasses cut into the flesh of his nose. His breathing was stertorous, broken and painful like an expiring rattle. He was beyond wishing for relief, only maintained a scrap of curiosity about how much more there was ahead of him.

"Delivery boy is here, Uncle," the recorded voice said from up close, followed by the soft slap of a heavy envelope on the counter.

Sol straightened slowly. He took the glasses off and rubbed the red mark on the bridge of his nose. Through the fuzziness of his impaired vision he could recognize Murillio.

"Take it in your hand," he commanded.

Sol shook his head.

"I have used a few minutes of my personal time to come here; I will not have it wasted."

Sol continued shaking his head. He sensed the imminence of release.

"For the last time, Uncle, take it!"

The head kept shaking.

"I warn you, and I think you know I am a man of my word, this is the end of you."

"You will kill me?"

Murillio nodded solemnly, without menace, indeed, with even the faintest cast of regret on his face.

"Ah then, if that is all you can do to me, Murillio, you are much weaker than I thought. Kill me then," he said indifferently, settling the glasses back on his nose. "I will be out of this, one way or another."

"You must be out of your mind," Murillio said, evidencing irritation for the first time. "Think clearly for a minute, will you? Dead, a bullet into you, then nothing, you're gone. You don't want to die, do you?" he asked, almost querulously. "Dying is ridiculous."

"And living?"

"I always thought you were a sensible man. Living is everything; what else is there?"

Sol smiled suddenly, an ancient expression of cerebral amusement.

"You seem to be trying to sell me on life. In any event, you are wasting your valuable time. There is nothing you can do to me. The only punishment you are capable of inflicting is impotent. I could learn nothing from it. And the threat of it is just a trifle. You don't understand, do you? It is a pity. What will you deprive me of? Look around at my kingdom. What is it? Would I miss it, even if I could in death?"

Murillio moved his eyes slowly, trying to see the store with the Pawnbroker's eyes, looking at it for the first time with curiosity, intently, searchingly, speculating on the profusion of gleams and lusters, trying to ascertain what all of it did to a man, what unpredictable strengths it gave, how it could armor a man against what he had always considered to be formidable weapons. The shop was silent around the dark-suited man with his white-lacquered face, and the Pawnbroker with his damp, gray skin, his half-concealed eyes. Old woods and tortured brasses, bits of glass and gold and silver, mother-of-pearl and tortoise shell, gut and steel and ivory surrounded them. Dust lay on everything, and it seemed like some rarely visited museum, a place of esoteric interest whose violences were far behind, whose sounds were only diminishing echoes. Finally Murillio moved his eyes back to Sol. For a moment he studied his face. And then he looked down to the tattooed arm, where he let his gaze rest a while in somber reflection.

Suddenly Murillio smiled, his eyes still on the blue numbers. "You know something, Uncle? I'm not a stupid man. I got instincts; that's how I got where I am. That's why I will go even farther. I don't yell, I don't stamp my feet, I don't kick corpses. And I will tell you this . . ." He raised his cold, slush-colored eyes to Sol's. "I believe you are right. I believe there is no point to killing you. One way or another I will get most of this investment back. But I see you can't be used for an example. No, I'm writing you off, not that you care. It's a pity, Uncle. You seem to be a interesting man. Most people that I deal with are stupid animals; they bore the life out of me. Too bad we couldn't have shot the shit once in a while. Who knows? Even I might have learned something."

Sol didn't answer him, and Murillio stood there for a few minutes longer, allowing the silence, as though trying to hear whatever peculiar sound it was that had cast the Pawnbroker into his reverie. And then he picked up the envelope of money, waved it once toward the Pawnbroker in a sort of farewell gesture, and walked out of the store.

And Sol said to himself, "So it isn't death that I am afraid of, although it may yet come to me today. Then what is it that makes me tremble and ache? Why does my breast distend and threaten to burst?" He gave a great moan as he pressed his hands to his face, and stood like that until Jesus returned with the food and coffee, whereupon he ate and drank just for something to do while he waited.

And Jesus went back upstairs to wait too.

No one came in. Sol felt an irrelevant petulance. He entertained the insane idea of a boycott, a sudden diverting of everything human. The store was a peculiar and grotesque tomb.

He picked up the feather duster and began twitching around among his merchandise, flicking the birdlike object at the horns and cameras like some devout witch doctor.

The smell of tar and frying entered the store and then was gone. From somewhere distant there came the odor of chocolate. Sol frowned, the feathers on the end of his voo-doo-stick duster trembling as on a breathing bird. And then the chocolate smell was gone, too, with inexplicable suddenness. Everything there was existed only in the store.

The store was full of minute sounds that Sol knew were

audible only to him. The fan, which gave a little plink at the end of each arc of its turn, pushed a microscopic breath through the bells of the trumpets, strummed with infinite delicacy over the strings of banjo and violin and guitar. His fantastically acute hearing picked up the rustling of his papers, the riffled edges of the ledger, and the various bills and tickets. Above him, the footsteps of his assistant in the loft creaked and thudded as though the slender figure moved under a burden heavier than himself, made sounds of restless, muffled regularity like the tread heard in a nightmare. Thump, thump, thump, dull, distant hammer blows, a counterpoint to the ghostly breath of the horns and the thrumming of the gut strings.

He was at the end of things now; at his back was the heatless press of the grave. His connection to life was the mere thread of light and sound. Only one thing remained to happen. He grew frantic with impatience for it to be over. Now the one tiny contact with living was an unbelievable agony, a white-hot pressure against his heart.

"Why does he stay up there? It's past time for him to leave. What is he up to? Does he think I don't notice he's still here? Oh, what a nightmare this world is! What a cruel joke God is! Oh yes, *kill us, kill us,* but ONLY ONCE, isn't once enough?"

What was he waiting for? He could bring about his own deliverance; his counters were filled with Black Forest daggers and pistols; death was within his reach all around.

Outside, the street gabbled and hooted, illuminated his doorway with a lively evening light. Cars glinted swiftly by, human figures made brief pantomimes in the frame of his vision: children in haunting insect-like bodies, women, varicolored men, each in slightly different costume, each enlivened by his own unique choreography. He tried to remember a time when he had been alive, but failed miserably. The perspective of time had eliminated his boyhood and youth, and all that remained was a diminishing façade of misery, the architecture of his recent years.

He went to the fan and pulled the chain that turned it off. Then he listened for a moment, the duster held like a fluttering weapon in his hand. The fan whirred to a stop, the instruments fell silent.

Thump, thump, thump went the human footfalls over his head. He raised his eyes to the ceiling in despair, the duster hanging uselessly from his fingers.

"Ohhh," he breathed. "Oh God damn this, God damn this," he whispered. Life fell like a shadow on his soul.

Slowly he let his eyes sink from the ceiling, down from the coiled tuba, down past the string instruments, the antique muzzle-loader musket, past the bongo drums on the shelf over the door, past the transom angled open to entice some air in from the street. Down until he was looking through the open doorway at the crazy sight of three figures just beginning to cross the street toward him.

They wore children's Halloween masks; one a doll-like girl's face with Cupid's-bow lips and neat red discs to represent rosy cheeks, one a green devil's face, and the third a clown with darkness showing through the upturned mouth in the midst of chalky whiteness.

And he stood with the feather duster in his hand, watching their approach with all the aplomb and rationality of someone watching a dream unfold.

## ✻ TWENTY-EIGHT

Sol backed up until he was against the counter where the wire grille was. The festive masks were on the sidewalk, in the corridor between the windows. Then they were crowding the doorway, inhuman faces which stared at him blandly. They came inside slowly, almost shyly. The doll face held back, its powerful body guarding the door. It seemed to be protecting Sol from the harsh outside. The devil face raised an ash-gray sleeve to reveal a shiny gun. It looked like a toy in the presence of the masks. The clown stepped forward with empty hands. Their breathing was loud and compressed behind the masks. Upstairs, there was silence, but the sounds of the outside were vivid and strangely sweet. "Hey, Ginger," called a boy's voice. "Where you goin', gal?" The clocks ticked out of step. Why hadn't he heard the clocks before when he had been able to make out the tiny sounds of the strings in the air of the fan?

"What . . . what do you want?" the Pawnbroker said in a dry, leafy voice.

The clown advanced, pointing toward the huge safe behind the counter.

"What, what, I don't understand your pointing," Sol said. He had the sensation of falling and tensed for the one instant of enormous pain that was the threshold of death.

"The money, the money," the clown said furiously. He came up close, and Sol could see the brown neck flexing passionately. "Open the safe, c'mon now. We not playin', open it fast." He cocked his white linen face toward the shiny weapon in the devil's hand.

"You are crazy," Sol said without inflection, dutifully playing out his part in the strange costumed charade. He waved the duster stiffly in imitation of anger. "You will be caught. Get out of here now, before you have real trouble."

The clown looked back toward the devil as though in amazement. The devil's bony brown hand flexed on the grip of the gun and he in turn looked toward the corner of the store where the stairway to the loft was. But there was nothing there. So the devil raised the gun up and then swung its barrel down with a sudden snapping movement, as though it were one of those cardboard guns that emit a "crack" as they display the word BANG in paper fire.

"No joke now, white man. Get that money outa that safe. We got no time. *Get it!*" And the devil leaned forward with a tenseness of body that culminated in the brown iron of his gun hand.

The clown seemed to lean backward, raised his arm a little as though against the impending noise. But the doll face near the door pointed suddenly to something behind Sol.

"Hey wait, the thing . . . the safe . . . it ain't . . . it's like . . . open. It *open!*" he cried.

Sol turned with them to look at the big safe door, which cast just enough of a shadow to reveal that it was not quite closed. He sighed wearily at the thought of having to provoke them again. And then, just ahead of the clown face, he slipped behind the counter and took up a stand with his back to the iron door. The clown face came behind the counter, too, but seemed cowed by the feather duster that Sol brandished at him. The devil moved up to the counter and put the barrel of the gun between the bars of the little teller's window.

"Step away, white man. Tangee, go get the stuff," the gunman said, gesturing slightly with the gun so that it clanked against the bars.

But Sol didn't move, and Tangee, behind his useless clown's face, looked helplessly at the devil. "He not movin', *Robinson*," he said.

"What for you want to die?" Robinson asked, with only the mildest curiosity, as he raised the barrel so it pointed toward the round, archaic spectacles. "That money mean so much to you?" He gestured at all the stock of the store, stopped for a moment as his eye caught the beautiful harmonica he had pawned, then went on as though having made a note to himself to get it later. "All this stuff, this junk . . ."

Sol didn't answer. They all fell into the slow steady slide toward destruction. Tangee stepped back slightly; Robinson made shorter and shorter arcs with the tip of the gun, arcs whose center was somewhere around the Pawnbroker's glasses. Buck White, at the doorway, began swiveling his head from them to the street outside in more and more rapid rotation, until he moved so swiftly trying to cover both views that he could not have been able to see anything; or else, bound by the limitations of aftervision, carried the image of the three figures of mutual doom to his view of the street, so that he could have had no idea, for the while, which way he would run to escape them.

Sol smelled the body sweat of one of them, identified it

as the rumored "nigger smell," and then drew a sardonic smile like a painful scratch inside himself as he realized it might be the odor of his own body. There was a creak from the direction of the stairway. It was like the sound of the peculiar silence into which they were cast. Sol raised the feather duster as though he were the commander of his own firing squad. It was all within his reach now. He savored it for a long minute as Robinson slowed the arc of the gun toward the motionless moment when he would fire.

But then Sol felt a sudden outrage. That his whole vast collection of experience should elude him now! He became incensed that his beginning and ending had no more depth and breadth than this shabby, littered shop. Suddenly he yearned for the drowning man's cliché, for some great distillation of everything. A vanity he had never considered made him demand recall, made him insist on even the myriad varieties of pain he had endured, the searing products of his sight and smell and hearing. As he stared at the stiff, linen faces, his heart silently called on the infinite subtleties of temperature, the pressures of all the hands and winds and wetnesses that had crossed the surface of his body. Furiously, in the shallow, death-rattle breathing of the four of them, he invoked at least the microcosmic view of all the faces as he would have glimpsed them through the tiny eyelet of those souvenir penholders so popular when he was a boy. But he could not even muster up the look of the penholder and he knew the faces would have been too small for him to see. And he became filled with the most incredible desolation, because his beginning and ending *would* take place in the narrow confines of this one empty hour, this one stifling and derelict room.

He swung the feather duster and sucked the last of life.

The explosion was deafening; it was as though a bomb had struck. He was blinded, saw only smoke. The echoes rang the brass bells of the horns. Numbness. Yet he was aware of the numbness . . . not death, then. What? Running feet. Reach out to touch . . . what was it? A human body, sliding slowly downward. Oh to see, to know! His hand pressed on the clothed, warm figure, tried to keep it from falling. It slid under his hand. Then he saw, in the doorway, Robinson, with the mask under his chin, the gun half raised, his face a horrible mask itself, the personification of that same desolation Sol had experienced. He faced the man with the gun calmly, his hand on the slipping body. And then Robinson wheeled and ran. Sol looked down, recognized from the back the slender form of Jesus Ortiz. A red stain was spreading over the yellow shirt back. He tried to seize him with both hands. Ortiz eluded him, slipped to the floor with a discreet little thump.

The echo of the gunshot made a diminishing ring in everything metal, drew itself out so finely he knew it would go on and on. Gently, he turned the slender body over, kicked some broken glass aside as he eased it down. Jesus stared at him, blinked a few times, but kept his eyes on Sol.

"It was crazy," Jesus said in a whisper.

Sol kneeled over him. "What happened? I couldn't know what happened. I thought he would shoot me. Then I heard the shot. . . . I was confused. You stepped in the way?"

"I told them no shooting. . . . It was just stupid . . . just a dumb thing."

"For me?"

"Don't be a goddam fool. . . . You goddam fool."

"Why, then?"

"It was dumb, dumb. . . ."

"More than that."

Jesus just shook his head stubbornly.

For a few seconds Sol stayed on one knee studying the youth's slowly whitening face. Then he stood up and began dialing for a doctor. Outside, there was an approaching babble of voices. A car pulled up. Someone shouted, and faces crowded the door. A policeman pushed through, looked in cautiously and then with puzzlement, because there was nothing to see. Sol pointed to the wounded man at his feet, and the policeman came over to see, widened his eyes at the sight, and shouted harshly at the crowd in the doorway as though to activate himself. Another policeman came in, and still another. Sol told the hospital where his store was. Several more policemen came in, one of them with sergeant's stripes on his sleeve.

"Do you know who they were?" the sergeant asked. "How many were there? Colored or white? You didn't see which way they went?"

Cars pulled up outside. The door was a wall of human bodies, which parted from time to time to let other men in. A policeman talked on the phone behind Sol, another in plain clothes asked him questions that he just shrugged at. And all the time he made a cover of his body over the wounded youth, kept his eyes on his assistant's eyes. There was a strange struggle between them, a silent tugging that left them both bewildered and dazed looking. From the floor, Jesus saw only the massive bulk of the Pawnbroker's hovering body, the great formless face that seemed to have meaning only because of the round spectacles. His world was reduced or enlarged to just that. He felt his body leaving him, the awful pain recede to a great distance. Only the Pawnbroker, with his secret, and the remote sounds of many people in the store. And the Pawnbroker stared just as yearningly as a freezing man stares at the last ember of a fire and suddenly sees how lovely the color of light can be. "What did you want from me, Ortiz?" Jesus just rolled his head on the floor. Ah, but the amazing quality of that brown skin, warm and pliable, full of little twitches and tremors. The eyes with their dark openings into mystery. What did they see? The lips shaped some silent words at him, a curse or a blessing or something else completely.

From far off, a siren approached. A woman's voice sounded hysterically in the street. Hands touched his arm. He shook them off. Something was breaking out of him.

His body felt full of the flow of some great wound. A rush and a torment burned him. He felt naked and flayed and he hung over the dying youth like a frayed canopy. A million pains raked his body, doubled him over so his face came down closer to the face beneath him. He wanted to say something but didn't know what it was. "Ortiz, Ortiz, Ortiz," he said. Everything he thought he had conquered rose up from its sham death and fell upon him. Ghosts mingled with the busy policemen in the store, and the voices were increased a thousandfold. "Ortiz, Ortiz," he pleaded. The dark eyes grew larger and more awful. "What will I do?" he moaned. *"Ortiz!"*

Someone pulled him forcibly away, and he tottered over to the loft steps, where he sat with his head in his hands. The siren sounded its expiring alarm right outside, and then the white-clad interns crowded into the narrow space behind the counter. A woman brought her screaming into the store.

"Jesus, Jesus, is it my Jesus?" the mother cried.

"I'm sorry, lady," someone said.

"Is he dead?"

Perhaps a silent nod.

"Ahhhhh, Mother of God, Lord help me. . . ."

And then the dry retching sound of weeping, growing louder and louder and louder, filling the Pawnbroker's ears, flooding him, drowning him, dragging him back to that sea of tears he had thought to have escaped. And he sat hunched against that abrasive roar, his body becoming worn down under the flood of it, washed down to the one polished stone of grief, of *grief.*

All his anesthetic numbness left him. He became terrified of the touch of air on the raw wounds. What was this great, agonizing sensitivity and what was it for? Good God, what was all this? *Love?* Could this be *love?* He began to laugh hysterically, and the voices in the store stopped. The mother cursed him from where she knelt over her dead son.

"He laugh, you hear, he laugh!" she cried wrathfully.

"Now, now, lady, he's probably in a state of shock," one of the policemen said soothingly.

"But he *laugh*. How could he laugh now?"

Oh no, not love! For whom? All these dark, dirty creatures? They turn my stomach, they sicken me. Oh, this din, this pain and thrashing.

The time passed in some strange, forgettable way. People questioned him. There was a coming and a going. They got him into the little glass-enclosed office and someone gave him some strong whisky to drink. All around him was a dazzle of faces and textures and voices. He nodded and spoke, negated and agreed, and had no idea of what he was saying. All around was the crush of warm bodies, the terrible stifling pungence of human smells. He had a glimpse of the white-covered body going out on a stretcher. Sometimes he thought he recognized a familiar voice and strained to see through the enveloping confusion some long-lost face. Once, he heard a woman's voice complain sorrowfully, "But I his girl, I got a *right!*" The phone rang many times. Someone asked him if he wanted to talk to someone. He didn't remember answering. For an instant he saw the immaculate face of Marilyn Birchfield and he said as in a dream, "No, no, I am too dirty; you must go away from me." And then she was gone, banished by his voice, and for a moment he thought he recognized the delicate shape of regret, until that, too, disappeared. His head rang like struck metal and his body was fantastically aged.

A man, possibly a doctor, forced him to drink something out of a little paper cup. It made him sleepy, and the doctor, a weary, sour-faced man, told him to come over to his office, where he had a couch Sol could sleep on for a while.

"A little rest would do you some good," he said.

Sol nodded in the buzz of voices around him but he held his hand up.

"I must make a telephone call first," he said. Suddenly he had found himself thinking in a muddled way about the store and Jesus Ortiz and his nephew, Morton, and he realized he had to straighten that out before he could sleep.

"I'll wait for you," the doctor said. "That sedative will make you very groggy. It will be better for me to go with you. Go on, make your call."

Leaning on the counter, Sol shuffled over to the phone. One of the policemen stepped out of his way and watched him curiously as he slowly dialed the Mount Vernon number. He felt drunk, and his body tingled with a need for sleep. In all the chaos of his stunned brain only this one chore took on any legible shape, and even it was rootless and indecipherable in relation to whatever it was he was going through.

"Morton, I want to speak to Morton," he said as soon as he heard the phone picked up at the other end.

"Sol?" his sister said. "Is that you? You sound funny. What's wrong?"

"Morton," he insisted. It was as though only that word kept the drowsiness at bay.

"What, what is it?"

"Give me Morton," he said thickly.

He heard the phone clunk down, and he rubbed his face to fight the sandy feeling of fatigue.

"What do you want?" Morton asked sulkily.

"Listen to me carefully, Morton, I don't want to repeat. Do not interrupt until I am through. I am very tired and I must lie down soon. There is a big mix-up here; it is bedlam. A terrible thing has happened. They tried to hold me up. There are police and everything. My boy, my assistant, has been killed . . . he is dead."

"What do you mean? How do . . . *killed?* Who, I mean . . ."

"My assistant, *Jesus* Ortiz, the *Shwartsa,* has been killed.

I am alone with this store. I cannot be alone with this place. I must say it simply. I want you to come here and work. You may continue to go to school; we will make arrangements somehow. But I need you to help me, I have no one."

"But how can I . . . I don't understand. You want me to come to the store every day? Where will I do my work? My mother . . ." Morton's voice was querulous and confused. Too much was being poured on his own misery, and he couldn't tell whether it was alleviation or aggravation.

"I *need* you, Morton," Sol said dully.

There was almost a minute's silence. Sol strained to keep his head erect. The doctor was a blur to his left, and only the center of his vision made a clear image of the tuba hanging from the ceiling. Finally there was the small phlegmy sound of Morton feeling for his voice.

"All right, Uncle Sol, all right. Tomorrow I'll come in to you in the store. I'll try. . . . You'll have to teach me."

And then Sol had only the vague memory of walking out of the store with the doctor's hand firm on his arm. He stepped outside and he was blind to the late sunlight, confused as to direction and sound. He was only aware of the movement of people and the bubbling din of their voices and he felt like a tiny ball spinning in a great, round wire cage.

He slept quite comfortably on the antiseptic quiet of the doctor's couch. For a while he was conscious of nothing except the vague sounds of his own breathing, which intruded on his sleep. And when he began to dream, he found the dream to be oddly without the usual horror and yet possessed of the greatest sadness he had ever experienced.

*He walked over a strangely desolate and overgrown meadow with Tessie and Morton. They were silent and seemed indifferent to him, yet they kept pace with him, step for step. The sky hung like a down-sagging green canopy.*

*There was no breeze, no sound of insect or bird. The silence was so intense that he imagined a long endless chord of music just beyond his physical ability to hear it. Even their footsteps were silent.*

*Ahead of them appeared the broken, rusty wire fence and the long low buildings blackened by weather and sagging under the years. A wooden tower leaned forlornly to one side, and the tall chimney standing in the ruin of a brick building was like a monument to a forgotten race. Nothing moved; no wind mourned the gaping windows.*

*They reached the fence and stopped there.*

*A black-uniformed figure came out of the nearest building. They waited for him to approach. There was no such thing as surprise there. He walked stiffly up to Sol and looked up at him with empty eye sockets; it was Murillio. Then he faced down to a slip of paper in his hand and he read:*

*"Your dead are not buried here."*

*Sol tried to object. He reached down for his voice but was able only to bring up an immense strangling pain.*

He woke up waving his arms in the dimness. The doctor was standing over him. It was dark outside.

"I must have been dreaming," he apologized. "How long have I been sleeping here?"

"Only about an hour. I'm surprised you woke up so soon. How do you feel?"

"I am all right. I must go now. There is the store. I just walked out without . . ."

"There are still police there, don't worry. If I were you, I would get home and try to rest. You have had a great shock, apparently. I'd like to give you a prescription."

"No, no, I can't know yet what I must do. There, see," he said, standing up carefully. "I'm all right now. If you will tell me how much I owe you . . ."

The doctor waved his hand indifferently.

"No, I insist. I am scrupulous about money matters," Sol said.

The doctor looked at him strangely. "I can see you are," he said. "Suppose we wait a day or two and have you stop back so I can look you over. That is, unless you have a family doctor. . . ."

"No, I have none. Very well, in a day or so."

He went down into the street and took a minute to plot his position. Then he saw the faint shape of the pawnshop sign and he headed for it.

The front door was open and the lights were on. Moe Leventhal and another policeman were inside, leaning on the counter. A man in civilian clothes was down on the floor with a flashlight and a little box of some kind. His pockets were filled with pads. It was quiet there, the store a lifeless tomb again.

"It's all right, Solly," Leventhal said gently. "We'll watch things. Why don't you go home now?"

Sol shrugged and looked around.

"Will you be all right?" Leventhal asked. "Can you make it home all right?"

"Yes, yes," he said and began walking out of the store.

"Oh, Solly, the keys, leave us the keys," Leventhal called after him.

He took the keys out and handed them to the policeman. Then he started toward the street again.

But in the doorway he imagined he heard the voice of Jesus Ortiz's mother screaming at him as she had before, and he turned back to cry out to the two policemen.

"All right, all right, I know what hurts her. I hear all of them screaming again. What does she want from me? Can't she see that I am weeping for her, that I am weeping for all of them now! Who asked for it? So maybe I love all of them, does it do any good? Doesn't that make it worse?"

Leventhal looked at his companion, and the man on the floor got up. They moved as though to restrain him, but he turned and hurried out.

For a minute or two he tried to think rationally about where he was going, what he was going to do.

Then he began to cry.

On his face was the wetness, in his mouth the strange saline taste. Blinded by his weeping, he bumped into people, was jostled by the bone and flesh of their bodies. In his head there was no stillness, no composure, only this terrible rushing, this immense fluid pouring. He thudded into people and felt them and took into himself their peculiar odors of sweat and breath, of dirt and hair, the smell of the great mortal decay that was living because it was dying. And when he tried to wipe his eyes, indeed, cleared them momentarily, he saw the ineffable marvel of their eyes and skins.

So he was caught in the flow of them as he tried to find the wellspring of his own tears. Until he realized he was crying for all his dead now, that all the dammed-up weeping had been released by the loss of one irreplaceable Negro who had been his assistant and who had tried to kill him but who had ended by saving him. For a moment he stopped on the pavement with a frown twisting his face as the people eddied past. What had impelled Ortiz to throw himself like a shield before him? Could it perhaps have been just the practical fear of not wanting the robbery to become too dangerous a venture? Had Ortiz himself had time to really know? He could not have had time to pick his way through the torturous litter of his soul to discover what *else* had prompted that act. And if it had been a mystery in the end to Ortiz, what right did he have to expect more? So his tears continued as he moved through the crowding filth of the people toward the river, dirty himself, mouthing his own salty tears, hopeless, wretched, strangely proud.

Then he was at the river, alone except for two men far

down the curbing that bordered the water. He wiped his eyes clear again and he stood watching the river as it slid obscurely under the bridges toward the sea, bright and glittery in the boat lights on its surface, so vast in its total, never anything here and now, as it hurried slowly toward the obscurity of the salty ocean; so great, so touching in its fleeting presence. The wetness dried on his cheeks and a great calm came over him.

The two men, Cecil Mapp and John Rider, came walking by. They said hello to him, but he seemed to be talking to himself. John Rider claimed he was counting all his money, but Cecil Mapp said, "No, man, that man suffer."

Actually, the Pawnbroker was counting his losses and forgiving himself as he watched the river.

"Rest in peace, Ortiz, Mendel, Rubin, Ruth, Naomi, David . . . rest in peace," he said, still crying a little, but mostly for himself. He took a great breath of air, which seemed to fill parts of his lungs unused for a long time. And he took the pain of it, if not happily, like a martyr, at least willingly, like an heir.

Then he began walking to the subway to take the long, underground journey to Tessie's house, to help her mourn.